Also available on

Sherlock Holmes and the
Sherlock Holmes and the Ghastly Gate
The Adventure of the Threatened New Yorker
The Byrne House Murders
Mary

Coming Soon:

The Case of Castle Atkinson
Sherlock Holmes and the Court of Time

The Specter at Painswick

Chapter One

In January of 1891, my dear wife Mary was often absent from our cozy home aiding a dear friend who had given birth prematurely. Mary had met Mrs. Abigail Mortimer through a reading club, and the two had become fast friends. The young girl and her husband were pleasant, as I quickly learned during their visits to dinner. Mrs. Mortimer went into labor three weeks early which frightened us all. I wasn't an attendant, not being a birthing doctor, but we were all overjoyed to see the baby and mother survive the labor with a good chance of a speedy recovery. The new mother was tired, however, and overwhelmed, and my sweet Mary was all too happy to spend her days helping her with the baby. It was only for this reason that on this wintery afternoon as I left my practice on Harley Street, I decided to drop by and give my old friend Sherlock Holmes a visit. Needless to say, I was enthusiastic about seeing my old acquaintance again. I had assisted him last year on that old Baskerville conundrum, but due to demands of work and matrimony, I had not seen him since.

Baker Street came into view outside the small window of my hansom cab, I cringed a bit at the deductions Holmes might make about me after so long a separation. Particularly, I worried about the half a stone I'd put on in the interim. Holmes was sure to notice; I imagined that almost childlike twinkle he'd get in his eye as he pointed it out and shook my head, letting out a soft laugh that I hoped my driver couldn't hear.

Holmes himself was likely to be exactly as I'd left him. In fact, despite a few laugh lines around those grey eyes of his, he hadn't seemed to age much at all in the 10 years I'd known him. I could picture him now, tall and lean, hunched over his chemical desk, hair in disarray, long fingers working deftly over his microscope and vials.

I hopped out of the cab and took a fortifying breath; as much as I was eager to see my dear old friend, interaction with Holmes was often a bit exhausting.

The scene that met me upon entering the sitting-room was not at all what I was expecting. Instead of the frantic energy of a man at work or the contrasting lethargy and moodiness of a man stuck in ennui, I found my old flatmate sitting comfortably on the divan, reading a novel.

At the sight of me in the doorway, he smiled broadly. So broadly, in fact, that I instinctively cast my eye around for that telltale morocco case that I so detested.

It was nowhere in sight, but Holmes caught the look, his smile dimming a bit. He swung his stockinged feet off the divan, his blue dressing robe fluttering about him as he stood. "My dear Watson!" he greeted, obviously choosing to ignore my unspoken but apparently abundantly clear thoughts, "What brings you to my humble flat on this snow-driven day?" He gave me one of those peculiar once-overs, and I'm sure he already knew every detail about my life and what had led me here instead of home, but I gave him a brief explanation of my wife's absence and my general disinclination to be alone.

"Ah," he murmured, "I see. And how is the lovely Mrs. Watson faring?"

"Perfectly well, now that her friend is out of the woods. In fact, she's fairly glowing. She enjoys being around the baby." I immediately realized I'd said too much, but Holmes merely smirked, thankfully leaving any comments about baby fever unvoiced. I settled myself in my old chair as Holmes sat down again, propping his feet up on the small end table.

Removing my gloves, I nodded to the book in his hand, "What are you reading?"

Holmes looked at the spine, as if he himself didn't know, "*The Man Who Would Be King*. Charming, if not heavy-handed, morality tale on British imperialism."

"I never took you much for a recreational reader."

"I enjoy the occasional novel. We must all be allowed our vices." There was an edge to his voice on this last bit that made me wonder if he hadn't been more hurt by my assumption about the cocaine. If so, he didn't give me time to respond, "Even so, this was a gift."

Holmes often received gifts from satisfied clients – jewels, opera tickets, even once an offer of marriage to a Lord's daughter – but a book seemed an odd boon. "A gift? From who?" I reached for the thing without asking. Holmes frowned a bit but made no move to snatch the item back.

"My brother, actually."

"Mycroft?"

"There is no secret third Holmes sibling, so, yes, Mycroft," he replied sardonically.

I ran my hand over the expensive leather of the cover. The lettering was gold-embroidered, the paper a fine quality. Not a cheap gift by any means, but I'd met the older Holmes brother before and a book seemed out of character for that torpid and inscrutable man. "Why this particular book?"

Holmes shrugged, "There's probably some meaning that I'm too dull-witted to decipher." Only in comparison to his brother would Sherlock Holmes ever be described as dull-witted. To be completely honest, I wasn't even sure that this was true in comparison to Mycroft – their intellects seemed much more equally matched than my friend believed. But the detective could benefit from a little humility, so I kept my tongue.

Flipping open the book, I quickly discovered the reason for his flash of irritation when I took it from him: On the inside cover was scrawled a neat and impersonal "*Many happy returns. Mycroft*".

I glanced up sharply at Holmes. "Is today your birthday, old chap?" Holmes bristled but didn't respond. I laughed. "I never knew when your birthday was."

"Yes, well now you know. Don't be too offended, Watson, I've saved you countless pennies on obligatory birthday gifts."

"It must be a nightmare shopping for you," I commented, though I was sure I was up to the task. Despite my jovial tone, I was a little stung that I was never allowed to purchase him something I knew he'd enjoy, like that nice Queen Victoria white clay pipe I'd come across in Manchester last year.

"Any interesting cases on the docket?" I asked as I handed the book back to him.

With a carelessness that made me wince, he tossed the heavy item onto the floor next to the divan and shrugged. "Nothing of note, unfortunately. Apparently, the snow has made everyone lethargic."

"So what have you been busy with?"

"I'm writing a monograph on fingerprints and the invaluable role they could play in crime-solving if the police would only use them. I'm also conducting tests to see if there is any way to detect ricin if used as a poisoning agent."

"Sounds fascinating," I lied.

"Indeed, it's kept me contentedly occupied for days. How about you, old man? Any interesting medical cases?"

Before I could answer, the bell rang, and Mrs. Hudson's light step could be heard at the end of the staircase. Holmes and I both held our breaths, unable to hear the particulars of the conversation but waiting to hear the telltale sounds of footsteps ascending the seventeen steps to our flat.

After a moment of hushed murmuring, two treads could be heard coming up the landing. Holmes's posture straightened, his eyes suddenly sharp and eager.

Mrs. Hudson admitted a tall, lean man nearing sixty with well-kept facial hair and a bowler hat.

"Mr. Holmes," he greeted amiably but in that aloof way that spoke of a businessman or broker and nodded his thanks to the gracious landlady as she left him in our care.

Holmes waved him into the customary client chair, forgoing niceties in that peculiarly rude but efficient way of his.

Our guest didn't seem deterred, settling down with an exaggerated grunt. "So pleased you're willing to see me, sir. I hope I'm not interrupting anything."

Holmes gestured nonchalantly towards me, "No, no. This is my good friend and chronicler, Dr. Watson."

"Ah, yes," he reached across, grasping my hand in a firm grip, "I greatly enjoyed your story in The Strand a year or two ago."

I flushed, still not accustomed to people praising me in Holmes's presence, something that would become more and more common as I published more and more of my case notes, much to Holmes' amused chagrin. "Thank you, sir. It was a humble endeavor, though I'm sure it's helped pad my friend's caseload a bit." Our guest and I laughed.

Holmes did not.

Clearing his throat, the newcomer finally introduced himself, "My name is Harris. I work for an investment firm in town, but I'm here on behalf of a good friend of mine. It may seem unorthodox, but the person I'm concerned for does not know I'm even here."

"It's not so unorthodox," Holmes replied, "though it may be a bit limiting. It's hard to help those who don't ask for it themselves."

"Yes, well, my dear friend I'm concerned for, though, may not be able to ask for help himself. He lives out in Painswick in his country estate. He's up in years, already in his late seventies, and his mind had deteriorated to the point that his wife has had to take control of their affairs, seeing as she's roughly 20 years younger and still in possession of all her faculties."

"And you believe there is some mischief on her part?" I surmised.

"No, indeed not. Mrs. Swift is a fine woman. The problem I'm going to describe to you is a much stranger tale than mere manipulation of an older man for financial gain. But I am worried about my friend's state of mind; I've heard some interesting stories about the estate."

The eager gleam in Holmes's eye dimmed. "Am I correct in assuming, Mr. Harris, that you want me to make a house call on your friend? That's more of the good doctor's area of expertise than mine."

"No, not at all." A tone of irritation crept into our visitor's voice. "It's the rumors I want you to look into. You see, Mr. Swift occasionally writes me. While some of his letters are confusing, he has rare moments of lucidity. At least, seeming lucidity."

"How can you tell?"

"His wording is surer, and he rambles less. But recently he sent me a letter detailing events that, were I not adept at reading his state of mind through his written language, I would be tempted to disregard as ravings of a sick man near his death."

Holmes leaned forward; while his movements were languid, I saw the tightening of his shoulder blades and recognized the spark of interest in his eyes. "Sounds promising. Continue."

"Richard writes me weekly. As of late, his letters have been a jumbled mix of memories. He clearly loses sight of what year he's in because of obvious dementia. That being said, despite his mental confusion, I can still easily recognize that he's not inventing his tales.

However, last week he sent me a new letter detailing what appears to be a haunting at his estate."

Holmes didn't look surprised at this revelation, but he was quiet for a moment. I remember his express distaste for the idea of the supernatural when that case of the Hound was brought before us. Finally, he held out his hand, "You have the letter on you, yes?"

Harris reached into his frock coat and removed a neatly folded letter and handed it over.

Holmes unfolded it, revealing two messily scribbled on pages, and scanned through the contents, occasionally letting out an unreadable noise under his breath. After he was done, he flapped it in my direction.

I took it and read it quickly. This Mr. Swift, in a swirl of both startlingly vivid details and vague, disjointed rambling, relayed that over the past few weeks, he had noticed unexplainable things going on in his home: the sound of footsteps at night, food missing, items moved about. The rest of the family had also noticed a few of the odd things but apparently discounted them as having some mundane explanation. This did not satisfy Mr. Swift, who was becoming increasingly convinced that his house was being haunted.

After I finished reading the letter and had handed it back over to our guest, Holmes was silent as he removed a cigarette from his engraved case and lit it with a coal from the fireplace.

"Do you wish me to go ghost hunting, Mr. Harris? Because that is hardly within my purview and, I'll admit, skill. I left my ghost hunting days behind me when I stopped roaming the hills of Yorkshire with my loyal dog."

"Hardly, Mr. Holmes. I'm not a superstitious man by any means. I put no stock in talk of hauntings. But I feel something is going on in that house. It's not a police matter, but you're not constrained by those rules and regulations. I was merely hoping ..." he sighed. "I can compensate you handsomely for just a few days of your time. God willing, the answer will be simple and to the point, and this matter can be cleared up in no time."

I knew that wasn't the wisest thing to say to my friend if one wanted his attention. I tried not to wince in sympathy for Mr. Harris, for he was sure to face a rejection any minute now. And rejections from Sherlock Holmes could be downright humiliating.

To my surprise, Holmes merely hummed. "Yes, indeed. It could be a simple thing." Holmes leaned his head back, swiveling his long pale neck to look at me. "Thoughts, Watson?"

I had not been expecting the inquiry, but as a medical man, I did have some thoughts. "Paranoia and confusion are both common symptoms of dementia. I spent a few months in Cornwall, at the St. Lawrence Hospital and personally encountered many patients suffering from these sorts of delusions. While I loath to diagnose anyone I haven't seen to myself, it does indeed seem like this may be, unfortunately, a very common ailment your friend is suffering from."

"I understand that may be true but ... I'm not sure how to explain it, gentlemen. All I can say is that something feels very wrong about the whole situation, and my fondness for the old man makes it difficult for me to rest without knowing something is being done to look into it."

Holmes rose, faced the fireplace for a moment, puffing thoughtfully on his pipe. Finally, he turned and began to unceremoniously usher our guest out. "Mr. Harris, I will think this matter over and contact you as soon as possible with my definite reply."

I expected some resistance, but Harris stood and gathered his belongings, thanking my friend for his time.

"So, Holmes," I said once we were alone, "what do you make of that?"

"Watson, you know how I feel about the supernatural."

"You don't believe in it."

"Indeed. The supernatural, if it exists, must be explored by the theologians and parapsychologists, Watson. My method of examination relies on logic and scientific cause and effect. If ghosts are real, I readily admit I'd be out of my depths."

"The idea is exciting though; you have to admit that."

"Yes, very exciting," he answered with a yawn.

"Come, Holmes, I saw your face when we first laid eyes on that fearsome and fiery Hound last year-"

He turned swiftly from the fireplace, eyes alight with an amused warning. "My expression was one of very normal amazement, Watson, and I do hope that if you choose to chronicle that little adventure – as I'm sure you will, considering the mass appeal of ghosts to the homespun populace – you'll accurately represent my *logical* and *rational* responses."

"I've never portrayed you inaccurately, Holmes."

He scoffed. "That's up for debate."

That wasn't a conversation I wanted to have at the moment. I diverted the discussion back to the topic at hand. "Harris doesn't seem like a man prone to emotion, though."

"No, indeed. Though men can surprise you. What's your honest opinion on the letter?"

"On just the letter? Dementia."

"Why do you say that?"

"Why do I say dementia?"

"No, why do you say *on just the letter*?"

Before I could give my reply, Mrs. Hudson bustled in – more accurately, *clanged* in – with a tray full of luncheon. "You haven't eaten all day, so I brought you up some of your favorite tea and sandwiches," she announced, sliding the noisy tray onto Holmes's breakfast table. "Doctor Watson, I brought enough for two if you're staying?" I nodded, and she smiled before her face scrunched up in distaste. She fanned her hand in the air. "My dear boy, this place smells like a gentleman's club when you smoke in here with all the windows closed." The dear, estimable landlady was one of the few people who could freely scold Holmes and get away with it.

He cracked a charming smile. "How do you know what a gentleman's club smells like, Hudson?"

She rolled her eyes, still waving her hand in the air. She strode over to the window, keys jangling on her belt, and pulled open the window. A nice, brisk, and clean breeze seeped into the room. "Crack the window a bit, please, from now on."

"Yes, of course. I apologize," Holmes demurred, pressing a kiss to her hand as she passed. She swatted at him reprovingly but laughed. "Behave yourselves, boys," she said by way of goodbye. I waited until her step could no longer be heard on the stairs before giving my friend a curious look about his strangely relaxed behavior.

He smirked, "I guess living alone has relieved some of my stress," he answered my unvoiced question. "You're not an easy man to cohabitate with, doctor."

"*I'm* not? Holmes-" I caught myself rising to the bait and took a breath. "So how will you respond to our potential client?"

"I'm not sure yet. You haven't answered my question."

"Question? Oh yes. It's just that Harris mentioned that the family had noticed some strange goings-on too, and I can't see how that would be true if it were only the old man's dementia. Of course, maybe the old man is the one moving things around and forgetting his own actions."

"Possible. In any case, I'll send word to him tomorrow about whatever I decide." He turned back to the fireplace, and I sat down to enjoy some supper. Holmes joined me a few moments later and ate in silent contemplation.

When he was done, he stood and lit a cigarette. "Are you staying the night, old man? Your room is still available."

"If you'd like me to."

"I only thought you may not want to be alone if your wife is absent," he replied a little too defensively. There was an edge to his tone that had me glancing around once more for that dreaded cocaine. He noticed, and this time he was less gracious about it. He waved his hand. "Stay or don't stay. Makes no difference to me." Then he plopped himself down at his workbench and began fiddling with his experiments. It was clear I had insulted or embarrassed him in some way.

It was best, though, not to address it directly. I stood as well and glanced out the cracked window. "It is late," I mused nonchalantly, "and hailing a hansom cab might be difficult. I guess I could stay here the night, if it's all right with you."

He waved his hand again, and I picked up his discarded novel and settled in for the evening.

Chapter Two

The next morning, I awoke and entered the sitting room to a bright-eyed and jovial Holmes already eating breakfast.

"Better make haste back to your own abode, Watson, and pack some clothes and a toothbrush. We may be a few days in Painswick."

"You've decided to take the case?"

"Indeed. I sent Harris word earlier this morning."

"May I ask why?"

He shrugged. "Bored. What's more, you're right about the letter. I wouldn't accept based solely on that piece of evidence, but the family has corroborated some of the story, and that intrigues me."

"And you wish for me to go with you?"

"Why of course. You did say your wife has been preoccupied. This seems like as good a time as any to take up a little adventure."

I wondered if Mary would object. She hadn't before, but it's best not to assume such things. I decided to discuss it with her when I got home.

"What time did you plan to leave?"

"There's a 2 pm train from Paddington Station. We could be at the Swift estate by dinner. I sent a telegraph early this morning and secured a room at the Falcon Inn. Before that, I'd like to take a trip to Somerset and look up the Swift's family, just to have an idea of them. You can accompany me there, if you'd like. We could take a bite to eat at the Grill Room, if it suits you." It was offered off-handedly but given Holmes's lack of interest in fine dining when on a case, I knew he had included that option as a way to lure me.

It worked.

Mary was usually home around 9 am, I could meet her and pack a bag and be back here before 11. I told Holmes this, and he nodded and told me he'd wait for my return. If I wasn't able to procure my wife's approval to leave town, I assured him I would send a telegram. Holmes smiled at this, but I sensed no mockery.

"Let her know I would be forever grateful to her if she let me borrow you for a few days," he replied nicely.

Mary was accommodating as ever, though she chided me teasingly that she may not be so compliant in the months to come. I kissed her and wished her a good day with her charge.

I must admit to feeling a thrill at the prospect of gallivanting on an investigation with Holmes once again. Marriage and professional duties were a balm to my soul, but it was nice to feel some of that old excitement, only experienced at my friend's side or during the rush of war battle.

Holmes was waiting patiently for me, and we set off at once towards Somerset house's General Registry Office.

There was not much in the official files besides the record of marriage and births. Richard Swift had 4 children with Emily Swift née Williamson: Emma aged 26, Richard II aged 24, Florence aged 18, and Jonathan aged 10.

Holmes pointed out that this was a positive development because more witnesses in the house would make the situation easier to clear up. I agreed, and we set off from the records house, making our way through the colonnade where we ran into a familiar face.

"Mr. Harris!" I exclaimed, "What a coincidence meeting you here."

"No coincidence at all." He shook his head. "Mr. Holmes here invited me to eat lunch with you."

"Splendid. Perhaps we could take this chance to hear more information about the Swift family."

"That was the intention," Holmes commented wryly.

"And, of course, to enjoy the pleasure of my company. Is that not so, detective?" Harris responded with gracious humor.

Holmes merely inclined his head and resumed his stride towards our waiting hansom cab. We fell into step with him.

"I admit I was very overjoyed to hear you'd accepted the case, Mr. Holmes. I've been an avid reader of the few cases the kind doctor has blessed us with in *The Strand*. I know public personas are not always the most accurate, but I feel very confident in your abilities to clear this matter up."

"You're very invested, if you don't mind my saying so," Holmes replied.

"I am indeed. Swift and I have been good friends for years. When he purchased the house in Painswick years ago, our contact naturally lessened, but his happiness is very important to me."

"Admirable," Holmes commented as he swung himself into the cab. "So it is not a family home?"

"No, recently purchased. Twenty years ago, I believe, or thereabouts."

"Can you tell us anything about his wife or children?" I asked as I settled into the seat next to my companion and pulled out my small notebook.

"I'll start with the boys. Little Richard – that's what he's called – is, to be blunt, a ne'er do well. The usual shenanigans these idle, relatively wealthy young men get up to. Gambling, whoring, and whatnot. He had a bit of a scare with a young woman a few years ago and that shocked him a bit onto the straight and narrow, but he still bets his money without much care. I believe he's in debt to multiple people." He took a drag of his newly lit cigarette. "The youngest boy keeps his head down; doesn't speak much. He's doing well in his studies. Again, to be blunt, not the most interesting person I've ever met, but he has a more stable future ahead of him than his brother."

He fell silent for a moment. I finished scribbling - a comforting habit albeit unnecessary since Holmes was able to remember almost anything ever told to him - and waited for him to continue. When no other information seemed forthcoming, I looked up and prompted, "And the women?"

He blew out a stream of smoke, aiming for the open window. "Ah, yes, the girls. Florence is the youngest. Strikingly pretty and well-mannered. Due to this, she's been courted a few times by gentlemen, and one or two less than gentlemanly suitors. As of now, I believe she's tentatively involved with a doctor. She's charming. Everything you'd expect a woman to be. Emma is the older and the opposite in almost every way. She's beautiful, don't misunderstand. But she is what the bard, and many of her neighbors, may call a 'shrew'."

Holmes shifted, fingers tightening a bit on his walking stick. "And what has she done to gain this reputation?"

"Very little, actually. She doesn't smile much and does very little to encourage attention. She can be blunt at times, nothing I've personally found especially offensive, but I'm certainly not a prospective husband. And you know how these young men are; for all their talk of 'courting', they don't actually want to work that hard for anything. In my admittedly subjective opinion, she's merely awkward and cursed with an intelligence that women are usually encouraged to hide. But there is a definite reason she is 26 and unmarried."

"And Mrs. Swift?" Holmes asked.

"She was a widow when she married Richard. She's always been kind and supportive. Also very intelligent, but she tempers that with those practiced manners and amiable conversation skills impressed upon women at a young age."

"Do you think any of them could be involved in tricking or

manipulating their father for any reason?"

"Not really. I don't see any of them being quite capable of that. Maybe Little Richard, if backed into a corner, but I can't imagine what he would gain from this."

"Are you aware of anything legal that may be connected to this? Any will or inheritance issues?" Holmes asked.

"Oh, you mean the insane delusion strategy to oppose a will? I believe Richard drew up his final will and testament years ago. If he has altered anything, I'm not aware of it. His solicitor is Mr. Davies. He lives in Painswick, and I'm sure he wouldn't be opposed to meeting with you. I take it this is your current theory?"

Holmes shook his head. "I have no theory. Theories are formed as facts come to light, and I do not have enough facts yet. It's easy to overlook relevant threads when your mind is already predisposed to a specific answer."

Harris nodded. "Where are you staying?"

"Falcon Inn."

"Nice place, good food."

"Speaking of food," Holmes commented as we came to a stop near our destination, "Let's enjoy some lunch together."

Chapter Three

A few hours later, we found ourselves disembarking the train and catching a carriage into the small town at the top of the hill. It was a quaint, old area built from Cotswold stone and supported mainly by wool.

I had dozed a bit on the train ride, and was now wide awake, watching the scenery roll by slowly as we bumped and jostled our way down the road. Holmes was absorbed in a book, leaving me to my own reflections. I was just thinking of Mary and mentally composing the telegram I was to send her after arriving at our destination when Holmes stretched his back and shuffled in his seat.

The light was dwindling, and he set his dog-eared book down – a small, cheap copy of *Jane Eyre*, surprisingly – and folded his long fingers together over his lap. He pushed his foot against his small traveling case. Holmes always packed lightly but managed to look put together no matter where he was. He was finicky about his appearance, a sharp contrast to the state of his rooms. Even now after a long day of traveling, he looked immaculate, his trousers perfectly ironed, his double-breasted dark green waistcoat in fashion and impeccably tailored. How he managed this with that small carpetbag as his only luggage – not counting his ever-present violin case – was no small feat. I myself only packed sack suits for these adventures, favoring comfort over style.

"Look at these charming houses."

"Nowhere in the world is there more moral degradation than those charming houses."

"I find that hard to believe. There are parts of London that are veritable cesspools of crime-"

"Indeed." He retrieved a cigarette from his case. "There are some things afoot in London that would give these isolated country homes a run for their money for cold-hearted violence." The strike of the match against the wood of the rickety carriage lit his face in a bright orange glow for a moment.

"Are you working on something?"

"Dabbling." He waved a pale hand dismissively and took a few contented puffs. He was silent for a moment, watching the dark, wet landscape as we rolled by. "You remember the Ripper killings?" he murmured.

What an absurd question. "Yes, of course," I replied patiently. "Were you called in on those? I didn't think Lestrade had his hand in that investigation."

"He didn't. Abberline. I looked into it a bit." There was a grave tone to his voice, so vastly different from his normal lecturing baritone.

"Any ideas? They never caught the man."

"I have an idea. The police didn't want to hear it."

"Do you mind telling me? You've piqued my curiosity, if that's what you meant to do."

"It isn't ..." Uncharacteristically, he trailed off, staring hard at me. At dinner with my wife once, I had off-handedly wondered about my companion's lack of romantic entanglements. Mary had helpfully told me that many girls didn't want to court a man whose eyes constantly looked like they were cutting right through you. It was much too intimidating. Mary herself confessed to still occasionally feeling this way in his presence, even after all this time. Here in the shadows of the fading day, his eyes were clear silver, brightly visible. He narrowed them at me, that familiar and frustratingly clinical look transforming his face.

"Mary is with child, yes?" he suddenly said. The words hung out there between us for a moment, awkward and entirely too blunt for any respectable gentleman to just blurt out.

"What? Good God, Holmes," I blustered ungracefully. This wasn't something I wished to discuss with him during a damp carriage ride. "How did you know that?" I demanded though I'm sure it was a simple matter of deduction. The only other person who knew of this development was Mary herself, and I hardly imagined she had informed Holmes or even spent any time with him outside my company. The very idea of that sent a frisson of what I could only, shamefully, describe as jealousy. That my wife would discuss such a private matter with a man-

"Not that hard to deduce," Holmes interrupted my train of thought, and I tried not to flush with guilt at how quickly my thoughts had turned combative.

"She's not that far along," I admitted. "We thought it best to wait before making any formal announcement."

Holmes looked puzzled. "Why ever for?"

"Sometimes it's too early to tell."

He was still frowning, uncomprehending. Would this blasted man force me to spell this out?

"Why?" he started, then caught himself as realization dawned. "Oh." He coughed uncomfortably. "I see."

Desperate to divert the conversation back to the topic before, I began, "You still haven't told me-"

"Name?"

"What?"

"Have you chosen a name?"

"We haven't thought that far ahead. She won't give birth until at least the end of June."

"June ..." he murmured. The queerest look came over his face, a sort of dim disquiet and then a complete blankness, like a veil falling

over his features. He nodded to himself, "Hmmmm."

"Why did you think of this? While we're talking about Jack the Ripper, of all things?"

"Jack the Ripper is merely a symptom of a much larger problem currently in London. A problem I'm working on that's dangerous."

"Yet you have time for this?"

"A vacation, if you will. But when this is over, I think it would be best for you not to come around for a while."

"I beg your pardon?"

"Stay at home and be with your wife. She'll need you more than I will. I'm not trying to be rude, old man. But I'm asking you politely to stay out of my company for a short while."

"All right. With a caveat – you will come to me if you desperately need help."

"Only if it's safe-"

"I don't care if it's safe for me."

"And if it isn't safe for Mary?"

"I trust you."

"You shouldn't."

"I don't believe you would let any harm ever befall her."

"Don't say such things," he replied testily. "I'm not a magician. I'm not even official police. Harm falls where it falls. People disappoint you, Watson. Best to realize that now."

"Ever the pessimist."

He pulled his violin case into his lap. Holmes had few nervous ticks, but I had come to recognize them. He often clutched at that thing when unsure. "I waded into the search for the Ripper without you for a reason."

"I'm a doctor. I could have handled seeing those crime scenes."

"No. The blood and viscera, perhaps. But not the grossly efficient sadism of the tableaus. That's what they were, like art. I confess I couldn't stay in Mary Kelly's room with her remains for more than a moment. Shamefully embarrassing. Even found myself stammering a bit talking to the detectives, something I haven't done since I was a boy … Have you ever seen a gas explosion, Watson?"

I had; a horrific sight that I had no desire to remember. I nodded.

"That's what that room looked like. In Miller's Court. We had patrolled the whole area all night to catch him. And I stumbled across his work by accident when I noticed the door ajar." A look akin to traumatized horror arrested the detective's face for a moment. "I had chased that thing through Whitechapel for a little over a month. And all it led to was that room-"

Uncharacteristically, he choked off and turned his head sharply to look out of the window. I hadn't accompanied Holmes on the case, but as a medical man and as a man whose name - though not as famous as Holmes's – was able to open some doors, I had requested information about the Ripper murders despite my own newly wedded bliss. I remember the photographs of Mary Kelly's death, and I shuddered to think of what it may have been like to stand in that room and see and smell the blood, offal, and pure evil that must have permeated it.

I saw the consequence of it on my friend's face for a moment. Holmes had an iron constitution and a detachment from emotion that was at times off-putting, but I could clearly see that those murders had pushed him past the limits of even his clinical dispassion.

"And the investigators won't look into your leads? They'd rather let that man, or thing, roam free?"

"He's dead."

"What?"

"Jack the Ripper is dead. He was merely a butcher, low-level on a rung of a ladder that climbs much higher than him. It's a long, complicated affair and the truly guilty party still sits in his web."

"A butcher?" I pressed.

"Not a literal butcher. Nor a bootmaker." He fell quiet as if debating how much to say. "Have you ever wondered, Watson, how the Ripper managed to spend so much time working on his victims?"

"With Mary Kelly, he had the benefit of being inside her rooms."

Holmes looked pained for a minute. "Indeed. In that case, he spent nearly two hours with the girl." His fingers tightened against the wood of his delicately stenciled violin case. "Two hours to smear her body parts all over the place. But the others were eviscerated outside, one in a yard with three entrances. How in the world could one work with such luck as to never get caught?"

"He must have a great understanding of Whitechapel's layout. It's alleys, its ins and outs-"

"The rotations of the police constables' beats?" he offered meaningfully.

My breath caught. "Holmes…" I ventured slowly.

He raised his eyebrow. "You might then understand why the government and police body may not have been keen to hear my conclusions." He seemed to visibly shake himself. "There's no use in talking about this. You said you were hungry. Let's get settled in our rooms and sit down for some dinner."

I was still a bit shocked but could tell the whole affair had strained my friend's nerves in more ways than one. I pushed away the last images of those police photos and coroner reports that I had sought out in an attempt to be prepared had Holmes knocked me up one night to join him in the hunt of London's monster. In retrospect, I had always been relieved that he had not, saving me from experiencing those horrors firsthand. I had not known that my dearest friend had been there himself, alone and threatened on all sides. I watched him dismount the cab and felt the urge to tell him how deeply it pained me to know what he had suffered, but the words fell silent on my lips.

We pulled up to the inn and entered the old, flat-fronted building. The ground floor held the welcome desk and a dining room connected to the kitchen. The rooms, of which there were only a few, took up the first and second floors above us.

Holmes checked in, and we were seated at a side table near a cozy fireplace. Holmes finished his cigarette and threw the stub into the flames.

"Have you ever thought about having children, Holmes?" I asked.

The detective was rarely caught off guard, but he seemed clearly startled by my question. He stared at me intently for a few moments, as I pretended to not notice his nails digging into the wood of the table. It wasn't a complicated question, in fact. He was 37 years old, after all.

After a moment, he scoffed. "Can you imagine me as a father, Watson?" It was a rhetorical question meant to dismiss the topic, but I answered honestly.

"Yes, I can. I think you'd be more than adequate."

He laughed, pulling out his cigarette case. "More than adequate? Glowing compliment, doctor. Thank you."

"In all honesty, Holmes. I think you'd make an excellent father."

"And husband?" he challenged.

I faltered. It would take an exceptional woman to put up with Holmes. We'd come across a few women who seemed tempted to try, but I doubted their ability to cohabitate with the detective long-term. Holmes could be charming, no doubt, but he could also be abrasive and cold, two qualities that often didn't mix well with the fairer sex. I'd also long accepted that my friend, beneath that sharp intellect, was plagued with that peculiar melancholy that afflicted some unfortunate souls. The medical community was growing in awareness and clarity about the condition, but remedies were vague and disputed.

"I'll take your long silence as an answer," he remarked ruefully. "And I agree with you. I would make any woman a terrible husband. And as it's unusual – and I daresay unacceptable – to have fatherhood without marriage, then I think you have your answer." He paused. "Why are you suddenly concerned with my domestic affairs? Do you have delusions of our children growing up together?"

"I hadn't thought of it," I replied. "I was just thinking that all men must feel the same level of doubt and stress I feel when faced with becoming a parent. Simply made me think of you and wonder."

I wanted to ask Holmes if he'd ever been in love with a woman, but the words were an awkward weight on my tongue. It wasn't something you asked so bluntly. In the course of a normal friendship, the answer would have already been clear. But our friendship was not normal, and much of Holmes' interior life was still hidden from me.

Holmes fell silent. The fire crackled soothingly as I waited impatiently for service. Holmes crossed his legs, gazing thoughtfully into the flames.

After a few minutes, his voice surprised me out of my thoughts. "A girl."

"I beg your pardon?" I asked, casting my eyes about instinctively for whatever form of the fairer sex might have caught my friend's eye. Perhaps I was more curious than a married man should be, but old habits die hard.

Holmes looked amused. "Not here. Your child," he clarified. "It's a girl."

"There's no way for you to deduce that, Holmes."

"Not a deduction. Just a feeling. You must allow me those occasionally." He smiled, and then finished thoughtfully, "A girl would suit you."

"A girl sounds terrifying," I replied ruefully. What would I do with such a creature that I know so little about?

"Yes," he agreed, lighting another cigarette, "I imagine it would be hard to raise a girl in this world that works so hard against them. But I'm sure you'd do your best to teach her how to thrive, not just as a woman, but as a free-thinking, intelligent member of the human race."

That wasn't at all what I had been thinking, and I felt another layer of worry settle over me. I only nodded though, hoping he wouldn't notice. The child was not even close to being born yet, and I was already panicking. It was normal though, wasn't it? Any sane man would panic a bit. Even Holmes would, if he were in my shoes.

The young waitress came over for our orders. I was famished and ordered a hearty plate of meat and potatoes, but Holmes waved her off.

"Do you have Beaune?" he asked instead. The girl nodded and left to get our requests in at the kitchen. I looked at Holmes questioningly. He smiled. "I'm all right, Doctor."

"You said you were hungry before."

"I've been put off my appetite a bit." I wondered if it were the talk of my future child or the memory of the Ripper gore. With Holmes, I imagined it could likely be either one. He looked up at me sharply, "Stop fussing."

"I learned long ago that fussing over you does no good." My dinner was placed before me, and I took up my fork and knife, careful to avoid staring at Holmes's wine glass being filled.

"You seemed worried about me when you came to visit me yesterday. Looking for a syringe lying around?" he took a sip of his drink.

"Of course not-"

"You needn't worry."

"I know."

"I'm aware of your thoughts on the matter."

"I know." I dug into my pork chop.

"You made them quite clear over the years."

"I know. And I'm sure you gave them great consideration."

"I did," he confessed. "Even in your absence. So when I tell you that you needn't worry, then you needn't worry."

I lowered my fork, shocked. "Have you ceased that disgusting habit finally? Have you rid yourself of that case and its contents?"

"It's been put away."

"It's still in your flat?"

"That's not good enough for you?" There was a dangerous edge of irritation in his voice, but I wasn't to be daunted.

"It's not wise to have it so close to you. Halsted-"

"I know what's best for me," he snapped, a little too loudly even for our private corner of the room. He caught himself, wincing. After a pause of awkward silence, he continued, "I apologize. I wish I could claim some deep wisdom and fortitude, but the truth is it has no effect anymore." As a doctor, I understood immediately what he meant. Many of the current medical articles discussed this very side effect. I nodded and hoped he'd go on. It was rare to hear him speak so honestly, and I worried he would clam up soon.

To my relief, he kept talking. "I had to up my dosage a few times, and I know that's not ..." He sighed. "I felt as if I were chasing after something always out of reach. It's not like the cases; they always feel the same. That hasn't dulled. Not much anyway." That worried me a bit. He downed his drink and tapped his cigarette into the empty glass. "Some of the alternatives I thought of to recreate the rush were shocking, unlike me. And after the Ripper affair, I found myself turning down cases in favor of ... well, in any case, I came to the decision that it would be best to simply forgo it completely."

"That is wisdom of fortitude."

He said nothing. We dined in silence for a while before he dropped his cigarette stub into the dregs of his Beaune and rose, gathering his coat across his arms. Before he turned to retire to his room, he tapped his fingers on the table absently. Finally, he looked me in the eye. "I don't want to be around your child like that," he confessed. His voice was completely serious.

Here now, a year later, penning this account, the remembrance of that confession pains me terribly. That night sitting across from him, I had no idea that in a few short months he would be snatched from my life forever. That his familiar smell of lavender and tobacco layered over sharp chemicals would be gone; that an almost tangible sense of void would strike me randomly as a bright flash of grief at the oddest times. That he would never meet my daughter, hold her, or speak to her.

I also didn't realize then that neither would I. The house now is painfully empty as I write. Mary's things are tucked away in a chest that I can't bear to let go of. Her absence is felt in the agonizing silence, the sounds of a once busy house now dead quiet. The only memory of my child a brief smell of her soft head before my whole world fell down. That's what Holmes said, didn't he? Harm falls where it falls.

In the space of a year, I would lose the only 3 people who ever meant anything to me.

Chapter Four

The next day we were up early and traveled by hansom cab to the Swift estate. It was a large double-story house outside of town. The cobbled pathway to the front door was wet with the winter rain, and our feet splashed in the puddles as we made our way up the few steps to the large porch.

We were welcomed into a large sitting room decorated with heavy rugs and warmed by a large fireplace. I was expecting to see the entire family, but there were only 2 young women waiting for us.

The girl perched attentively on the divan drew my attention first. "Soft" is really the only apt word to describe her. Her face was soft, her figure was soft, and her smile was soft. She sat with her hands delicately laid across the folds on her skirt. The firelight made her skin glow and her eyes appear a dark inviting green.

The other occupant of the room was nearly the opposite. Pretty, but wispy. She stood stiffly by the mantle, one hand firmly grasping the other across her waist. Her face was freckled, her jaw gently curved but sharper than the other woman's jaw. Her eyebrows cut a no-nonsense line across her wide brow. Her eyes were dark and deep-set, and the quirk to her strong mouth impressed upon me a sort of detached intelligence. If I was correct and this was Emma, she looked much younger than her 26 years.

The seated woman stood for a moment and inclined her head, "Mr. Holmes and Mr. Watson, pleased to meet you. Please sit." We removed our gloves and shook their hands. I hesitated with the older sister; her own hand was bare.

I could see Holmes twitch impatiently, never one to enjoy drawn-out, polite chats. But he sat on the edge of the seat offered, elbows on his knees and fingers laced together.

"You are Mr. Holmes, yes?" The girl sat, gesturing at my friend with a curious look between the both of us. "Did I deduce that correctly?" Her eyes twinkled with self-awareness at how trite her joke was. It was a joke that would normally exasperate Holmes, but he merely smiled.

"Yes, I am Mr. Holmes and this is Dr. Watson."

"Oh! Doctor? That's right, isn't it?" She pressed a hand to her stomach in shocked regret. "Please forgive my manners, doctor."

I waved a hand, utterly charmed by her. "No worries, miss … Florence?"

"Oh, you hear that, Emma?" She cast a quick sidelong glance at her sister. "They know about us. I hope nothing too unpleasant."

"Nothing but complimentary-" I began, before being cut off by Holmes, who had obviously reached the end of his social tether.

"That must mean you are Emma?" He pointed, a bit rudely, at her. She merely inclined her head.

"You know," Florence began, eyes lingering on Emma before directing her gaze back to the detective, "You look nothing like those pictures in The Strand."

Holmes grunted with a wry mix of irritation and amusement, "Thank goodness, I must say."

"That's an actor," I supplied, "He poses for the illustrator. We didn't want too close of a resemblance to avoid undue attention in our daily lives."

"I see. Well," she smoothed her skirts, "I think those stories are just delightful. I've read all of them. You do plan to write more, doctor?"

"As long as Holmes is willing. I have a few I'm writing up now. I'm glad you enjoy them."

"My sister and I both read them. They're so exciting."

I looked at Emma. Her face was unreadable, but I remembered what Harris had said about her. "I'm glad you enjoy them as well, miss. May I call you Emma?"

"If it pleases you," she said matter-of-factly. After a pause, she continued. "Your stories are enjoyable. Though I find it hard to believe they really took place as you say. Some of the crimes are too bizarre to not be exaggerated."

"Emma," her sister scolded. "Forgive my sister-"

"It's completely all right," I assured happily, "Holmes says the very same thing. But nothing is exaggerated, I assure you. At least, nothing about the crimes. I don't quite have the imagination needed to invent those."

"How does Mr. Holmes tell you the same when he hasn't read them?"

My smile faltered a bit at her strange comment. I tilted my head, "Yes. Yes, he has."

"No, he hasn't," she insisted.

Miss Florence coughed awkwardly,

I glanced at Holmes, confused. He was staring intently at the older sister, a small, inscrutable smile on his face. Some communication seemed to pass between the two before Holmes pursed his lips and looked down at his clasped hands.

Miss Florence sighed, "Forgive my sister, once again, she thinks she's the detective now."

Holmes laughed a bit ruefully. "Don't apologize. She's right. No, I haven't actually read them." He looked back up at her, "Your deductive reasoning alludes me in this, and that's not something I say often."

I leaned back in my chair, shocked and a little hurt. Holmes had lied to me about reading my work. I bit down the urge to say something impolite to him here in front of mixed company, but from the set of his shoulders, I could tell he was aware that we would have words later.

"It wasn't deductive reasoning," Emma was saying, "I just understand how terrifying it would be to read about yourself through someone else's eyes. Like stepping outside yourself. I would be scared to experience that too."

Her younger sister laughed with that sort of loud awkwardness that often plagued those more aware of social manners; she stood quickly. "I'm sure the detective is not scared of anything, Emma. Now let's get some tea in here for our visitors. We're being rude." Holmes was forced to lean back as her skirts passed him on the way to the bell-rope, and for a minute he looked utterly confused and out of his depths.

I decided to brave on. I had lived with Holmes for years; I was accustomed to strange social encounters. "Miss Emma, Harris told us you were learning the piano."

She shifted a bit on her feet, looking a little less stiff suddenly. "Yes. I learned some when I was young, but I've taken it up again. I take lessons in town with Mrs. Knight. She runs a very small music school."

"Harris says you're very good."

"I'm not perfect."

"Hardly anyone is perfect."

A servant girl came in then, holding a tray of tea and sandwiches.

Holmes obliged to a cup of tea, sipping it dutifully before getting to business. "Now, I'm sure you're aware we're here because Mr. Harris asked us to come."

"Yes, to check on father."

"I suppose that is one way of looking at it. In fact, we're here to see if there is any validity to his claims and, if so, discover the reasonable answers."

"You mean you don't believe in ghosts, detective?" Florence smirked, raising her glass daintily to her lips.

"Indeed not. Nor do they factor into my work, even if they did exist. Have either of you noticed any of the strange happenings that your father has noticed?"

"No."

"Yes." The girls' two voices overlapped, and they each looked at each other with irritation.

Surprisingly, Emma had answered in the affirmative, so Holmes directed his attention to her. "What have you noticed?"

"Items out of place in the morning."

"Trifles," Florence sighed, "Nothing that there couldn't be a rational explanation for."

"I do believe there is a rational explanation, but that does not mean I did not observe what I observed."

"Like what?" Holmes asked.

"Here," she gestured for him to join her. He stood and approached the fireplace. With Holmes now standing next to her, I was struck by how short she was, barely to his shoulder. She pointed to the mantle. "This clock was moved, like this." She pushed the large brass clock a few inches to the left. Her sister laughed.

"Emma, a clock moved a few inches is hardly something to get so worked up about."

"I'm not worked up. The detective asked a question, and I'm answering it." She picked up the clock. Her hand was small, and I saw her struggle a bit with it. "Feel how heavy it is, Mr. Holmes." He took the clock out of her hands and hmmmmed a bit. "All these items are heavy," she continued, gesturing to the few ornaments, "Most made of brass. These items do not move on their own. Here, you can even see the worn marks on the mantle where the clock always sits."

Holmes ran his hand over the place. "Your maid doesn't move these when she polishes the wood," he remarked. "You're right, I can feel where the clock has sat for a considerable amount of time." He set the item back, carefully arranging it in its spot. "Have you noticed anything else?"

"Other items moved, food missing. One piece from a set of pens is missing from the study. No one can find it."

Holmes glanced at Florence. "You do not believe any of this?"

Florence fluttered her hands airily, "I do not believe or disbelieve. But I do worry about indulging what may simply be my father's fancies. He is old and getting older. And I don't want him to be a laughingstock."

"I hear things too," Emma continued before we could reply. "At night, like shuffling. And doors creaking."

"I've heard that too," Florence nodded. "But it could very well be father roaming or Richard coming and going without wanting all of us to know."

"Once I was here on my own, reading in my bedchambers, and I swore I heard a loud scraping. Agatha, my lady's-maid, was with me and she heard it too. We came down here to the sitting room but there was nothing here."

"You came down here on your own?" I commented, "With just your maid?"

"The butler and servant boys were already in bed. Agatha and I were the only ones here."

"And why were you here on your own?" Holmes asked.

"Oh, Emma abhors balls and social events of any kind. A sort of misanthrope," Florence supplied, a twinkle in her eye and a mischievous glance at her older sister.

Emma sighed, "I do not dislike people. I merely find all of it exhausting."

"All of what?" I responded, curious. "Dancing?"

She looked frustrated for a moment, searching for the right words. "No, I-" she broke off and gave Holmes a knowing look. "He understands what I mean."

Holmes raised his eyebrows in surprise. I turned to him expectantly, as if waiting on an interpreter to translate some foreign language. He merely nodded at her, looking a little off step.

"You're very forthcoming," he murmured after a moment. There was no censure in his voice. Yes, she was. I had immediately noticed that sort of sharp logic behind her eyes – very unsettling in a woman – and had recognized how similar she was in that regard to my friend. But in this aspect, they were opposites. Holmes was not a forthcoming man. He never felt obliged to express his thoughts or feelings, and could erect a façade so impenetrable that even a close ally like myself had given up trying to find my way around it. Now, with her relatively innocent observation, he seemed on edge, like a game animal hearing the rustling of paws in the undergrowth.

At the tenseness of his tone, Emma looked uncertain for a moment. "Yes, I've been told this. Another reason I choose to forgo many social events. I have a hard time understanding why people find my conversation uncomfortable."

"Oh, she's always just so honest!" Florence explained with affectionate disappointment. "Really puts men off." She broke off with a blush when she realized that she too was being perhaps a bit more honest than socially acceptable at the moment. "I mean … Oh, I'm sorry."

Holmes smiled. "It's all right. This isn't a social event, and my bread and butter relies on forthright honesty. On that note, is your father-"

The doors opened at that moment. A tall distinguished man, the butler, I assumed, entered. He was trailed by a very robust man in a wheelchair and an elegant woman.

"Mr. and Mrs. Swift." The butler bowed and left promptly, closing the double doors behind him with a soft click.

Holmes strode forward and clasped the man's hand. "Sherlock Holmes. My colleague, Doctor Watson."

Mr. Swift shook vigorously and then shooed my friend out of the way. His wheelchair was large, and we struggled to move to allow him space to navigate between the furniture. Holmes stepped aside, crowding the girls a bit. The older gentleman made his way to the couch, opening a cigar box and lighting it. Mrs. Swift sat next to him, arranging her skirts and smiling pleasantly at us.

Florence sat next to her mother but Emma stood at her father's shoulder, like a protective sentinel. We introduced ourselves to the lady of the house, who expressed her thanks for our call.

Holmes and I sat. "Mr. Swift," the detective started, all business, "We were asked to come to visit you by your friend Mr. Harris."

"Yes, yes. Michael, the old chap. I haven't seen him in years. But it's good to see you, Mr ..." he trailed off, looking confused.

"Holmes, sir." The detective hesitated, then continued, "You don't know me, Mr. Swift. We've never met before."

The man across from us looked relieved. "Quite right. I knew that."

"Of course," my friend answered smoothly. I saw Florence and her mother exchange worried glances. "Can you tell me a bit about the events that worried you enough to write to Harris?"

"Oh, you mean the haunting?"

Holmes faltered, then glanced at Mrs. Swift. "Yes, the haunting, if you will. What have you noticed?"

"Things moved. My dressing gowns worn and rumpled. Once I do believe I awoke to the ghost standing right over me. By the time I woke Eloise to help me sit up, it had vanished."

"Vanished?" Holmes leaned forward. "What did it look like?"

"A dark amorphous shadow. With spindly arms coming towards me."

Holmes sat back. This was certainly untrue. The imagination of a sick man. The detective was quiet for a long time.

"Papa often misremembers things, but they are not pure imagination," Emma supplied.

Mr. Swift grabbed her hand affectionately but shook it with reproof. "Hush, hush, dear. I do not misremember things at all! You all simply do not pay attention to what is happening around you. I try to explain the obvious, and you lot all look at me like uncomprehending dolts!"

Mrs. Swift settled her fingers against his arm, casting us a rueful glance that spoke of apology. "Dear, our guests are likely busy men. Let's continue our story before they need to leave."

"And you, Mrs. Swift?" Holmes asked, "Have you been paying attention enough to notice any of what your husband speaks of?"

She took a deep breath. "I have noticed some things moved about. But we have servants, so it seems to me that the most likely explanation is simply wayward help moving about the house after hours."

"How many servants do you have?"

"Twelve. A parlour-maid, two cooks, a governess for Florence, two lady's-maids, a valet, a butler, two gardeners, and two stable boys."

"I used to ride before this damned chair!" Mr. Swift broke in.

"But you still keep horses?" Holmes responded, carefully sidestepping our host's burst of frustration. I understood it perfectly; I felt a stab of pain for the older man, so clearly once full of vigor and now suffering the cage of a broken body and disjointed mind.

"Florence and Emma still ride," Mrs. Swift explained.

"I ride side-saddle but Emma doesn't," Florence offered, grinning.

"Florence!" her mother scolded.

"Sorry, mama."

Holmes cleared his throat. "Any person or persons you can think of that may be playing a cruel joke on you? Any enemies?"

"We had to let a few servant boys go last summer because…" Mrs. Swift seemed unsure how much to reveal. Holmes arched an eyebrow at her expectantly. "Well, they were involving our son, Little Richard, in some gambling, and we felt it better they be removed."

"What became of them?"

"One moved to Lancashire and got employment there. The other, I believe, made his way to Scotland."

"And your son? What is he like?"

"Oh, a black sheep and a loafer if there ever was one!" his father declared. "Gambles away money like it's worthless. Then takes any winnings he has and spends them on whores."

"Papa," Emma hushed.

"What, what?" he waved off, "The doctors here know what whores are."

Florence poked her mother in the side, eyes wide.

Holmes twisted his hat in his hand, clear amusement on his face. I could see he was fighting not to laugh. I, for my part, felt my face flush with embarrassment.

"Indeed, I think we all know," Holmes reassured. "Does your son still engage in this lifestyle?"

"Well, he almost got a little servant girl in the family way a few months ago. Thankfully, nothing came of it. Her parents packed her up and sent her to her aunt in Bath. I think it jostled him a bit, especially knowing I would not have tolerated his abandoning the poor thing. He's been better-behaved, I suppose."

"Reformed?"

"I wouldn't go that far. I'm sure he'll grow restless soon enough and cause us more trouble. A bit like his grandfather. That man was incorrigible! One time, he left for an entire month-"

Emma placed her hand gently on her father's shoulder. He broke off from his reminisces and sighed. "My family thinks I ramble too much about the past. Sometimes it feels more real than anything in the here and now." Emma's fingers tightened reassuringly. He patted her hand. "In any case, as much as a disappointment my namesake has proven himself to be, my two girls here are my pride and joy. Such sweet things. Even if Emma here will never give me grandchildren."

Emma sighed and removed her hand.

"Oh, that's not-" I began, moved to defend the young girl.

"It's all right," Emma cut me off.

"It's absolutely not all right!" Mr. Swift argued. "A pretty girl like you! You should have suitors breaking down my doors, and yet none want to give me grandchildren." He looked at both of us, the peculiar unfocused look in his eye that I recognized as a sign of his deteriorating cognitive functions. "Either of you would have children with her, would you not?"

Holmes, who until that point at watched this all with that sparkle of amusement in his eye, now flushed and stammered for an answer. I couldn't help myself, I laughed, more in disbelief at the absurdity of the whole ordeal, but Mrs. Swift's face twisted into pained chagrin, and she leaned forward as if to block her husband from our view.

Florence stood suddenly. "I think we could do with a fresh pot of tea," she declared and weaved through the room, saving us all. Holmes leant back and then stared at Emma, who seemed the least flustered. When she caught Holmes's eye, she shrugged a bit.

"I apologize for my husband," Mrs. Swift began, as Florence settled back onto the settee.

"Don't apologize for me." Mr. Swift's voice sounded small, almost childish. After a long moment, he started again, "I can apologize for myself ... and I do. I forget my manners at times. I get too familiar and speak out of turn with complete strangers ... you are strangers?"

Holmes nodded solemnly. "Yes, we are. You don't know us."

"Right, right."

"Do you have a personal doctor?" I asked, more to the lady of the house.

"We do," she answered. "Doctor Rikes. He's here often in the day and is on call for any issues that may come up."

"How long has he been engaged with your family?"

"About 2 years. I contacted him when I first started to notice," she glanced at her husband, "some decline. He has experience with both back ailments and dementia."

"I don't have dementia," her husband muttered. "And I'm tired," he declared, louder.

Mrs. Swift stood. "I don't feel we've given you the welcome you deserve, gentlemen, but my husband is ill, and I'd like to bring him to bed for a small nap. We do appreciate you being here, and I and my children will supply you with whatever you need to help put my husband's mind at ease, whether it be resources or information."

We stood and thanked her. Emma and Florence stayed behind as she wheeled him out into the hall. Holmes turned to them. "Where is your brother now?"

Emma shrugged. "Likely out at the pub."

"It's early. Does he have a particular place he goes?"

"The Fox Tail, a bit in town."

"Is that just a pub?"

"Pub. Gambling," she explained dully. "The usual 'gentlemen's' club."

"Do you mind if we have a glance around the rest of the house?"

Emma nodded and led us out into the hall. "This is the hall," she announced unnecessarily.

"Indeed," Holmes commented wryly.

"I can show you my room, if you'll follow me." We went up the stairs. "I can tell my mother was embarrassed by my father's behavior. I tell her that she shouldn't be. He cannot help it. He was always a very talkative man, but his social graces have disappeared, and he can be a bit crass at times. It doesn't really shock us but polite company can find it unbearable."

"You admitted you were forthright, Miss, but your father strikes me as-"

"Impaired?" she finished or me. "Indeed. I do have the social awareness to avoid some topics in public," she explained drolly.

She turned to us at the landing. "My maid will be in my room; let me go in and mention to her that two gentlemen are entering." She went into the first room on the left. I inhaled a whiff of jasmine and honeysuckle when her door opened.

Florence came up the stairwell. "Is my sister escorting you around the house?" she asked.

I nodded towards the door. "Went to warn the maid of our presence."

She frowned, apparently confused by her sister's consideration for the help.

"Tell me, Miss Florence, what do you really think of your father's claims?" Holmes asked.

Florence smiled. "I think he's old but his imagination is as active as ever. You know, he loves ghost stories and bizarre mysteries. You should see the stack of books he has by his bed."

"So just a creative mind no longer able to tell the difference between imaginings and reality?"

"Perhaps."

"That's an interesting perfume you have on," Holmes commented suddenly.

The young lady knit her brow, "I have no perfume on."

Holmes frowned but let it drop. Instead, he gave her a discerning once over and asked, "How long have you and the doctor been courting?"

She stammered, "How-how did you know anything about that?"

"Harris mentioned that you were seeing a doctor and when your mother mentioned Dr. Rikes, your hand tightened. At first, I thought it was a negative reaction, but now I see it was more that you were attempting not to give anything away … common mistake. We expose ourselves more when we try not to react."

Something like irritation crossed the young girl's face, but Holmes was already looking back at the door as if curious what was taking so long for Emma to reemerge.

I felt sympathy for Florence, being so summarily deduced and dismissed. I stepped forward. "Miss, your sister has offered to show us around the home, but would you like us to call upon you when we get to your bedchamber?"

She nodded. "I'll likely be in my bedchamber, so simply knock. I have some embroidery to finish, so I'll bid you both farewell for now." I kissed her knuckles before she moved down the hall. Holmes gave me an annoyed look.

"What?" I demanded.

"Your doting is a bit much, doctor. What would Mary say?"

"That's not humorous, Holmes."

He shrugged. "I wasn't actually attempting to be. Developing preferences for members of the family at this early a stage seems unwise."

"Holmes, this is barely a case. And I haven't developed any preferences. I was just raised a gentleman. As were you – at least I'd hazard to guess you were."

The detective tilted his head at me. I wonder if the insult had dug into him at all; with Holmes, it was often impossible to tell.

Emma opened her door and bid us entry before we could continue our spat.

Her room was dimly lit by gaslight and warmed by the stove. I imagined in the springtime, it was very airy and well-lit by the rising sun. It was traditionally decorated and very neat. Her lady's-maid sat on the divan, absorbed in mending, though she cast an appraising but shy glance over the two strange men who were occupying this usually private space.

Holmes glanced around the room, moving over to the cold fireplace. It looked like it had been unused for some time. "You never light this?"

"No," she replied. "It doesn't work well when the downstairs place is lit. Besides, the stove warms the rooms much better."

"This shares a chimney with the sitting-room fireplace?"

"Yes."

He nodded, then lightly rapped on the marble and the wood of the wall.

"What are you doing?" Emma asked.

"I'm seeing if the ghosts answer," Holmes responded, smiling good-humoredly. The maid lowered her mending and let out a surprised giggle. Holmes winked at her and she looked down, resuming her work and blushing furiously.

"You prefer the city, Mr. Holmes?" Emma asked, apropos of nothing.

Holmes looked mildly surprised but conceded, "I must confess to feeling most at home in the heart of London."

"But it's more than feeling at home – you dislike these country houses."

Holmes hummed, looking under the bed without asking for permission. "Too large," he answered, voice muffled, "easy to hide things. In my experience, the most heinous abuses have always been behind the walls of these old sprawling estates. Too much privacy affords us too much secrecy."

"That's an interesting viewpoint. I trust it's not shaded at all with a cosmopolitan arrogance against country folk?"

"I grew up in an estate much like this. Nothing I think formed out of ignorance." He rose gracefully.

"Yes, I believe you. I suspect ignorance isn't one of your flaws."

He made a look of exaggerated affront. "Who's to say I have any flaws?"

"We all have flaws, Mr. Holmes. I suspect you have your fair share."

Holmes laughed but didn't contradict her. Instead, he asked, "Do you know the details of your father's last will and testament?"

I glanced at the maid, but Emma waved her hand airily. "Don't mind Agatha. You can speak freely in front of her. To answer your question, no. I presume he'll leave everything to mama, with some set aside for each of his children."

"But you don't actually know for sure? You've never discussed it with him?"

"No. Never felt the need to."

"Is it possible your father may leave all the inheritance to his firstborn son?"

"Not likely."

"It's extremely likely. Common, even."

"With the way my brother handles money, I don't imagine my father would let him control the estate."

"And how would you feel if he did?"

"I'm not sure. It's such an impossible idea. But my father would never leave any of us without security."

"Some fathers do so on purpose, to their daughters, that is, in order to force them into marriage," I interjected gently.

Emma shot me a perturbed frown, "My father would never be that cruel."

"If that's cruel, many men are cruel," Holmes commented. He seemed to be watching the lady closely.

Emma was quiet for a long time, but her silence bore an air of defiance. Finally, she raised her chin and declared, "Perhaps they are."

Holmes stared back for a moment before nodding. "They are," he agreed, "normalized cruelty is still cruelty, I believe." There didn't seem to be anything appropriate to say in response, so we let the silence settle as he examined the floorboards.

Finally, he stopped his examination of the room and leaned on the mantle. "How much money do you expect to receive?" he asked.

"I haven't thought of it. I don't think my father is near death – perhaps in this way, I'm too emotional. I understand he is very old – and I've never been without and don't expect to be so after my father has passed. He loves us, and he treats us equally. If anything, I'd suspect he may rethink little Richard's claim as a precaution."

"How would Richard respond to that?"

"Sulk. Brood. Soothe his hurt feelings with nights out at the pub."

"Do you think he'd find a way to fix it?"

She took a moment to work out his meaning and then waved her hand. "I don't think he's smart enough, to be frank."

"Of course. I appreciate your frankness."

"You're not offered a lot of honesty in your work, are you, sir?"

"Not particularly. I wouldn't make any coin if people were generally honest."

"Your clients must be honest though? Disassembling would be counter-productive."

He scoffed. "You speak too rationally, miss. People cling to their secrets, even if it makes my job harder. Even if they're asking for my aid." He looked down. "What's beneath us?"

"The ground floor."

He gave her a wry grin. "I meant beneath the house. Is there a cellar?"

"Yes. For coal and food. The gardener also keeps his tools there."

"May I see it?"

"Of course. We'll look around the grounds after you're satisfied with the house."

"Have you had any strange occurrences in this room?"

She shook her head. "No, sir. Any unusual things seem to take place near the sitting-room."

"But your father claimed someone was in his room?"

"A nightmare. Or maybe Wells starting the morning fire."

"Wells?"

"The butler." Emma snapped her fingers with sudden recollection. "Oh, Agatha, do you remember what you told me a few days ago?"

The poor girl looked like a fish at the end of a hook, gaping dumbly at the sudden attention. "Um, yes, yes, um …" Holmes shifted his weight and gave her his full attention. She faltered and fell silent, then drew herself up admirably and finally spoke without stammering, "I went up into the sitting room early one day because Will – one of the servant boys - told me that he was worried he hadn't cleaned up the soot well enough the night before, and I wanted to check before anyone noticed. And, um, there were two empty but used glasses on the sideboard that were not there when the master and missus retired for bed."

"And what do you make of that?"

"I thought it might be little Richard and a late night guest."

"Do you often correct Will's work?"

She smiled, "He's very young, sir. I see no reason to withhold aid from someone still learning. He needs this position, sir."

Holmes nodded, apparently satisfied. "How did you know the glasses were used?"

"Obviously, the glasses still had some small amount of liquid in each."

"The same amount left over in each?"

"Yes."

"Did you notice any other detail? Anything at all that could be a clue as to who the secretive partakers could be?"

"Um … no, I don't believe so."

"No lip rouge on the rim?"

"Not that I remember, sir."

I could see frustration brimming under my friend's calm exterior. He loathed relying on others' recollection of details, rightfully suspicious of their observational skills. He had spent years with me attempting to sharpen my mental clarity and strengthen the accuracy of my memory recall, and he still would not rely on my narration of an event or scene if it were in his power to view it himself.

Before he could interrogate the poor girl anymore, I large blur of white flew out from behind one of the decorative pillows on the bed and began tussling with the mending materials trailing on the floor. I drew back with a startled noise, and Holmes laughed.

Just a cat. I sighed, irritated at my own reaction in front of the two women.

"I apologize, doctor," Emma offered, sincerity belied a bit by the twinkle in her eye, "She likes to sleep under my pillows. I should have warned you all. She flies around like a little tornado when she's rested."

Holmes bent down and stroked the cat for a long while, scratching under its chin and speaking softly to it.

"Beautiful creature," he commented. The maid drew her legs back a bit, blushing, obviously ill-at-ease with a gentleman so close to her. The cat, intrigued more by this new person than the thread that was previously putting up a worthy fight, rubbed against my friend's legs, loudly purring.

"Oh, she likes you," Emma murmured.

"Animals like Holmes more than people do," I joked.

Holmes shot me a good-natured glare. "Most animals are more intelligent than people."

"Oh, I'm sure that's not true at all, doctor Watson," Emma countered with that unnerving no-nonsense tone of hers. "I like Mr. Holmes very much. As does Agatha."

I didn't think the maid could turn any redder. Holmes cast her a small glance, smiling slightly, and stood. The cat weaved itself around his ankles. We exited, leaving the poor girl to her mending without our distracting presence.

Chapter Five

Florence was not in her room, despite her previous announcement that she would be. Emma showed us around, but her room too was styled in the innocuously ordinary design of most girls of her age and status. We were not able to enter the master bedroom seeing as Mr. Swift was too ill to allow us entry at the time. Little Richard's bedroom was locked. Emma informed us that no one, not even the servants, were allowed to enter his room and the only key was always on his person. When Holmes asked if Emma believed he was hiding something, she flapped her hands in a way that told me she had grown accustomed to ignoring her brother's behavior.

I know Holmes could easily pick the lock. I saw his eyes dart over it, tempted, but he moved on as Emma led us downstairs to the dining room. Holmes ran his hands over the tables, the sideboards, tapping on all the walls and floors. He seemed dissatisfied and asked to see the rest of the house.

The kitchen was spotless. The cook was there preparing lunch. She was a sullenly unresponsive thing, obviously annoyed by our presence. The only pertinent piece of information we received from her was that food items had gone missing. She too believed it was Richard feeding late night guests.

"Have you seen the young master with secret visitors late at night?" Holmes asked.

The cook nodded, brushing Holmes out of the way of her way to get to a counter strewn with the makings of some very delicious looking tea sandwiches. I wondered if we'd be invited to dine with them. My stomach rumbled a bit.

"When? How often?"

"That impertinent little servant girl from the Bamford estate. She was always scurrying about with him after hours."

"The one sent away to Bath? Have you seen him with anyone after her departure?"

The cook shook her head. "No, but I'm sure the lad is still up to his old games."

Holmes looked around counters, opening the doors and pushing around cutlery and pots and pans. With an intense stare, the cook seemed to beseech Emma for a reprieve from my friend's intrusions, but the young girl merely nodded at the older woman.

After a thorough search, Holmes closed one of the cabinets with a bit more force than necessary.

"What are you looking for, Holmes?" I asked.

He sighed. "I'm not entirely sure. How many other rooms are in the house?"

"The music room and my father's study, though he hardly uses it anymore except to draft correspondence. Outside there are the stables, the cellar, and the atrium."

"Atrium?"

"It's very modest. I like to grow and tend to plants and flowers. It's right off the patio connected to the sitting room. It's a lovely place for solitude and reflection."

"It does sound lovely. I would like to see it, but first let's examine the last two rooms available to us now, even though I suspect they will be as fruitless as the rest of the house."

As we made our way back towards the music room, Holmes perused the portraits and paintings in the hallways. He didn't comment on them, though he did stop near one and lightly tug on the frame.

"What are you looking for?" I repeated, feeling like a broken record. Holmes obviously had something on his mind, but I wondered if it was Emma's presence that made him keep silent about it.

He sucked on the inside of his bottom lip. "Nothing very imaginative, Watson," he finally conceded. "It just seems likely that someone is able to make their way into this house undetected. But I can't find any clues as to where these secret entrances are."

"Maybe the son is simply letting someone in," I theorized. Holmes glanced at Emma, standing patiently by the music room door, but the girl had no strong reaction to my words.

Holmes gave her a searching, curious glance. "Emma, do you know what the insane delusion void is?"

She thought for a moment. "No, sir," she admitted. "I do not believe I've ever heard that before."

"It's used to contest wills."

Understanding dawned across her lovely face. "Oh, I see. So if you can argue that a person is not fit mentally when they draw up a will, you can contest it?"

"Indeed."

"And you believe someone may be attempting to do this with my father? Push him to make outrageous claims so they can try to contest his will?"

"Considering his age and his sickness, this seems like a possible theory."

She frowned. "Has anyone ever succeeded in that tack before?"

Holmes nodded. "I'm not sure what the data says, but I knew of one very old man who left his entire estate to his very new, very young, wife. The children contested that he was not mentally fit, and she had coerced him. Legally, they didn't actually win, but the woman grew tired of the conflict, forfeited most of her inheritance, and retired to a modest place in the country."

Emma opened the music room door, her expression thoughtful. "I must say, I feel conflicted over this. I can understand not wanting your loved ones to make decisions under mental duress or incompetence, but it also seemed disrespectful to fight against a deceased person's wishes."

Holmes hmmmmmd as we entered the room. "Yes, context matters," he murmured, already distracted by the new environment, his eyes darting here and there, taking in details that I would never notice on my own.

The room was not large. The main component was a large grand piano. Next to it, there was a modest divan with comfortable pillows. The windows of the room looked out into the surrounding countryside. It was a very idyllic and soothing view.

"Who plays?" Holmes asked, examining the lock to the French doors closely.

"I do. Florence attempts, but she's much more suited to painting and embroidery, two skills I lack, I'm afraid."

Holmes jiggled the doors loudly. "Music does have a certain allure to it that many other forms of art lack, in my opinion."

"Do you play?" she asked, looking not a whit perturbed by Holmes's roughness with their expensive doors.

"Violin, mainly. But I can play the piano. My mother was pianist."

I looked sharply at him; I didn't know that. I was aware his mother's side was French and came from a long line of painters, but this tidbit had somehow remained unknown to me even after 10 years of companionship. Holmes was indeed an oddly enigmatic man. I wondered if I would ever really know him.

Instead of keeping silent, as I normally would, I remarked, "I've never heard you play the piano, Holmes?"

He turned from the doorway, looking upwards towards where the walls met the ceiling. "I don't really have room in Baker Street for an instrument of that size. Besides, my violin is my forte."

He walked over to the piano bench and sat down. Casting me a playful smirk, he positioned his hands carefully on the keys and began a competent rendition of Beethoven's Symphony 7, Allegretto, a personal favorite of mine. I had heard his version of this song on his violin many times, but was impressed by his skill on the piano as well.

He trailed off, and Emma gave a small clap. "Very proficient, sir. I can see you practiced quite a bit growing up. I sense though that you are not very interested in it."

Holmes arched an eyebrow. "As I said, the violin is my forte. I appreciate all music, but to play and create my own, nothing feels the same as my Stradivarius."

"How in the world did you get your hands on a Stradivarius?" Emma exclaimed with an energy completely lacking the normal social restraint a young woman was meant to display in conversation with a man.

Holmes laughed, grinning widely. "Now that story, young lady, may make me seem very clever but perhaps a bit ruthless. Let's just say some poor pawnbroker with very little knowledge of musical instruments may have missed out on a great sum of money by offering that violin to me for 45 shillings. In my defense, I did consider telling him the value of what he had, but ultimately acted in my own self-interest."

"I would have done the same!" she declared, smiling.

"The study is nearby, is that right?" Holmes asked, rising from the piano bench.

"Oh yes," she nodded, "Jonathan will be in there with the tutor right now, but I think we can interrupt for a few moments." I had nearly forgotten there was a younger son, but this would be the normal time a youth would be engaged in various studies.

The study was large and richly furnished with books and desks and neatly arranged but obviously used furniture.

The tutor was a young man, roughly 20, who answered our questions perfunctorily. The young student in question, Jonathan, was sitting at attention at the desk, at work on some math equations, though he stared at my friend with barely disguised fascination.

Holmes did his usual examination of the room, ignoring the look of irritation the tutor kept sending his way at the disruption to the day's lessons. Holmes spent a few minutes at a hanging portrait, pulling it from the wall but seemed frustrated when he turned around.

His eyes alighted on the young boy. He stepped towards him. "Are you the master of the house?" he asked, and the boy giggled.

"No, sir, I'm only 10. Are you Sherlock Holmes?"

Holmes looked a bit surprised, "Yes, I am. Have you heard of me?"

The boy stood up excitedly and came up close to my friend. His tutor reprimanded him, but Holmes waved him off, leaning over and bracing his hands on his thighs to come eye level with the boy.

"You're the detective from the story!" Jonathan exclaimed, bouncing with barely restrained excitement. His sandy blonde hair was feathery like Emma's, and he shared her same pleasantly mellow hazel eyes.

"The story Dr. Watson wrote?" Holmes asked, nodding at me.

The boy's eyes widened even more upon realizing who I was. "Emma has read me your story at least a dozen times! It's so exciting!"

Holmes laughed. "What was your favorite part?"

"The part with the handcuffs!"

Holmes laughed again, straightening up and clapping a hand on the boy's back. "Yes," he winked, "that was clever, wasn't it?"

"Do you have handcuffs on you right now?" the boy asked; he reached out and fiddled with the edge of Holmes's jacket.

"I'm afraid I don't, but maybe someday you can visit me in London, and I can show you all the interesting tools I have. You seem like a bright boy who would find them intriguing."

I thought of some of the odd tools Holmes had collected over the years and made a mental note to supervise any visit of that nature.

"Oh yes, yes! I would love that Mr. Holmes." The boy was all exuberance now.

"Master Jonathan!" the tutor reprimanded. "I didn't give you permission to break from your studies nor to bother the detective with your prattling."

The boy looked chastened but still pressed a bit closer to Holmes's side. "Can't Mr. Holmes be a part of my studies? I want to be a detective as well."

"Being a detective is not a suitable profession-" the tutor snapped before catching himself. He flushed when he realized his blunder.

Holmes looked amused but annoyed. He patted the boy's head. "No matter your future aspirations, young man, math will do you good. In fact, I'm going to tell you a secret: all knowledge is vital to the detective."

The boy looked gobsmacked, glancing at his tutor for confirmation. The other man nodded, and we all watched as the boy scampered eagerly back to his desk to pick up his lesson with a renewed vigor.

We apologized for the disruption and exited to the hall. "Did you notice anything of interest?" I asked.

Holmes frowned. "None of the portrait frames have been dusted in quite some time, but one had a small portion on the lower right side that was dust-free."

"What does that mean?" Emma asked.

"I thought it indicated where someone would put their hand to move the painting," he mimicked the gesture with his right hand, "but there was nothing behind it. I saw something similar in the other hall near the music room as well."

Emma frowned. I could see her quick mind running full steam; it reminded me of my friend as he worked out one of these mysterious problems. "Perhaps there is something adhered to the back of the paintings?"

Holmes shook his head, "I thought of that as well. But no. Just ordinary paintings."

"So what other reason could there be for that?"

Holmes's grey eyes sparkled with excitement. "Someone is trying to mislead me."

Chapter Six

The stables and the atrium did not seem to interest my friend much, though he did spend time with Emma looking at her plants and listening politely and intently to her as she spoke at length about the seeding and growth process. Her work was indeed very fruitful and the atrium, with its tall windows streaming the afternoon light and beautiful foliage, was fragrant and very calming.

Once we'd spent an appropriately polite amount of time listening to her thoughts on horticulture, Holmes gently prompted, "The cellar?" It was the only room available to us that we had not yet seen.

"Yes," she nodded, though she seemed inclined to linger in her little sanctuary.

We met Florence coming across the yard as we exited. She waved at us as we approached her. "I was looking for you," she explained. "I suspected that you may have departed already, but Jonathan told me you had ventured outside."

"I was showing them my atrium," Emma explained.

Florence gave her an amused look. "Of course, I'm sure it was fascinating."

"It was," Holmes reassured. "I only beg your patience for a bit longer to look in your cellar. Tomorrow, I may return to resume my examination of the house."

"I can lead you to the cellar," Florence announced happily, but Emma insisted on coming along as well. Both girls walked ahead of us, shoulders bumping companionably.

"What do you make of them?" Holmes asked me quietly.

I watched them for a bit longer. "Both intelligent. Florence has a much better grasp of manners. Neither are overly demonstrative of their feelings, but I believe they care for one another deeply."

Holmes hummed in assent, but a frown still creased his brow. I wasn't able to question him further once we reached the cellar doors. Emma leaned down to open them, but I moved forward and took over for her.

They swung open to a much smaller room than I imagined. Fruits and vegetables were neatly packed away on shelves, and a wine rack only half full spanned the back wall.

"This doesn't extend under the entire house," Holmes commented.

"No," Florence answered. "The house is on a hill. This cellar is only under the elevated part."

Holmes spent a long time in this room as I attempted to engage the young girls in conversation. Florence spoke easily of the latest opera that she had seen months ago in a trip to London, but Emma sat on the cellar steps and watched my friend work. He moved shelves, examined the crease where the wall met the floor with care, and tapped on the cellar ceiling for long enough that even Florence broke off from her polite speech and frowned at him.

"What do you know of the history of this house?" Holmes asked, hopping down from where he had been balancing on an apple barrel.

"Nothing at all," Florence answered.

"Well, I think it was built a long time ago. But beyond that, we know little. The last family sold it to my father about 20 years ago," Emma supplied.

"And the last family was descended from the original owners?"

"I'm not entirely sure. My father would know … if you can get the answer from him."

Holmes pursed his lips thoughtfully. "Well, I think I've seen all I can see for the day. Would you mind if we visit again sometime tomorrow? When your brother is home?"

"He should be home after midday tea. Speaking of, would you and the doctor like to stay for lunch?"

Holmes waved Florence off and thanked her for her offer. "Watson and I have much to do, but we appreciate the invitation. Perhaps we could accept for tomorrow?"

"Of course. Would you like us to see you out?"

"No, no," Holmes gently pushed me, "We can find our way. Have a lovely day, ladies."

Once we were comfortably ensconced in our four-wheeler, I bravely decided to ask about our own lunch.

"I was thinking we could stop at The Royal Oak – nice little 16th century pub – and then head into Stroud to see Mr. Davies," Holmes responded. "What do you think of the case?"

"I'm not sure, Holmes. By all accounts, it seems that the old man is imaginings things."

"I'm curious, though, about the paintings. Seems as if someone was laying false clues. And you realize the implication of that?"

"I'm afraid I'm not following you."

"It means someone knows my methods. They can not only lay clues, but cover over them as well."

That was certainly an interesting idea. "But still, to what point? Nothing criminal has taken place. Nothing even overtly harmful. Just seems like the pranks of someone very bored."

"Unsettling a sick old man isn't completely harmless."

"That is true," I agreed.

"And that's the thread we'll have to pull. It must revolve around the master of the house."

That seemed to be the most logical route. I nodded and tapped my cane on the floor absently. "Was the cat important?"

"What?"

"You spent a long time examining it."

He laughed. "I was simply petting the cat, Watson. But I applaud your attempt to pay close attention. The devil is in the details." Evidently noticing my embarrassment, he continued after a long pause. "You're aware I had a terrier hound when I was a child, but when I lived on Montague Street, I had a cat – as far as anyone can 'have' a cat. They admirably defy ownership. Large fellow, a lot of hair. He came into my window one day and never left. He was very old, his joints already touched with arthritis. He died roughly 3 years later. He had such a calm disposition. He would lay his chin on my leg as I worked on my experiments or played my violin; nothing disturbed him." He gave me a sly look. "Really was an ideal roommate, I must say."

I shot him a congenial glare but didn't rise to the bait. "Did you name him?"

"Paganini. I called him Pags."

I snorted. "I can't imagine you keeping company with a cat."

"Why is that, old man?"

"Ones who have similar personalities often chafe against each other."

This time he glared at me. "Cats are delightfully independent and intelligent. And they rarely suffer fools. Therefore, I will take your ribbing as the compliment you didn't intend it to be." He shot me one of those bright, disarmingly pleasant smiles.

"If that appeases you," I shrugged. "How is Toby, by the way?"

His smile dimmed a bit. "He's in the land of the living but certainly slowing down. I offered to take him off of old Sherman's hands for the last years of his life, but the man didn't want to part from him." He looked peeved by that.

"Mr. Sherman takes good care of his animals. Besides, it might cause the old thing undue stress in his old age to be relocated."

Holmes looked begrudgingly convinced. Holmes's soft spot for animals was a strange contradiction to his professed adherence to cold, rational logic. His Achilles' heel had always been the defenseless, and I suppose animals inspired the same feeling as the children and maltreated women who had crossed our paths.

"A complication, Holmes," I ventured, "You say this person knows your methods, but anyone who reads my work will know your methods."

Holmes hummed discontentedly. "Yes, an unfortunate side-effect of your little stories."

"The 'little stories' you haven't read, you mean?"

He felt for a cigarette. I wondered, not for the first time, if he were aware of his own tells. "Enlighten me, doctor, why would I need to read your accounts? Either they are events I already experienced, in which case I have nothing to gain from them, or they are not. And in that case, I again have nothing to gain from them but an inaccurate representation of my work."

Or rather an accurate representation of you, I wanted to say, but I bit my tongue. "You're not curious at all to understand my thoughts and feelings on a case?" At his blank look, I continued playfully, "No interest in seeing what our adventures are like to a mere, common mortal like myself?"

He grunted, realizing he was out of matches. "I'd hardly call you common, Watson. Mortal? Yes. A fact I'm painfully aware of."

I wondered at that last sentiment but had no time to pursue it as we pulled up to The Royal Oak, a quaint pub with low ceilings and stone floors attached to a historic inn.

Holmes stepped out to send a wire to the lawyer announcing our visit while I found a table and ordered us some bread and cheese and the very strong Darjeeling tea that Holmes favored.

We were sipping the last of the brew when a small boy delivered us a message from the lawyer assuring us he would be available and willing to speak to us.

The town of Stroud was charming, with a lively market and steep narrowed streets.

Mr. Davies was a private lawyer working out of the attached office of his small home. He was in his early 50's, greying but still youthful around his dark eyes. He welcomed us warmly and once we were seated in the two plush chairs facing his desk, he retreated to a small corner of the room and retrieved Mr. Swift's legal documents from his safe.

"Typically, I wouldn't entertain inquiries about my clients, but I'm aware of who you are, Mr. Holmes. Are you working in an official capacity?"

Holmes nodded, "In a sense. Mr. Swift himself called upon me."

"Is that so? For what purpose?"

"It may be nothing, but the information you can provide for me could be invaluable for the thread I'm pulling. When was the last time Mr. Swift amended or altered his will?"

"Two years ago." He looked down at the papers in front of him. "Two years and 4 months, to be exact."

Outwardly, Holmes made no reaction, but I could see the sparkle of excitement in his eyes. "Is that so? May I ask what changes he made?"

"I want to be clear here. Mr. Swift isn't under any kind of suspicion is he?"

"No-"

"Because he's a very good man," he continued. "He may be a bit rough around the edges, now but he is the epitome of integrity."

Holmes waved him off, "I assure you, sir, we have no intention of causing problems for your client. In fact, I was very sincere when I said we were here on his behalf."

"Very well then." He started to read, "On September 13, 1888, Mr. Swift amended his will as follows. The previous will stated that upon Mr. Swift's death, half of his estate would be given to his widow. The other half would be split evenly between his four children, with young Jonathan's portion staying in trust until he comes of age. The current will now stipulates that half the estate be given to his widow and the remaining half be given, in full, to Emma Swift."

Holmes froze, obviously taken by surprise. I could see his mind processing this new information. He leaned forward, "Did Swift explain to you his reasons for altering the will like this?"

"I believe it had something to do with his son. He did not trust him to manage his own money. I believe he felt Emma could be responsible enough to provide allowances for her siblings while protecting the money."

"That seems a strange and awkward position to put young Emma in," I cut in. I tried to imagine young Emma leashed to her siblings in such a manner. The resentment this would cause would certainly hinder her and impede her happiness.

"Have you met Miss Emma?" Davies said by way of explanation, one eyebrow cocked wryly.

"I have."

"Then you may understand his reasons. In any case, none of the family were aware of the changes to his will."

"Was the lady of the house aware?" Holmes asked.

"Yes, she was fully apprised of the legalities of the last will and testament and, as far as I could tell, completely supportive."

"And does Mrs. Swift have her own official wishes noted?"

"Yes, upon her passing – presuming her death proceeds her

husbands – her half of the estate will also pass in full to Miss Emma Swift."

Holmes leaned back, falling deep in thought for a long while. Davies waited patiently, apparently used to long stretches of thoughtful silence. "And if all the family passes away? What becomes of the estate then?" Holmes finally inquired.

"Well, it passes to me. I'm instructed to donate certain sums to certain charities with a lump sum being left to me for my own use."

"A large sum?"

Davies shook his head, "A modest sum."

"And you're sure the children had no knowledge of these changes?"

"I'm only sure they did not learn it from me. But Mr. Swift is …" he searched for a diplomatic word, "… mixed up lately. It's not impossible to imagine he may have inadvertently revealed something in the fog of confusion."

Holmes tapped his fingers on his knee. "What exactly about the young Mr. Swift's behavior would have motivated his parents to cut him out of the will?"

"It's a well-known secret around here that little Richard spends most of his time at the Fox Tail, gambling and …" Davies cleared his throat loudly, "spending his money. He loafs about with a group of boys, some of his class but many from the servant pools of various houses in the area."

I could see Holmes filing that new information away. "Is the Fox Tail a pub?"

"Yes, nearby. Its activities are run by a shady little foreigner. Satine, I think." He eyed us critically. "Are you thinking of visiting there?"

"Perhaps."

"You may not feel at home?" he waved at our attire.

"Young Mr. Swift feels at home," the detective pointed out, "We'll be fine. What sort of gambling takes place there?"

"Boxing."

Holmes's face lit up.

Chapter Seven

The Fox Tail was on the outskirts of Stroud. It posed as an ordinary, if rough, pub, but led into an underground boxing ring through the stairs behind the bar.

It was loud and obnoxiously blanketed with a stagnating layer of cheap smoke. The floor was composed of dirt and peanut shells. There was a makeshift bar with barrels of whiskey, a cluster of tables with men dressed in that sort of gaudy expensive fashion particular to conmen and criminals, and a few doors leading off to private areas. The middle of the room was mainly taken up by a large circle pen wherein two men were currently doing their best to knock each other's teeth out. The crowd around cheered and booed, rattling the wood and stamping their feet seemingly in an effort to make as much noise as possible.

It was a horrible place, and I instantly wished to leave. Holmes was scanning the crowd and grabbed hold of one of the barmaids and asked her where Satine was. She directed us to the cluster of tables, and we wove our way towards it, dodging women serving drinks (and offering other wares) and drunk men.

The man in question was a tawny little thing, barely up to my shoulder. He rubbed his delicate mustache and looked Holmes up and down impudently when we politely asked him for some information. "Pretty boy and his bumbling sidekick will get no information from me. I have better things to do, money to make. Good day."

"I beg your pardon?" I growled.

"I said I am a busy man," he repeated slowly, as if we were stupid.

"I can make you some money," Holmes offered simply, unfazed. I wondered at how he tolerated the man speaking to him in this way.

The man turned back, guarded interest in his greedy little eyes.

"And how will you do this, little bird?"

I scoffed, blatantly eyeing the man's height in a way that I hoped made my thoughts obvious. Holmes looked over at the boxing ring. "I'll take your best boxer. Put all your money on me."

The man laughed, hand coming down on the small betting table, coins rattling. The other men followed his lead, guffawing as if just told the funniest joke in the world.

"You win this money, eh?" Satine remarked, pressing a finger into Holmes's chest. "How, little bird? You will get your nice suit ruined, *n'est-ce pas?*"

Holmes smiled, unperturbed. "Put your money on me and I'll make you rich. If I don't, I'll pay you what you lost." He cocked his head. "If anything, you'll get the pleasure of watching this coxcomb get his jaw smashed in."

"Ah, a shame," the man smiled. "It's a pretty mouth. But that would be entertaining, I think. I accept." He turned to his bookie, "Put Mr....?"

"Holmes."

"Put Mr. Holmes in the ring next. With Caruthers." The other man smiled gleefully, and Holmes and I moved away.

"Really, Holmes. This seems ridiculous. Just pay him."

"I don't have enough money to pay him, Watson," he responded, shucking off his coat and unbuttoning his waistcoat.

"Then how do you expect to pay him if you lose?"

He snorted, pulling off his fingerless gloves. "I don't plan to lose." He folded his clothes onto a barrel near the makeshift bar, and whipped his tie off. "I know men like this; they'll pick the largest fighter believing size means a sure win. I can fight men out of my weight range. I've done it before." He flashed me a winning smile. "Easy-peasy."

"Holmes, I do believe you're looking forward to this."

He smiled again, now down to his undershirt. "Boxing is a gentleman's sport, Watson. You don't have to look so scandalized."

"Not boxing of this sort, Holmes. It's beneath you."

He frowned. "This isn't new to me, Watson. It's a harmless diversion." He unbuttoned the top two buttons of his undershirt. "Especially since I always win. How do you think I helped pay for rent those first few years before your stories made me so sought after?" He put down some money on the bar and slung back a glass of whiskey that was handed to him.

"Yes, but I thought you were past these sorts of things."

He frowned, an edge of irritation stiffening his shoulders. "I think you're conflating things that needn't be conflated. I can box, I can drink. I can do whatever I please, doctor."

He turned and faced the ring with me, breathing out some of the tension he was feeling at what he obviously perceived as my mothering. He glanced at me. "Put some money on me," he ordered.

"I'm sorry?"

"Put some money on me," he nodded over to the bookie table. "Might as well make some profit for your concern."

"Holmes! I'm not putting money on you like you're a prized pony."

"And why not?"

"Just no."

He shrugged but looked a bit annoyed.

I did end up betting on him though. As he moved over to the ring to enter the next fight, I decided it would be practical to do so. If he won, we'd have more expense money. And if he lost, well then, I could always remind him of it for years.

Holmes was right. His opponent was the largest fighter in play, a hulking, shirtless man who looked as if he conversed purely in grunts and growls.

Holmes entered the dirt ring, flashed his opponent a winning smile, and just stood there as the other man took up a fighting stance. The countdown to the fight ended, and the giant moved forward, immediately going in for the kill. Holmes, surefooted and by all appearances already having a great time, simply danced away.

I wondered if his plan was really to just tire his opponent out. Surely, he couldn't win on physical strength. I had never seen Holmes fight, but no amount of training could allow him to deliver a knockout blow to a man with a head this size.

Holmes did indeed dance and dodge for the first few minutes. I moved up closer to the edge of the ring and watched him duck under what would have been a dismayingly powerful punch. He flashed that smile again and laughed when the other man growled in frustration.

"Are you going to fight, *beau ténébreux*, or ballet around for hours?" Satine yelled from the other side of the circle.

Holmes mock saluted him and dodged another blow, laughing as the other man's fist hit the wood of the ring with a loud crack. He shook out his hand and rushed my friend, who sidestepped him like a matador with an old bull.

This was fine and lovely and all, but if Holmes thought this man was simply going to pass out from exhaustion, this match was going to last forever-

Holmes swung under an outstretched arm, spun, and delivered a punch to his opponent's kidneys that made the whole crowd quiet in shock before letting out a collective sympathetic groan. Caruthers hissed but rallied, spinning again to do a one-two punch. Holmes didn't duck this time but blocked both attempts easily with his arms. Gone was the carefree demeanor from before. Both men were sweating, and the fight was now well on.

As I said, I'd never had the pleasure – if that's what it could be called – of watching Holmes fight before. He moved like the ring was his home, blocking punches easily, the thud of flesh against flesh loud and unpleasant even over the drunken clamoring of the crowd, which was growing more and more annoyed. It seemed most had bet against the newcomer and were slowly realizing they may be out of all their money in a minute.

The man managed one hit against my friend's face, but Holmes merely laughed and spun away, spitting out a bit of blood.

And then it was over – Holmes took two steps forward, too quickly for the giant to react, and swung a right hook with the force of a man twice his size and sent Caruthers to the floor, unconscious.

Silence.

And then the crowd erupted, mostly in anger.

I thought the detective may be in real danger from the losing betters, but Satine succeeded in hushing them, barely managing to contain the glee on his face.

Holmes exited the ring and was nearly side-swiped by one of the 'ladies' working the bar. She hugged herself to my friend's side and pressed a bottle of whiskey into his hand, which, to my surprise, he took a large swig of. I worked my way to him. He didn't have his arm around the girl, but he didn't push her away, smiling at me.

"I told you, Watson. A prized pony, indeed!"

He seemed happily wound up, and I eyed him a bit disapprovingly before staring hard at the girl. "Ma'am, thank you for the drink but I'd like to speak to my companion alone."

"Oi," she laughed, "I think he wants to celebrate, eh? Man, with a lot of money to spend!"

Holmes pushed her away, his eyes still bright with drink and the win. "Actually, my friend here is the one with all the money." He winked at me. "Pay the girl for the bottle of whiskey, Watson." He shoved the girl at me and made his way over to his clothes, still taking large swigs of alcohol.

She latched onto me, and I fumbled to pay her from the small bills I had while keeping my eye on my friend. She gave me an annoyed huff when it was clear the whiskey was all I was paying for.

Holmes was at the bar, shaking out his shirt, so I picked up my winnings from the bookie table and made my way over to him. He was buttoning his waistcoat and laughed when he saw the bundle of bills in my hand.

I flushed. "Well, you told me to bet on you!"

He clapped my shoulder. "Indeed, I did. And you listened. Wisely."

Satine accosted us as Holmes was shrugging on his coat. "*Mon Dieu! Tu étais magnifique ! Le joli homme est un bon combattant, non ? Qui l'aurait deviné?*"

Holmes smiled but some of the twinkle had left his eye at the impertinence of the man and the way he had sidled up too close to Holmes's side.

"*J'ai besoin d'informations sur un homme qui vient souvent dans votre établissement,*" he responded tightly.

"*Oui, oui. En effet, vous avez besoin d'informations. Bien sûr. Je vous donnerai tout ce que vous voulez. Vous m'avez fait gagner beaucoup d'argent et je crois que je vous aime bien!* But I must say, I can hear your English in your French, sir," he laughed.

"I can hear your French in your English," Holmes responded amiably, but I could see he was irritated by the implication that his French was anything other than perfect.

"You were raised speaking French?" the man asked.

"My mother was French," Holmes responded coolly.

"Yes, yes. I can see some Gallic in your look, eh?"

Holmes nodded curtly. "Will you answer the questions I put to you?"

"Yes, Mr. Holmes. As I said, little bird, I will give you anything you want."

"I'm only seeking some details about a man who often comes here. Richard Swift. The young one."

"Ah, of course, the young one. The cripple is not a regular customer," the man laughed

"Have you met the older Mr. Swift?" Holmes asked.

"No, but I hear he looks down on me for taking his money. As if I force his son in here to spend all his coin on whisky and three-penny-uprights."

"How much debt is the young Swift in now?"

Satine answered immediately, "250 pounds."

I whistled.

"Does he often pay off his debts?" Holmes asked.

"Yes, yes. It may take him some time, but he always pays up in the end, with a nice sum of interest," he grinned.

"And he's getting this money from his father?"

Satine shrugged, looking irritated. "How should I know this? I do not ask as long as I get my money."

Holmes bounced a bit on his heels, growing impatient. I saw him cast an appraising glance around. "Does Swift have a favorite companion here?"

Satine clapped his hands delightedly, "*Oui, oui*! Madeline. She speaks only French, but Swift and his companions always request the pleasure of her company, yes?"

"Is she here presently?"

"Yes, and for you? I will give you a discount. You want the private room?"

Holmes nodded, and I frowned, pulling at his sleeve as Satine moved away to fetch the girl.

Holmes dislodged me with a roll of his eyes. "She may have more information than Satine. One thing you can count on men to do around women is brag. Stop fussing."

The proffered girl was stout but pretty. She smiled, but it did not reach her eyes.

Trying not to be embarrassed, I passed Holmes some bills from my new winnings, and he began to move off to a back room with the girl.

"You will not join them?" Satine asked.

I walked away from him in disgust, grabbing a perilously rickety stool at the bar and slapping some coin down for a strong glass of whiskey. I hoped the robust smell would cover over the rank of sweat and other unpleasant things, but it merely mixed with it and put me off. I swung back the drink.

I kept my eye on the door Holmes disappeared through, but it was an intolerable half of an hour before it opened. The detective paused with the girl in the doorway, speaking intently to her. There was no trace of coquettishness or coyness in the way she stood or conversed with him. She nodded, responded with some vigor, and he evidently thanked her and wove his way back towards me.

"We can go now, Watson. You've been the spirit of patience," he murmured and pressed my elbow to turn me towards the exit. He glanced over my head, saw Satine walking towards us, and urged me quicker, obviously eager to avoid another conversation with the impertinent businessman.

Once safe in a growler headed towards our inn, I asked Holmes what the girl had told him.

He took out his handkerchief and wiped at his mouth where some blood still lingered from his impromptu fight. "Quite a lot. She's been seeing – to put it politely – young Swift for roughly a year now. He comes often with another lad that she believes is a servant of some sort. They drink and gamble and then spend the night with her, often paying her very handsomely from their winnings or promising Satine that they will pay soon. She's not fond of him or his friend. She says they speak too much and snore and will not let her leave. They prefer her to sleep the night with them. She's complained to Satine because it prevents her from seeing other clients, but Satine says they pay handsomely and makes it up to her each time. They speak in English around her, thinking she does not understand anything. Her grasp is limited, admittedly, but she knows they are involved in some sort of club, though she could not make out any more than that."

"She told you all this willingly?"

Holmes shrugged. "I paid her to tell me these things."

"And that's all you paid her to do?"

Holmes laughed. "Ah, Watson. What would I do without your constant concern for my everlasting soul?" He tugged on his gloves. He was smiling, but he seemed displeased at my implication. "Of course that's all I paid her for. Don't be ludicrous."

I felt shamed by that; Holmes had his foibles, but I knew him better than that. My nerves were strained by the noise and smell of the pub, and it was affecting my mood. "Who do you think this other man is?" I asked, trying to bypass the uncomfortable moment.

Holmes huffed. "The uptight little peacocks from good families who are dead set on getting up to no good often find compatriots in the desperation of the working class. The poor drink and carouse to appease their pain; the rich do so for pure enjoyment. They know they will suffer little consequence and always have a warm bed and security to come home to," he explained with some heat. He pointed to the soft webbing between his index finger and thumb. "Madeline also said that both men had a tattoo on their hands. When she asked what it was, they made up stories, mocking her, so she never asked again."

"We can perhaps get a peek of it tomorrow when we meet the young man."

"Yes," he agreed, "but now, let's retire and have some dinner. I have a suspicion that our meeting with the young Mr. Swift will be exhausting."

Chapter Eight

We dined for lunch with the family the next day. We spoke little of the case, listening politely to Mr. Swift as he regaled us with tales of his youth, which he spoke of with a clarity that seemed to pain his wife.

His namesake did not appear at lunch, and we weren't entirely sure if he was even home.

After dining, we went to the master bedroom, in truth 2 separate rooms, one belonging to Mrs. Swift and the other to her husband, conjoined by a small living space and personal dining area.

The women of the house escorted us and watched with similar looks of cool curiosity as Holmes set about analyzing every inch of the room with deft fingers and a magnifying glass.

"You don't share a bed?" Holmes asked bluntly, on his hands and knees examining the carpet.

Mrs. Swift blushed. "We have always had separate rooms, Mr. Holmes."

"On the night your husband described the spectral intruder, were you in your own bed?"

I glanced apologetically at the woman, but despite her and her daughters' vaguely uncomfortable expressions, she answered, "I was in my own bed, sir. I heard his exclamations and some rustling that alarmed me, so I entered his quarters to calm him."

"Did you see anything amiss?"

"I did not, but I did take time to put on my robe and slippers." At his questioning look, she explained, "My husband is often restless, I did not think it an emergency."

"Do you think enough time elapsed between his distress and your attendance on him for someone to have slipped out of the room?"

"Yes, it's possible. They would have been quick, however."

After a moment, the door opened and a young servant boy, I would guess his age to be about 13 years, entered and looked startled at the mixed company.

Mrs. Swift made some elaborate gestures at him, and he moved off to begin loading the fireplace. "William is starting the fire for my husband's daily nap. Forgive him."

Holmes turned to the boy and caught his eye, gesturing for a while in sign language.

"What happened to his hearing?" he asked once the boy had responded.

"Childhood injury, we think," Emma answered. "He doesn't remember it himself. He's always spoken with his hands."

"And all of you know how to speak to him?"

"My mother and I do, but everyone generally makes do with notes."

"He reads?"

"Yes, though with some difficulty. Where did you learn his language, sir?"

"A long time ago," he answered vaguely.

"How many languages do you speak?" Emma probed persistently.

"Fluently? Six. Seven if you count William's language. English, French, Norwegian, Romanian, German, and Latin. I know only a smattering of Arabic and Tibetan, but I have little opportunity to practice them."

Emma looked astounded, sharing a significant look with her mother.

Holmes lobbied a few more complicated hand gestures towards the young man, who looked thrilled to find another who spoke his language. He responded with vigor, his side of the silent conversation lasting quite some time. Holmes watched intently, gestured 'thank you', and turned back to the women. "He says a few nights, he saw footprints in the fireplace soot around the stone hearth. He thought nothing of them and cleaned them up."

Florence shrugged. "That could have been anyone in the house. We don't clean the fireplace after use, as it's the servants' job."

The boy came and tugged on Holmes's sleeve, gesturing more. Emma and her mother watched interestedly. Holmes nodded. "He says he's sure they were men's boots. But he didn't pay any attention to the size or type of sole," he explained for my benefit. Holmes's mouth quirked into a grin, "He says he'll pay attention from now on and report to me without delay."

"Why does he know anything about this?" Florence asked, a note of irritation in her voice. She turned to Emma, "You need to get control of Agatha. She's becoming a gossip."

"Girls," their mother reprimanded softly. "Do you need anything else, Mr. Holmes? I want to prepare my husband for his bath."

Holmes shook his head, "No, I'm quite satisfied here. Excuse our intrusion."

We exited, followed by the daughters and then William, who had quickly stoked the fire, obviously more interested in following us than remaining in the room. He grasped Holmes's coat once again, already entirely too comfortable, in my opinion, but Holmes seemed unbothered.

He listened with interest to the boy then nodded. "Yes," he said out loud, signing to him, "Keep your eyes open and report anything suspicious you see here. I'm counting on you."

William looked absolutely thrilled, but Florence protested. "Sir, I know that this might be of aid to you, but I'm not sure I agree with you encouraging servants to be busybodies."

"Not busybodies, miss. Merely observant. I understand your

perspective but my own requirements for my work supersede our strict code of manners." He signed all of this as he spoke, in a touching show of consideration for the deaf boy.

Florence still didn't look entirely convinced.

"Besides," Holmes continued, "William understands this is not carte blanche to spy about on people's private affairs willy-nilly. Isn't that right, young man?"

William nodded eagerly. Holmes gestured for him to be on his way. He scampered off with a definite skip to his step.

"Oh, that boy's going to be insufferable now," Florence said with rueful affection.

"Speaking of, is your brother home?"

Florence didn't catch the insult, but Emma smiled. "He's in his room, we can attempt to gain entry."

She led up back up the stairs and knocked at the locked door we had passed the day before.

It was opened by a good-looking young man, though in a tall, ungainly grasshopper sort of way. He was pale and the small heart of his mouth was pinched and arrogant looking.

He gave his sister a withering once over. "Yes, my dear?" he asked sarcastically.

Emma glared at him. "These two detectives are here at father's request. They wish to take a look around your room."

"And I must submit to this?"

He spoke as if we weren't there, declining to make eye contact or shake our hands. Holmes gave me a knowing glance out of the corner of his eye.

"Papa wants it," Emma insisted.

"Well, whatever papa wants, yes?" he opened the door more but did not move aside to let us in. Instead, he leaned on the door frame and eyed us rudely. "So you're the famous detective?"

Holmes smiled tightly. "I'm a detective. Not sure which famous figure you're referring to."

"Oh, you're not Dupin?"

"No, indeed not," my friend responded amiably.

"What an interesting hobby of yours, Mr. Holmes. Running around poking your nose in other people's private affairs. I wonder what we could turn up about you, if one was so inclined to dig around."

Holmes held up a staying hand. "No need for threats, Mr. Swift. I'm quite capable of ruining my own reputation. We're merely here to help put your father's mind at ease."

"My father's mind is a jumbled mess. I think you're fighting a losing battle there."

"That may be true, but there's no harm in taking him seriously for now. Besides, you'd be surprised at what complicated schemes these little problems sometimes reveal."

"I may be a young man, but I'm no child. I'm wise to the world, as I can see you are." He gave my friend a sly look. "Though perhaps not in the same manner," he laughed.

Holmes swayed almost imperceptibly towards Emma and away from the impudent young man. I'm sure it was unconscious, but it always struck me – for all Holmes's occasional exasperated comments about the fairer sex, I had always detected a slight preference for their company. He was more comfortable in the company of women and had always appeared guarded and wary of other men, myself and his brother excluded.

"You can come in," the little brat finally moved aside. He blocked Emma from entering. "Ah, ah! Just the men, darling." He closed the door in her face.

I didn't comment on his rudeness, feeling it would be a fruitless endeavor. Holmes moved around the room without permission, looking closely at the fireplace and the picture – an inoffensive landscape – above it.

"Do you use this fireplace often?"

"Whenever I'm home." He came around the small table and chair and stood next to my friend at the front of the fireplace.

"Have you noticed any strange things going on in the house?"

He scoffed. "Besides my father wheeling around and babbling incoherently? No, nothing but the banality of domestic life, sir."

Richard suddenly leaned forward and smelled my friend's neck with a certain obscene pleasure. Holmes jerked away and then tensed, realizing he had fallen for the bait and given the young twit the reaction he wanted. "You smell like my pub," the young man smirked, "Have you been checking up on me? It's not like I couldn't ask around. You cut a memorable figure, you and your little friend here."

"What would you do if your father disinherited you?" my friend asked bluntly.

The boy shrugged. "He wouldn't."

"You sound very sure."

"I am."

"With the allowance you get now, do you save? Invest?" I inquired, tapping my cane on the ground.

Another blithe shrug. "A little here and there. But I think money should be spent."

"So you waste it?"

He gave me a contemptuous glare. "You cannot waste money. Its sole purpose is to be spent."

"And what do you spend your money on?" Holmes asked, turned once again to look at the painting with the cool curiosity of someone not actually interested in the conversation.

"I spend my money on what I desire, which are things all men desire." He gave Holmes another sly look. "Yes, Mr. Holmes?" he needled. He gestured at my friend's person, "I see your waistcoat and frock are very expensive. Well-tailored and fashionable."

"Your point?"

"My point is that you obviously do understand what I mean. You want something, you buy it, spending the money you have a right to spend because you've earned it."

"You've earned it?" I echoed incredulously. This young man had clearly never worked a day in his life.

"Yes, I've earned it," he responded with no shortage of heat. "Forgive me if I don't have to scrounge for change by slinking about with criminals and the underworld."

"No, you do that for sport," Holmes answered smoothly.

"Ha! I like you, old man." A calculating look overcame his face. He looked the detective up and down. "Emma does as well. Strange little creature, isn't she? But she looks at you like she looks at that piano of hers. Like she wants to get her hands on your keys."

"Sir!" I interjected, "That's your sister."

"So? She's still a girl. She'll eventually get herself bred like all women do. If it's what they're meant for, I'm not sure why we dance around it so much."

Holmes flinched with unconcealed disgust. Turning to me, he remarked meaningfully, "There's nothing of interest in this room."

Young Richard laughed again. "Have you been to Emma's room?" He flounced onto his bed, the picture of indolent relaxation. "Did you like it?"

"You seem to have an unhealthy fascination with your sister," Holmes commented.

A dark look flashed across the boy's face. "She saunters around here like she thinks she's a man. I keep telling father to marry her off and be done with it, but he will not listen. Curious what sort of gentleman will be able to untighten her screws and get her out of this house."

"Are you eager for her to marry well in hopes your father will no longer feel the need to leave her any of the estate?"

"I don't think that would hold my father back. He has some unhealthy attachment to those two thornbacks. I merely wish to be rid of her. Florence is slightly more tolerable, and she'll be married off soon enough."

"That's an interesting tattoo you have," Holmes commented, apropos of nothing.

Swift looked down at his hand, surprised.

"What is it?" I asked.

He smirked, "A Caduceus."

Holmes hummed lightly under his breath and then turned to leave without a goodbye, closing the door a bit more roughly than necessary behind us.

I took a deep breath, happy to be free of that room and that annoying boy's company.

"What an ass," I muttered.

Holmes laughed and patted me on the back.

Emma was no longer in the hall, and we saw ourselves down the stairs and towards the voices in the sitting area.

Holmes froze at the doorway, shoulders suddenly tense. I wondered at the shift in mood and stepped around him to peer into the room. Florence and Emma were standing near the hearth with a man in his late 30's, perhaps early 40's.

Dr, Rikes, I would presume. The man was tall and broad-shouldered, a shock a dark red hair on his head and very green eyes. He turned to look at us, and I saw clear recognition in his eyes when they landed on Holmes.

Holmes seemed to shake himself and strode forward, smiling. His congeniality would have seemed natural to anyone else, but I saw the underlying edge of discomfort.

"Dr. Rikes. Of course. I feel foolish I didn't recognize the name right away."

The doctor shook his hand vigorously, but his gaze darted across the detective's face as if looking for something. "Yes, Florence told me that a detective was here, but she failed to mention it was the famous Sherlock Holmes. I've been following you closely in the papers. I meant to write to you many times-"

"That's quite all right," Holmes waved off quickly. "How have you been, doctor?"

"Getting along splendidly!" he assured, but he still had that strangely intent look on his face. "And how are you?"

"Do you two know each other?" I interjected.

Holmes looked a bit uncomfortable. "We've met once or twice. Very briefly. I had some dealings with a mentor of his, Dr. McClaren."

That named seemed familiar. It took me a second to place it. "Oh, McClaren? The alienist?"

Holmes and Rikes shared a meaningful glance that I did not understand.

"You know of him?" Rikes asked.

"Yes, I'm a medical man myself, though my expertise is strictly with the body. But I'm keenly interested in the science of the mind and the growing field of psychology. He's been around for quite some time, yes? He runs a school for troubled boys still?"

"Yes, in Wolverhampton," Rikes answered. He was silent for a long moment. Then, "He mentored me, though I moved into the field of cognitive decline. I met Holmes here when he was using McClaren as a source in a case a few years back."

He and Holmes shared another strange look. "Yes," Holmes eventually agreed. "Very interesting case. I'll relate it to you sometime, Watson."

What in the world was going on? Holmes was being, at least to me, obviously disingenuous.

"Doesn't Dr. McClaren specialize in suicide and self-mutilation?" Emma interjected.

"Yes- yes, I believe," Rikes stammered.

Florence took her sister's arm, "Emma, goodness, this isn't proper conversation for mixed company. Please excuse my sister. We'll leave you gentlemen to catch up with each other in privacy."

Emma scowled at her sister but gave Holmes a curious glance as she was led out of the room.

Rikes cleared his throat. "Are you here to look into the master's mental decline?"

I was still feeling ill-footed from the strangeness of the whole encounter. I wasn't sure if he was addressing me or Holmes.

Holmes answered, "Mr. Swift seems convinced there are spirits at work here."

"You don't believe that, do you, Sherlock?"

I frowned at the familiarity, but Holmes didn't seem to notice or didn't wish to draw attention to it. "I do not. But I wonder if there isn't something more earthly going on to torment the old man."

"As a professional, do you think Mr. Swift is prone to hallucinations or delusions?" I asked.

Rikes shook his head. "Absolutely not. He struggles with time. He gets past and present easily confused. He also forgets his manners," he commented ruefully. "He rows with his son with abandon. No veneer of the English gentleman there anymore."

"What do they fight about?" Holmes asked.

"Money, of course. And the young man's attitude is atrocious."

"Yes, we've experienced it," I commented dryly. "How do you and the young man get along?"

"Honestly, I don't speak to him," Rikes shrugged. "He's unpleasant, and my job here is to evaluate and take care of the old man. That's my sole purpose. I guide him through mental exercises meant to strengthen his memory. I also administer morphine when he needs to relax or calm down."

"Not your only purpose," Holmes pushed gently.

"Ah, yes, I remember that nothing gets past you," Rikes demurred. "Yes, Florence and I are … well, I guess we're courting. Though it's been very slow and undefined."

"You're much older than her," I offered, hoping my tone didn't imply any insult.

"Indeed, and that does give me pause. But she's made it clear she's interested and has a good head on her shoulders."

Holmes frowned, either in disagreement with his statement or discomfort with the ease with which he involved himself with someone so young.

"But that relationship is inconsequential to your case," Rikes asserted.

"Do you have any reason to think anyone would purposefully be tormenting your patient?"

Rikes looked surprised at the suggestion. "Certainly not. I mean, Mr. Swift has no enemies. He's always been a pleasant and fair man."

"Pleasant and fair men can have enemies. Usually, other men who are not so pleasant and fair."

"That's true," the doctor conceded. "I've only been working with the man for about 4 years. But in that time, I've seen no evidence of any scandal or grudges. As I said, he and the son argue, but little Richard seems, to be blunt, too lazy for this elaborate of a prank if he's getting no real benefit from it."

"If he were getting benefit from it, do you think he's capable?"

"Yes … and if you suspect this has something to do with the will or money, I'd suggest you visit Mr. Davies and see how the estate stands. Now, I have another patient to see and must be on my way. It was a pleasure speaking to you gentlemen."

We shook hands and bid him adieu. At the door, he turned and looked meaningfully at Holmes. "Very glad to see you again, too, sir. I was very pleased to see you find your path. I would have thought to encounter you again as a famous musician, but I see now that detective work is your true purpose. You look very well."

I glanced sharply at Holmes, intrigued by the strange tone of this conversation. Holmes nodded, and the other man made his departure.

An awkward silence fell. Left alone in the room, Holmes glanced around and, his eyes alighting on the carpet between the sofas, let out a happy exclamation and fell to his knees. "See the indents, Watson?" he asked, pushing the table aside and pulling up the rug.

He hadn't given me time to see anything. He carefully examined the floor, knocking on the wood and digging his fingernails into the cracks. After a moment, that exuberance faded into frustration. He wrapped his knuckles hard against the planks one last time and tossed the rug back down violently.

"Nothing," he muttered.

"What is it, Holmes?"

He pulled the table back where it was, then pointed at the rug. "See there? You can see the indents where the legs have flattened the grain, but the table was moved a few inches away. It should indicate someone moved the table to raise the carpet, but there is nothing there."

"What does that mean?"

"It could mean the table just happened to be moved in the course of cleaning – unlikely – or someone moved this table to tempt me." He paused. "Or mock me ... either way, I am not amused."

Chapter Nine

We ordered dinner in Holmes's room. He picked at his food listlessly, his mind obviously elsewhere. After a long stretch of time, he gave up even pretending to eat and plucked absently at his violin.

However, his mind was not on the mystery, evidently, as when I dared to interrupt his thinking with an inquiry about the case, he seemed uncharacteristically confused and distracted.

"I was saying, Holmes," I repeated, "that this whole thing really strikes me as simply the younger son playing games to bother his family. Hardly something worth our time."

He removed his coat and rolled up his shirtsleeves. "I'm inclined to agree with you, but yet I find myself … intrigued."

"By the girls?"

Holmes scowled at me. "No, not just the girls. Watson, you really must learn to stop thinking like a romantic. Not every woman is a damsel in distress like in those adventure novels you read so often."

"I only meant that they don't seem the type to be easily fooled."

"I'm more interested in that tattoo. A Caduceus is the symbol of Mercury."

"The god of messengers?"

"And outlaws," he added, raising his eyebrows at me. "Seems an odd symbol for a group of young men to adopt, especially a wealthy young man. Unless it has some meaning to them."

"Young Richard seems overly enamored with a rebellious lifestyle. It may be a vain youthful wish to be associated with a more rough and tumble crowd. Madeline did say his companion seemed lower-class."

"That very well could be, but I wonder." He fell silent for a long while, staring into the fire. The flames reflected in the water glass at his elbow. At last, he pulled out his engraved cigarette case and retrieved one.

"Holmes," I dared, "what was the conversation with you and Dr. Rikes about?"

He rolled up a piece of paper and thrust it into the fireplace. He used the flaming end to light his cigarette. "What do you mean?" he asked, tossing the fiery thing into his water glass.

"You didn't consult with Dr. McClaren on a case, did you?"

He frowned at me, confused. He inhaled on his smoke, his hollowed cheeks lit sharply by the shadows of the fire. "It was before your time, Watson. Why are you so hell-bent on disbelieving me?"

It was a strangely defensive tone, considering that I had not questioned him about this before. "Because you're lying about something," I stated frankly.

He blew smoke in my direction, his eyes flashing with uncharacteristic anger. He didn't respond beyond that intense, intimidating stare.

I wasn't to be deterred though. "Were you a patient of Dr. McClaren, Holmes?"

"Don't be ridiculous," he snorted.

"How do you know him? It wasn't a case, I'm sure…"

He stood suddenly, cutting off my ruminations. If he had been any other man, I would have thought I was in danger of being hit. He looked angry, though controlled, and stared down at me. His hackles, and his guard, were well up.

"It's none of your business, Watson. Stop asking."

"It is my business. I'm your closest friend — your *only* friend, if we're being honest. Yet you keep so many things from me."

"You're not my only friend," he snapped. He stepped away from the table, pushing his chair as he moved. It scraped shrilly against the floor.

I wondered at this strange behavior. I had upset him, perhaps even insulted him. I tried to gentle my tone. "What I mean, Holmes, is that to be a friend, there's a deeper level of intimate knowledge expected. I only wish to understand why you reacted the way you did to Dr. Rikes today. It obviously means something to you."

He turned away from the window, stubbing his barely smoked cigarette out into the ashtray on the mantelpiece. "Get out."

"I beg your pardon?"

"Get out. I'm tired, and I don't wish to speak to you anymore."

"Surely, you must be joking," I spluttered, indignant.

"I'm anything but joking," he said levelly and then turned back away from me with an overt air of dismissal.

I threw down my napkin huffily. "Just fine, then, Holmes. Of course. I should have expected you to react this way." I stood. "Perhaps you do need to speak to an alienist," my shot was aimed to strike, and it did. He turned his head sharply to me, a startlingly clear look of hurt flashing over his expression before turning into cold fury.

"I'm sorry, I didn't mean that," I sighed.

"I said get out." His tone brooked no argument, and I moved wordlessly to the door, my throat catching on a sudden surge of regret. That had gone wrong too quickly; I was given no time to rectify it or change course.

Back in my own room, I heard him play a few jarring strings on his violin before an ominous silence fell.

I reviewed the interaction in my mind to understand what happened. Holmes never responded with such ire and hostility. If he did not want to discuss something, he merely refused or wrangled the conversation more to his liking. His unflappability was steady and reliable. To show not only anger but a moment of what I was sure was just barely restrained aggression was so out of character that it gave me a sharp pang of worry.

Something about Rikes was a sore spot. The men had clearly not met during a case; indeed, they had clearly not met only a few years ago. I remember Rikes's parting words about expecting Holmes to be a musician. That did not fit with their story.

I rang the bell and ordered a glass of whiskey, feeling the need for a little extra help sleeping. As I sipped on it, I did some deducing of my own. Holmes must have encountered Rikes before he was a detective which placed him early in Holmes's life. He also met him more than simply once or twice, as Rikes had gone so far as to indicate he meant to write to him. There was also the use of the strange *Sherlock* – the familiarity was obvious but almost paternal. This was also odd seeing as Rikes appeared to only be a few years older than my friend.

The late hour, the whiskey, and the stress of conflict made my head fuzzy and tired. I decided to retire, hoping in the morning I would realize that this was all a bad dream.

I slept like a rock, dreaming of nothing. I was awoken in the late morning by a tentative but persistent knock on my door. The sun was already high in the window, unfurling pale wintry columns of sunlight over my bed and night table. I groped for my pocket watch next to my empty glass of whisky and was surprised to see it was already a quarter past eleven. Stumbling out of the tangled covers, my head pounding, I wrapped myself in a robe and opened the door. Holmes was there, and I found myself unconsciously holding the door closed so he could not enter.

If he noticed, he said nothing. Instead, he looked a little rueful. "I took the liberty of ordering our breakfast to my room, if you'd like to join me. I called out for some newspapers, so I may be a bit absorbed. Your company would be welcome, though."

I recognized this as his idea of an apology. Or at least an attempt to move past the conflict without the unpleasant ordeal of addressing it. I nodded and asked for a moment to wash and dress. He returned to his room without a word.

I took my time, no small part of me happy to make him wait. When I finally entered his room, he had spread his newspaper across the settee and was, as he warned, absorbed in them. Breakfast was still warm, and it didn't appear that he had eaten anything at all besides a cup or two of coffee.

He looked freshly bathed, his silken dark hair pushed back from his forehead and his collar crisp. Over his shirt and waistcoat, he had tossed on a dressing gown, but he was clearly ready to depart at a moment's notice. There was a very small nick on the corner of his jaw from shaving, a slipup that made me pause because it was unusual for him to be careless. It was the only sign in his immaculately styled grooming that indicated anything was troubling him.

I made him a small plate of eggs and rashers, bringing it to him and placing it by his coffee cup. He looked up and frowned but thanked me quietly.

"What are you reading about?" I asked as I retook my seat at the breakfast table and dug into my own food. If he chose not to speak of our clash the previous night, I would follow his lead for now. But I made a mental note to return to the topic and not let it go as I let so many other things go in my relationship with the enigmatic detective.

"I had a realization last night that I was overlooking one obvious possibility," he told me, looking at me over the top of his paper.

"And what would that be?"

"Robbery," he said simply. "That would be one common reason why someone would want to gain entry into a home at hours when the family is not awake."

I chewed my food thoughtfully.

"But there is no evidence of theft at the Swift household."

"Perhaps not, though Emma did mention a pen set missing. I can't imagine it was worth much if they didn't report it." He wiggled his paper. "But there has been a string of burglaries among some of the surrounding estates. Minor thefts of silverware, jewelry, etc. The police are working on it but, to no one's surprise, they seem at a loss."

"You think it's connected?"

"It may be. In any case, I may visit the local constabulary today and endeavor to gain some more information on these events."

"What do the papers say?"

"Disparate accounts. One theft took place during a party. A wealthy widow's safe was opened and a treasured necklace stolen. Another house was robbed late at night, though there were no signs of a break-in which suggests an insider was involved. In that case, a very valuable silverware set was nicked. Another happened as the family was at Sunday services; a rare statue of Hermes that time."

"The method and items are different, but it does seem coincidental that so many thefts would take place in the same area."

"Indeed. The universe-"

"- is rarely so lazy," I finished.

He glanced up at me and smiled faintly. "Yes. It seems unlikely that this is all just a coincidence." He folded the newspaper and placed it aside, reaching for his coffee. Sipping contentedly, he eyed his plate of food with disfavor but snuck a glance in my direction and pulled it closer, eating dutifully.

He valiantly made it through more than half the meal before pushing it away, but I was touched by the effort. Taking up his violin, he started a lovely rendition of Tchaikovsky's sadly lambasted Swan Lake. It was a haunting piece and had captured Holmes's attention when we saw it in London a few years prior.

The melody was interrupted by a knock, and I rose to allow in the proprietor's daughter. She handed Holmes a telegram. "Just delivered, sir." She paused and then continued, "If you keep making those lovely sounds, sir, we may be obliged to compensate you for entertaining the rest of our guests."

Holmes laughed, unfolding the telegram as I gave the girl a few pennies for her trouble.

I closed the door behind her and turned around to see Holmes standing near the hearth. He was staring intently at the missive, all cheerfulness wiped from his face.

He read the wire at least twice and then leaned down and tossed it into the fireplace.

"What was that, Holmes?" I asked.

"Just a wire from Mycroft about some business in London."

"How did Mycroft know we were here?"

"I can keep in touch with my brother," he snapped.

I ignored his tone with valiant effort. "Is it about a case?"

He turned to me from the fireplace. There was a look of contrition on his face. "Yes, he's keeping me up to date with things unfolding there." His voice was much more level.

I debated asking why he felt the need to burn it but bit my tongue. I was in no mood for another round with him. I hadn't known him to get wires from his brother on a regular basis, but pressing matters clearly was not the strategy if I wanted any real answers.

I sat back down, my good-humor suddenly gone. I was once again reminded of last night and his stubborn refusal to treat me as anything more than a dutiful hound following him around, helping him track clues.

I ate some more eggs, even though they were cold and rubbery. "What is the plan for today?"

He stared at me for a long time, seemingly aware of my change of mood but unsure how to proceed in the face of it. Finally, he chose avoidance.

"I was going to visit the local police station and see if there are any details about these robberies that are not in the papers." He sat back down, drinking the dregs of his coffee. "Would you like to join me?"

"That's why I'm here."

He evidently didn't know how to respond to that, so he stood and removed his robe, gathering his frock coat and adjusting his collar in the small mirror near the bath.

"Whenever you're ready," he announced brusquely.

We could only catch a hansom cab and seated close to each other, we fell into a terse and uncomfortable silence. Occasionally, I was under the impression that Holmes was on the verge of saying something, but he would simply continue staring out at the damp but fresh-smelling scenery as if deep in thought until we rolled up to the small police station.

Constable Miller was a short, stocky man who looked at my friend with unrestrained awe when we introduced ourselves. He dropped his papers as he reached out to shake the detective's hand, fumbling to catch them with a curse.

Holmes leaned down to help him gather them, looking tickled by the attention.

"I'm so sorry, sir," the constable apologized, sweeping the reports back together in a jumbled mess, "You surprised me, that's all. I never would have expected Sherlock Holmes to simply walk in here and introduce himself like it's not at all out of the ordinary!"

Holmes stood and handed him the last of the pile. "It's perfectly ordinary to me," he commented pleasantly.

"Sit, sit, please. Doctor Watson, I presume? I am such an admirer of your work!"

I waved him off and took a seat next to Holmes at the cluttered desk we were standing next to.

"What brings you from the hustle and bustle of London to our little province, Mr. Holmes?"

Holmes tugged at his gloves. "I was reading some of your town's past newspapers and noticed some articles on a smattering of burglaries over the past few months. I was curious what more information you could provide for me?"

"Oh, yes. We actually got one of the thieves. A servant boy who worked in the kitchen of one house was caught red-handed trying to pocket some fancy plates. But he swears up and down that it was a crime of impulsivity and nothing more."

Holmes narrowed his eyes. "You think there's a wider conspiracy?"

"I'm not naïve enough to believe that pilfering isn't a common occurrence amongst the servant classes, but it does seem odd that there seemed to be a sudden rash of them over the last few months and within one province. All of them seem to be inside jobs happening at night or when the family was away – except Mrs. Lawry, whose necklace was also interestingly returned – so it's clear it has something to do with the help, but I think it's a more concerted group effort, if you will."

I could see Holmes had already had the same thought. "So a burglary ring with members of various households?"

Miller nodded.

"Have you checked the pawnshops nearby to see what items may have been hocked?" I asked.

"We did, and we found some earrings that had been reported missing but the pawnshop owners obviously have no incentive to reveal anything to us. In fact, snitching about their clients certainly doesn't help their businesses."

"Of course."

Miller gave Holmes a curious look. "Why exactly are you looking into this? It seems a petty thing for a man of your talents."

"We're actually investigating some strange happenings at the Swift estate."

"Things missing?"

"Just strange nightly movements, sounds, etcetera. A pair of pens missing but hardly anything concerning."

"Interesting. You think it's connected?"

"Possibly. Tell me, did the boy you arrested have any tattoos?"

Miller looked startled. "Yes, a strange one on his forearm. It was all windy, like snakes."

Holmes gave me a sharp, knowing look, before turning back to the constable. "What do you know of the young Mr. Swift? Richard the second?"

"Little Richard? Or 'Dick' as he's affectionately called by some," he said with an impish twinkle in his eye. Holmes and I laughed. "We don't hear much about him beyond rumors. We know he gets up to some gambling, a pastime we try to get control of around here, but it's not really our top priority."

"Yes, that's about as much as we know about him as well."

"I wish I could provide more help."

Holmes straightened, a signal we were readying to take our leave. "Can you give me the address of Mrs. Lawry?" he asked. "I wonder why the stolen item was returned. Seems very odd."

We were duly supplied the address and directions but once outside on the pavement, Holmes told me that he was going to head to the local library and parishes to research the history of the house.

He hailed a four-wheeler but did not follow me into it. "I think this part of my investigation will be uneventful for you. There's a lovely walk across Juniper Hill and into Slad village that I'm sure you'll enjoy. Perhaps we could meet together for dinner at the inn? Let's say 5pm?"

He didn't give me much time to argue or decline, promptly directed the driver and giving me an amiable wave as I was carried off.

Chapter Ten

I wasn't very interested in a walk, and especially averse to giving in to Holmes's dictatorial decision making.

Instead, I toured around St. Mary's for a while before returning to the inn and settling in for a few hours of peaceful reading. I was distracted and found myself rereading the same chapters twice; therefore, I missed lunch and dutifully entered the inn's restaurant to meet Holmes at 5 pm.

The clock struck 5 and then half past, and I tried to push aside my impatience. Normally, I would wait for my habitually tardy friend, but I was hungry and a bit cross, so I ordered a roast and butter potatoes with a nice sweet cabernet.

It was nearing 6 when I heard the door to the inn open, bringing in a gust of cool wind that I could feel even by the fireplace. I looked up, expecting to see Holmes, and was surprised to find the tall, ruddy Dr. Rikes standing in the threshold. His eyes landed on me, and for a second, he looked like he was going to turn tail and run. But then his face cleared, and he politely made his way over to my table.

"Doctor Watson," he greeted. "I was just coming by to see if Holmes wanted to dine with me."

"Holmes is currently ensconced at the library doing some very exciting research. I'm sorry you missed him."

The other doctor looked disappointed. "Oh … very well, then. Sorry to have intruded on your meal. Have a lovely evening."

He turned to leave, but I stopped him. "You can sit if you'd like. Holmes claimed he'd be here for dinner, but I'm sure he's been distracted. Dine with me, and maybe you'll catch him when he finally makes his appearance."

I got the distinct impression that the man was looking for a way to decline my invitation but could not think of an excuse that was not rude. He finally nodded in acquiescence, taking off his coat and gloves.

He sat with mild discomfort; I was not in a very charitable mood, however, my conflict with Holmes still chafing at me. I smiled amiably, though, and tried to put him at ease.

He ordered the beef roast as well and, as we dug in, I calculated how to begin.

"Holmes must have made quite an impression on you all those years ago," I commented, hoping my voice was the appropriate level of neutral curiosity.

Rikes smiles, stabbing a seasoned potato with his fork, "I imagine Holmes makes an impression on most people. Even just as words on a page."

"Oh? Have you read my tall-tales?"

"I don't think there's anything tall about your tales, doctor. But of course I have. I was very interested in what Sherlock was getting up to. I wondered if he would find his way to the musical arts."

I cut a bit of my roast and then rested my wrists on the table, narrowing my eyes. "You said Holmes came across you when he was already a detective working a case."

He flushed. "Oh, well … he was just starting out."

"When was this?"

Rikes looked startled. "Early 70's, I believe. My memory is not so good with dates."

"And what was the case about?"

Rikes made a show of trying to remember. "Let's see. He came to Wolverhampton looking for a missing boy. A runaway."

I put down my knife and fork. "I must warn you, I'm not as unobservant as one may think from reading my stories."

Rikes stared at me for a long while before slowly cutting into his own food. "Of course. That must be an advantage in your work with Sherlock, hmm? They're so worried about his attention, they don't see you at all."

I resumed eating. Now that we had gotten these trifling lies out of the way, I felt prepared to continue. "So if you did not meet in Wolverhampton due to a case, did you attend Oxford with Holmes?"

He cleared his throat and took a sip of his red wine before answering. "No, I received my degree a few years before him. I did overlap his brother very briefly, but we spoke little. We knew Mycroft was meant for something great. The Holmes name was pretty renowned already. Which is odd because I have no idea whatever became of him."

"Minor government official."

He looked unconvinced but smiled. "I see. Minor, you say? That's interesting."

"Sherlock never took his degree. He left in the last term."

"Well, I hardly blame him after everything."

I latched on to that but carefully avoided making any reaction to indicate I did not already know what he was speaking about. "Yes, after everything," I echoed, meaningfully.

He chewed his food and nodded, "It really was the best for everyone involved."

"Yes, everyone."

There must have been something in my voice that gave me away. He squinted knowingly at me. He fell silent, eating and drinking mechanically, mind obviously elsewhere but attempting to appear natural. I followed his lead, my own mind searching for a way to keep the conversation going.

Finally, he drew me out of my thoughts. "I understand, doctor," he started, crossing his knife and fork on his near-empty plate, "that

Sherlock can be quite reserved about his private life. At times to his own detriment. However, this isn't my story to tell. You put me in an awkward position."

I sighed and leaned back heavily in my chair. I spread my palms in a gesture of helplessness. "I've never even met his parents."

"His parents are dead."

The plates rattled when my hands fell dejectedly onto the table. Rikes seemed to realize his mistake and rushed to cover it. "His mother died years ago. I would imagine it's a topic he doesn't bring up casually after all this time. His father ... his father died about 5 years ago, I believe."

"So while I knew him."

Rikes looked rueful. "I only heard this by accident."

I gulped down my drink, feeling irritated and strangely rejected. "I would have gone with him to the services."

Rikes shrugged. "I don't believe there were any services. Mycroft handled the burial arrangements efficiently and quietly."

"Why?"

His face became guarded again. "I'm sure they had their reasons. Where did you receive your medical training, doctor?" he asked suddenly, with the overt air of someone clearly changing the subject.

I gestured to the girl for another glass of port. "St. Barts and The University of London. I was then trained at Netley as an assistant surgeon in the British Army."

"Your medical knowledge must come in handy in your cases with Sherlock."

I scoffed. "I'm more useful as the designated carrier of the Webley."

"Ha! Yes, Sherlock is a terrible shot."

"Indeed. He can tell the minute differences in red clay well enough to track them to their exact origins, but long-distance? He's hopeless. His left eye gives him trouble."

Rikes's smile dimmed. Something dark crossed his face for a moment. "… Yes, that's true … So tell me how an army surgeon comes to be invested in medical matters of the mind?"

I wondered at the momentary shift in mood, but I was growing tired. Interrogation was Holmes's milieu, and I was weary of it already. I also felt a pang of regret for pushing for private details behind my friend's back. No matter how irritable we may be with each other at the moment, my behavior was becoming inexcusable. "It's always been a passing interest for me, but in my adventures with Holmes, I've often come across people who make me wonder … what has to happen to some to turn them into these monsters capable of such horrific acts? I know the prevailing belief is that it is genetic – that evil is passed down in families – but I'm not convinced."

"There has been some research to indicate that behaviors can be genetic. It's the old debate, yes? Genetics versus environment. I think it's both. That's why two children raised in the same household, under identical circumstances, can still vary greatly in personality."

"You too still seem invested in the field of psychology," I noted.

"I am. My father devolved much as Mr. Swift is at present. He was much younger, however. This shifted my motivation and focus out of the field of psychology. It's an ignoble way to die, and I wish to help others." He leaned forward, "Have you read *The Principles of Psychology*?"

Our conversation settled into a discussion of medical books and the current discussions around neurological studies.

We were on our third glass of cabernet when Holmes returned to the inn. His coat and the bundle of papers under his arm were damp with rain. When he spied us at our table, he stepped over to us cautiously.

"Watson. Dr. Rikes," he acknowledged, eyeing our wine glasses warily. Rikes stood and embraced him which Holmes allowed with a sort of bemused amusement.

"Have a seat with us," I pressed. "Rikes here came to visit you, but I commandeered him to dine with me."

Holmes shucked off his jackets and laid them over the back of his chair. He seemed at a loss for how to stow away his papers but ended up folding them neatly and setting them on his plate. He declined dinner but asked for wine. "I have some catching up to do," he said jokingly, gesturing at the glasses, but I sensed a double meaning to his words.

He tugged off his gloves as the barmaid placed his drink in front of him. "You both seemed engrossed in conversation. What's the topic?"

"Esoteric psychology research. I'm sure I'm boring your friend here," Rikes answered smoothly. "But I really want to know if you still play, Holmes? Oh I know doctor Watson here described your violin playing in his stories, but are you still serious about it?"

Holmes shrugged. "Depends on your version of serious. I don't intend to take it up professionally, but it's a favorite pastime for me."

"I'd love to hear you again sometime. Your playing was magnificent, especially the music you composed."

I thought of the occasionally screeching concerts I had been subjected to when Holmes was in a particularly dark mood and took a casual sip of my wine.

"If I had my violin, I'd offer. Maybe if you ever get up to London." I looked sharply at Holmes and thought of the Stradivarius currently in his room. There was a caginess to Holmes's demeanor around Rikes that seemed even deeper than simple discomfort at my presence. At the same time, both men seemed to like each other, if the ease with which Rikes approached my friend was any indication. It itched at me, not knowing the history between the men, but I clearly had to resign myself to knowing only that which Holmes was willing to confide to me. Which was sadly very little.

"Ah, that's a shame," the man commented and downed the last of his cabernet. "I once saw him playing Bach, Partita No. 2 in, what is it?" he struggled.

"D minor," Holmes supplied.

"Yes, that's right. Bach – Partita No. 2 in D minor. I'm no musical expert but it was one of the most amazing things I had ever heard," he told me. Then to Holmes: "You remember you had that little boy sitting at your feet? Simply entranced. I think you may have changed his life that night."

Holmes gave me a side glance but smiled a little sadly.

Rikes, understanding that he may have said too much, neatly folded his napkin and stood. "Well, I've dawdled for longer than I intended, thanks to your friend's absolutely charming and lovely conversation. Perhaps I'll find some time to visit you again before you leave, if that's acceptable to you."

Holmes nodded, another look passing between the men that I couldn't decipher. He leaned his crossed arms on the table and watched the other man depart.

Holmes stared at the door he left through, but he didn't seem to be really looking at it. He reached for his wine glass, and I noticed the slight tremor of nervous energy in his hands. I felt suddenly sorry for him.

"Are you going to order dinner?" I asked casually.

"You've already eaten," he observed. "I apologize for being late, I lost track of the time."

"I can sit here with you. In fact, I heard they have some very nice cider cake I might try," I beckoned to the girl and ordered a slice and a coffee with cream, and Holmes asked for the same.

"Did you find anything of interest?" I asked.

He pulled the little bundle of notes towards him. "Not really," he lamented, despite the fact that there were plenty of notations on the papers. "It's a very old house, built in the 16th century by a wealthy family. Very little is known about them, and the house stayed in the family until it was sold to the Swifts in 1870. Even then, the house had remained uninhabited for roughly 40 years because the last of the original family lived in Kent in a larger estate. They were childless and apparently felt no need to hold on to so much property if it wasn't going to be handed down in inheritance in any case."

The cider cake smelled heavenly, and I dug in with gusto even though I was not at all hungry.

Holmes ate slowly, deep in thought.

"You like it?" I asked, and he nodded.

"It's one of the better cider cakes I've had," I continued inanely.

The discomfort was palpable, and Holmes gave me a patient look. "That's enough of that, Watson. We don't need to make light conversation, and we don't need to dance so inelegantly around each other." He took a long sip of his coffee. "Tomorrow, I think we should visit Mrs. Lawry. Something about that case was different – someone regretted stealing that necklace or at least stealing it in that manner or at that precise moment. That may give us a clue."

I wanted to tell him that we would not need to dance so inelegantly around each other if he wasn't being so infuriatingly and clearly secretive, but instead, I said, "The timing of the theft must have given something away. Perhaps they returned the item in hopes the widow would assume she overlooked it before."

"My thoughts exactly, my dear Watson. Did you enjoy your walk?"

"I went to St. Mary's instead."

"Oh?"

"Yes, I like to make my own plans."

He ate the last bite of his cake and nodded, not rising to my bait. "I hear it's beautiful. Maybe I'll find some time to visit once this mystery is cleared up. But, if you don't mind, I'm going to retire to my room and ruminate a bit. I wish I had my pipe."

"I'll stay down here for a while, it's warm and relaxing."

He nodded and stood. "Don't forget to wire Mary in the morning," he reminded gently, and I saw it for the olive branch it was.

Chapter Eleven

We visited the widow Lawry in her comfortable flat near Slad. She was very elderly, evidently in her late 70's. She lived alone with one servant and seemed happy to have company. She bade us welcome very warmly, decked in warm furs. Her hair was styled with a smooth, old-fashioned middle part with tight curls framing her elderly face. She pressed a familiar kiss to our cheeks, flustering Holmes who never appreciated being pressed into prolonged physical contact without a fair amount of warning.

There was no recognition on her face when we introduced ourselves. She let us into her drawing room, and we sunk into her expensive, high back floral chairs.

"Sherlock Holmes, you say? Are you here on some personal business?"

Holmes seemed pleased with the moment of rare anonymity. "Not as such, ma'am. We heard about your trouble a few weeks ago, with your necklace?"

"Where did you hear of that? It was hardly in the papers."

"The local police."

"Are you a policeman?"

My friend's face twisted with momentary distaste. "Absolutely not. Can you tell us what happened the night the necklace was stolen?"

She waved her hands airily. "Well, that's just it. I don't believe it was stolen."

Holmes's posture straightened. "Can you explain that?"

"Well, I reported the necklace stolen, but when the nice constable came to look into it, we opened the safe, and it was right there! Like magic!"

Holmes tugged absently on his gloves, face hawk-like and intent.

"And what do you make of that? Are you sure it was gone when you looked before?"

"I was quite certain it was gone. But then it wasn't, so I suppose I may have simply had a moment of confusion. They happen as you get older. You'll understand someday." Holmes frowned at that prospect but moved on quickly.

"What's the size of your safe?"

"Roughly one foot by one foot."

"Seems hard to overlook something in a safe of such a size."

"As I said, the mind ages with the body."

He smiled charmingly, "I'm not so sure there's anything amiss with your mind, my lady. Would you object terribly if I examined the necklace?"

She looked suddenly cautious. "You wouldn't be attempting to do anything nefarious, I hope?"

Holmes twisted a nonchalant wrist in the air. "Ma'am, we're gentlemen."

"You have to be cautious when you're a woman on your own," she explained. "Wait just a moment." She disappeared up the stairs, her tread slow and labored.

Holmes glanced around, taking in the clean furniture and pleasantly large windows that looked out onto the pavement. "This isn't about timing, Watson," he murmured. I did not have time to ask him to clarify, hearing the creaking of the floorboards as the widow returned holding a dainty but considerable necklace with a dark gemstone pendant.

Holmes took it from her gently, splaying it out over his large palm. "Is this gold?"

"Yes, the chain and the setting for the stone are all pure gold," she leaned over and ran a weathered finger over the chain. "The gem is a 3 karat black opal. It's been in my family for generations."

Holmes looked consternated, a crease burrowing between his brows. He carefully handed the necklace back to her. "It's a beautiful piece," he said simply, but there was an odd tone in his voice that the older woman did not notice. We left soon after, assuring her that all was well and that the whole affair was likely a misunderstanding, as she said.

On the kerb, Holmes raised a graceful hand to hail a cab, still frowning.

"What are you thinking, Holmes? I can tell something bothered you about the necklace."

A four-wheeler trotted past us without stopping. Holmes looked irritated, never one to tolerate being ignored. "It was a fake," he answered.

"Dear lord, are you sure?"

"Very sure."

"Why didn't you tell her?"

"I felt a bit sorry for her." He looked down the street, waiting for another cabbie. "A moment of weakness," he admitted, looking chagrined. "Besides, knowing something your opponent doesn't know you know is always preferable, so I'll keep it close for now. I'll inform the constable when the moment is right."

"By that time, her necklace could be irretrievable."

"It's been nearly a month, Watson. The necklace is likely very far from here. If it's still even in one piece. The gold could be easily melted down and the gem peddled separately, or perhaps put in another setting. It makes me wonder about our clients. I think a visit would be in order."

"You suspect that they may be victims of theft as well, unknowingly?"

"That's what I suspect. I hope they don't mind an unannounced visit." A hansom cab finally pulled over to pick us up.

At the Swift home, I was surprised when Emma opened the door.

"I saw you through the window," she explained.

"Are you here alone?" I asked.

"Only the servants and I are in. My mother took my father to the rococo garden for fresh air. She takes him out whenever he feels up to it. It's good for his mind and constitution to get out of the house every once in a while. My sister and Jonathan accompanied them. Little Richard is out doing who knows what." She stepped aside, "You can enter, gentlemen." Holmes slid in, but noticing my hesitation, she cast me a wry look. "It's quite all right. Please, don't stand on ridiculous ceremony, doctor. I understand you're here on official matters."

She closed the door behind us. "Has something happened?"

Holmes, never one for frivolities, asked, "What would you say is the most valuable bric-à-brac in your home? The items not under lock and key?"

The young lady looked caught off guard. "Oh, well, the vases in my mother's bedroom are crystal. I'm not sure what they're worth; they were here before I was born. In the drawing room, there are porcelain ornaments. And the raven figurine on the mantelpiece is gold, I believe."

"I assume your mother has valuable jewelry?"

"Oh, quite a bit. And my father has some very expensive cufflinks. They keep it in a safe in my father's room."

"Who has the key?"

"Only my mother."

"Has she worn any of the items recently?"

"Yes, she had a nice pair of earrings on this morning, so she must still be in possession of the key."

"And do you know where she keeps the key when it's not on her person?

"No."

"What if you wish to borrow a piece of jewelry?"

"I don't wear much jewelry, sir." She reached up and touched the small pearls she was wearing, "These earrings were from my grandmother but they are not worth much. My sister wears more jewelry than I do, but her items are mostly costume. Any pieces of actual worth that my sister and I own are also kept in the safe. My mother retrieves them if we are going to a formal event."

Holmes seemed to accept this, humming quietly under his breath. "May I see the items in the sitting room?"

"Of course." She led us back into the room, following Holmes as he immediately crossed over to the mantelpiece and picked up an ornamental gold raven figurine attached to a small square of marble. He examined it closely and then seemed to weigh it with both hands.

Instead of expounding on his thoughts, he gave Emma a curious look and handed her the item.

"Hold this," he commanded." Tell me what you notice."

She turned it around in her hands, then held it in both palms much as the detective had done. "It's lightweight," she finally concluded.

"What does that indicate?" Holmes pushed, an eagerness to his tone that I didn't understand.

"It's not real gold."

Holmes nodded, appearing impressed with her quick mind. He took the item and replaced it on the mantle. "The vases?"

She led us to her mother's room, and Holmes once again examined the vases on the coffee table between the divan and the chairs.

"These aren't real either," he declared.

"They were taken and replaced with fakes?" Emma asked.

"Nice way to cover one's tracks."

"But that means the thief was very familiar with the items in advance, to have time to replicate them," she mused.

"Your deduction is correct. And very significant."

"The servants?" She paused. "Not Agatha." Her tone was decisive and sure.

"Why not Agatha?" I pressed, wondering about her confidence with the maid.

"She's been with me ..." she trailed off. Then her face grew even more stubborn. "Just no, not her," she repeated with finality.

Surprisingly, Holmes seemed to accept this. "What of the other servants?" he asked.

"There's almost always someone in the house, so they would have to be stealthy. Plus, I trust most of them. Of course ... we do not know when the items were replaced. We did let two workers go a few weeks ago because they were caught up in little Richard's gambling."

"Gambling debts are a good motivation for making quick money."

"So they may have stolen from us before we released them from our service. They're far away now," she concluded, looking displeased.

"The items are gone too. Likely pawned. I think your possessions are now sitting comfortably in some bookie's pocket."

"Do you think your brother may have aided them? I hear he habitually wracks up serious debt as well?" I inquired, wondering why Holmes had not already pointed this out.

"I would not be surprised," she answered. "I put very little past him."

"Has he always been this way?" I asked.

"He was always willful. But I believe if my parents had used a firmer hand with him, he likely could have grown up much more humble than he has. I love my parents dearly, but I do not think they knew how to deal with him. He's spoiled and entitled, and he gets away with it because the rest of us are too exhausted to butt heads with him. Trying to scold him simply leads to worse behavior."

Holmes hummed again. "Sometimes it is easier and more practical to put one's head down and simply bear through," he murmured.

"Besides, men are allowed, are they not?" she declared boldly.

I cocked my head at her. "Your meaning?"

"They're allowed," she repeated. "They fight and they gamble and they whore and we wink at it because it's allowed. Because it is behavior all men engage in, isn't that right?"

Holmes's mouth twisted into an expression of distaste. "I know that's not entirely true, but I understand your opinion." He moved out of the room. "You've been an enormous help to me, Miss Emma. We'll return later in the evening to discuss these developments with your parents. We'll see ourselves out. Have a good day."

"Were you offended by her speech?" I asked as we closed the front door behind ourselves.

"Hmm? No, not at all. Let's head back to the inn."

Earlier, he had requested some more newspapers, and they were waiting in his room when we entered. I called up for a pot of tea while he gathered them at the foot of his chair and opened one across his side of the table.

I watched him read, smoothing the back of his hair down absently. "What are you searching for now?" I asked.

"I'm perusing the personal columns."

I smirked. "Well, I've often urged you to expand your social circle, Holmes, but I didn't think you'd so quickly resort to the matrimonial ads," I teased.

He looked up, glaring good-humoredly at me. "My interest lies in ciphers, dear Watson."

I picked up my teacup. "Matrimonial ads written in ciphers?" I exclaimed. "Well, that does sound like it might capture your affection … if anything can."

He dropped one side of the newspaper and rested his chin in his hands, staring patiently at me. His eyes were twinkling with amusement. "Are you quite finished? I'm looking for any indication of secret messages being sent to and from the members of our possible little band of thieves."

"Have you found anything?"

He resumed his browsing. "Not particularly. Just innocuous requests for governesses and trite love missives. *Kitten, I hope you are happy,*" he read mockingly, *"I am most miserable. Do write to our house before Wednesday next; I cannot bear a year. Pray let me see you for old love, which is still stronger.* What drivel."

I agreed, but sipped my tea and attempted to be understanding. "I'm sure they feel it very strongly."

"Today," he muttered.

"What was that?"

"They feel it today," he repeated louder, turning the page. "The romantic inclinations of man are fickle and shift with the slightest breeze. Women are more consistent, but that's no less a flaw, I suppose, all things considered." After a long pause, he looked up. "Present company excluded, of course," he clarified hastily.

"Of course," I agreed smoothly. After contentedly sipping my tea for a few more minutes, I observed, "Advertising through the personal columns only seems necessary if communication otherwise is difficult. That may not be true in this case. Servants talk to other servants in different houses, a line of communication that's untraceable wouldn't be too difficult to achieve."

"Indeed. I'm inclined to agree with you. But I shall leave no stone unturned."

The paper was spread out on the table, and he was curled over it, one hand supporting his head. I took him in, wondering not for the first or last time about my friend. His shirtsleeves were pushed up, and the firelight was not forgiving to the numerous aged needle-marks dotting his arm. There were times when I wished to … well, I'm not entirely sure. The medical man in me wanted to cure, to solve. The friend in me wanted to comfort, to understand. But neither of those things were in my capacity.

Always observant, he felt my gaze and glanced up, a small frown creasing his smooth brow. I was struck by how little he had aged since the day I met him 10 years ago, when he first stuck out an elegant but scarred hand and shook mine with a confidence that had nearly bowled me over. Neither of us were even 30 yet.

When he looked back down, I decided to bravely venture forth. "I didn't mean to upset you before, Holmes." I hoped my voice was properly contrite but neutral. "It wasn't my intention to pry."

He didn't raise his eyes from the newspaper he was studying. "Then what was your intention?"

I spread my hands with frustrated helplessness I couldn't contain. "To feel that I perhaps know you, just a little."

He looked up at that, staring at me for a moment with a mix of confusion and regret. After a moment, he continued his search in the articles in front of him.

So that was that, then. I sighed and took up my cup, sipping quietly and staring out into the damp but vibrantly green scenery outside our little window.

After the clock had ticked nearly a quarter of an hour, he inhaled loudly and cleared his throat. He leaned back, bringing his paper up and shaking it out with forced, casual air. "My childhood was less than ideal," he started, shocking me a bit, but I covered it with a steady sip of my tea. I didn't respond but gave him my attention, hoping he didn't retreat into the aloof reserve he assumed like a second skin.

Thankfully, he continued. "I grappled with some things. Dark moods, I guess you'd call them." He gave me a brief smile. I wondered at the use of past tense; Holmes still grappled often with dark moods. Even though he would attribute them to mere boredom and lack of mental stimuli, as a medical man I knew the truth. I wondered how bad they must have been in his youth for him to be willing to label them more honestly than his present bouts of melancholy.

"We had money and a modest estate in Yorkshire, so I didn't really want for anything," he explained, "but my father was ..." uncharacteristically, he struggled for the right word, "a rough man. And paranoid. He got in it in his mind when I was very young that I was not his child." He laughed at this, but it was tinged with bitterness. "Caused a great strain in the family and specifically on my mother. But she bore it with admirable stoicism. Mycroft always took after her more. To put it succinctly, my father didn't like me very much. And the feeling was mutual."

"When you say 'rough'?" I gently pressed.

He shrugged and continued without clarification. "I went to a boarding school when I was 15, so my contact with him became thankfully limited. Then I was accepted into Oxford."

"But you didn't take your degree."

"No, you know I left before the final term." He inhaled deeply, looking over the top of his paper to a corner of the room for a heavy moment. "My mother died that year, and I was already struggling."

He went silent again. Not wanting to push too hard, I decided to encourage him on the safer route, leaving the news of his mother for now. "Struggling? Not academically, surely."

"No. The other students – much like my father – didn't like me very much. Seems to be a common theme wherever I go." He smiled like it was a blithe joke.

"I like you very much."

His smile faltered a little. "Strange, that," he murmured. He closed his newspaper and took out one of his comforting cigarettes. "My mother died in a riding accident. Mycroft was home and witnessed it. The horse spooked and fell. She had the bad luck of being under it." He lit his smoke and took a few fortifying puffs. "Death was fortunately instantaneous. I had declined to visit for the Christmas season, so I hadn't seen her in a year's time." He stared off, eyes distant and turned inward.

I felt awkward, not knowing the best way to respond. I had asked for this, however. "Mycroft was riding?" I asked gently, hoping to distract him for a moment from the assuredly unpleasant memory of his mother's death.

He smiled slyly, but it was forced. He was playing along with me. "This may shock you, but my brother was not always the robust man you're familiar with. That development didn't 'bloom' – pun intended - until he was working for the government. Brainwork took over. The corporeal became secondary."

"Are you certain it wasn't also a response to your mother's death?" He shrugged again, and I sensed his guard rising. Despite their reserved demeanor towards each other, I suspected Holmes was protective of his brother. I veered to a different path. "Why didn't the other students like you? Did you reveal some embarrassing facts about them upon introduction?"

His gaze fluttered away for a moment, and I realized that the other students not liking him was perhaps more serious than I thought.

"It was a lot of things. It culminated in my besting one of the more popular – and more intolerable – students in a boxing match. He was the head of a little clique of very well-to-do and coddled boys. I broke his jaw."

"Good for you," I declared.

Holmes looked a little startled, perhaps expecting my disapproval. "I regret it. I didn't mean to harm him to that degree. It's unwise to spar with someone you dislike; it's easy to let things escalate. In any case, it was a victory short-lived. In response to my maiming of their leader, they started a scandal about me that threatened expulsion."

I couldn't imagine Holmes embroiled in any sort of scandal. He was rude and blunt and obnoxiously obstinate at times, but he was essentially a man of integrity and morals that, while maybe not always strictly aligned with our often unforgiving society, were nearly impossible to shake. "A scandal of what nature?"

He rolled his eyes. "Our chemistry professor had a research assistant – his wife. I often met with her to work on some projects after class hours. And gossip is powerful."

I flinched back in disgust. "How petty." He hummed in response and took a more contemplative drag of his cigarette. I narrowed my eyes at him suspiciously. "What was the nature of your relationship with her?"

"I beg your pardon?"

"What was your relationship?"

He scowled at me. "She was a married woman. Fifteen years my senior."

I noticed he hadn't answered the question, and he had become defensive as if I meant to imply something untoward. I decided to let it drop, no need to pick at a wound that may have been a very common wound typical of young men. "They were willing to ruin her as well, just to put you in your place?"

"They resented a woman being there in any case. That coupled with my mother's death led to … some worrisome behavior." The phrasing gave me pause, but he moved on before I could react. "After one incident, Mycroft rushed to help. He sent me to McClaren's institute, but I wasn't officially a patient. I was much older than his usual lot. I spent a year there. When I left, I chose not to return to university and instead dedicate myself to matters more suited to my strengths, much to Mycroft's chagrin."

"What was the incident?"

He waved his hand dismissively. "It's not important now."

"Holmes-"

He snubbed out his smoke. "Are you never satisfied?" he snapped but then seemed to reign himself in with effort. "I do not wish to dwell on it," he explained softly. There was a subtle beseeching tone to his voice, and I felt a surge of sympathy that moved me to let it go.

Instead, I commented, "I can't imagine Mycroft rushing to help in any context."

"He knew I was to be expelled and the scandal would spread, ruining the reputation of the Holmes name and the lives of others. He also cared about me. He wanted me to get help, and he was progressive enough to understand the best way to do so. For my part, I was willing to let Mycroft take control of the situation. I wasn't in the right frame of mind to handle things rationally on my own."

"So McClaren did help you?"

"Right as rain." He pushed his sleeves down, fastening his cuffs. I wondered if he realized the significance of his action or if it were unconscious. "So now you know the dreary, mundane drama of the Holmes family," he concluded with no shortage of sarcasm. He stood a little abruptly. "I hope I satisfied your curiosity."

"It's not lurid curiosity, Holmes," I started, irritation creeping into my voice. "Knowledge is required for intimacy."

He moved over to the settee, rifling through more of the papers strewn about there. "No, knowledge is required for power. We strive to know things and know people so we feel in control of them."

That drew me up very short. I wasn't insulted, though I knew I had justification to be; instead, his words concerned me. How did you move through the world with a viewpoint like that? How lonely it must be to believe that. Is that how he perceived my concern?

I watched him gather together a few more pieces of paper and retake his seat across from me.

"What became of the research assistant? Did she come out unscathed?"

He tugged on his ear. "The last I heard of Mrs. Isla MacGowan, she returned to Edinburgh with her husband when he took up a teaching post at the university there. She was untouched by the gossip, thanks to Mycroft's quick actions. Which he never fails to remind me of." He muttered the last part with a touch of sullenness.

After a moment, he reached over and pressed his hand to the cold teapot. "I'll call up for a fresh pot," he said.

I stood first, thankful for the excuse to do something else. "No need, I'm closer to the bell."

I'd barely rung it when the door swung open. I started to wryly comment on the swiftness of the service when I realized it was young William who had unceremoniously burst through our door without knocking.

He began gesturing wildly to my friend who stood abruptly, rattling the table and the teacups.

"What?" Holmes exclaimed, signing the word urgently at the same time. "When?"

A few more moments of excited gesticulating and the detective lurched across the room, gathering his coat. "Come, Watson! There's been a murder."

Chapter Twelve

The house was already full of policemen milling about. The murder had taken place in the drawing room. Through the crowded forms of the bobbies, I could see a figure lying between the tea table and the divan. We were let through by Constable Miller, who I suspected would have cleared the way for us as if we were royalty if Holmes had not stilled him with a firm hand on his arm.

Upon closer look, the victim's head was framed by a circle of blood, and I realized that it was little Richard. I glanced sharply at Holmes who looked puzzled for a moment. Apparently, this was a development he had not expected.

Otherwise, the room was pristine. From the way the body was sprawled, I would have expected the table to be off center, or even overturned, but it was in its exact spot. The only thing that seemed to indicate a fight was the vase between the chairs was upended, shattered across the floor, leaving soggy flowers and water seeping into the corner of the carpet.

I spotted Emma standing by the fireplace, hands clasped tightly across her shawl. Beneath that, she wore a simple flannel robe and socks. Why the police had not escorted a lady from such a room of gore could perhaps only be explained by how quiet she was.

Holmes sidled up next to her, removing his gloves. "Miss Emma, no surprise to see you here, observing."

"*Observer* is the ideal location in life, don't you agree, detective?" she murmured, eyes still forward on the scene in front of us.

"Mmmm," Holmes hummed. "Depends on context, I'd assume."

She nodded briskly. The fire crackled gently behind us for a few moments. I felt left-footed here with her, as always, my condolences sitting uncomfortably on the edge of my mouth not yet verbalized.

Holmes remembered himself as well, saving us both from the embarrassment of my impending bumbling. "I'm sorry for your loss," he said quietly. "Forgive me for my rudeness in not saying it as soon as I approached you. Forgive us both."

She shrugged. "We are not acquainted enough with each other for your condolences to be anything but civil manners, so do not worry about forgetting them. You have not insulted me."

I flushed up at her bluntness, but Holmes nodded. "I understand your perspective, but I assure you that we are acquainted enough that my feelings of sympathy are sincere."

For the first time, she looked up at him and made eye contact. The sight of it made me realize how rarely she did so. Now, she kept the connection for far longer than would be modest, her eyes flickering quickly and confidently across my companion's face as if measuring him. He must have passed some sort of test; her tense jaw relaxed back to its naturally gentle curve, and she broke eye contact to gaze stoically back at the scene in front of her.

"Then my thanks are sincere as well, Mr. Holmes."

We fell silent. I wondered what Holmes was accomplishing here instead of examining the crime scene, but I trusted my friend's strategies as I always did and remained by his side.

"When do they remove the body?" Emma finally asked.

Holmes was silent for a moment. "Once the police – and I – are satisfied that all evidence concerning the body has been found and documented, they will bring him to the local morgue for an autopsy."

"We can't keep the carpet. The blood will be impossible to get out." For the first time, I heard her voice crack. She tightened her shawl around her shoulders and quickly excused herself.

"We will need to speak to you later," Holmes advised as she passed us, "We will be as efficient as possible so as not to cause you further discomfort."

She jerked her chin down in brusque acknowledgment and disappeared into the hall.

"She seemed awfully unaffected by the whole affair, Holmes. That's her brother lying there, and she shows so little emotion."

"I wouldn't measure her guilt by shows of emotion, Watson. I don't believe that is the wise approach with a woman like her."

"You sound as if you admire her."

He glanced at me, a moment of genuine surprise melting into irritation. "I said nothing of the sort. I'm merely avoiding drawing an erroneous conclusion."

"I did not say you said it. I said you sounded as if you admired her."

"This isn't one of your writings, Watson. Stop romanticizing things."

I frowned, suddenly annoyed. "No need for such a defensive attitude, detective. I was merely *observing*. You have the right to admire or not admire whomever you please." I moved away from him, determined to look at the body if just to avoid arguing with him here in front of people. To be so prickly about my comment after haranguing me about "doting" on miss Florence! My friend's audacity at times was unbearable. Unbearable enough that the dead body I approached was preferable to dealing with his moods.

"Excuse me, gentlemen, I am a doctor. May I be allowed to examine the body?" The policemen assented, making room for me in the circle. After a few minutes, I felt Holmes come up behind me. His presence set me on edge, but when he leaned down next to me, coats removed and shirt-sleeves pushed up, that familiar focused and analytical look on his face, I felt my frustration bleed away.

It was only Holmes; the same man I'd shared rooms with for

nearly a decade.

He pointed a black-gloved finger at the body, balancing his forearms on his bent knees. "What do you see?"

I gently rotated the head. The hair was matted with blood, hanging limply over the collar. "Looks like one hit with a very hard object. He was struck right where his neck meets the back of his head, a very fragile spot. I suspect death was pretty much instantaneous."

Holmes shifted forward, one knee pressing into my side as he balanced precariously over the body, his quick eyes darting to and fro, noting and cataloging rapidly. I often wondered what it might be like to be Holmes. The world must have seemed very loud to him.

He stood, his long legs bringing him around the body and to the other side of the table in two long strides. He didn't do any of his usual contortions to look at the ground, nor did he pull out his magnifying glass. His eyes narrowed as he examined the carpet, and then he turned and picked up a few items from the mantle and turn them over carefully in his hands.

I couldn't read his responses to anything he was seeing. I returned to my own examination, satisfying myself that there was no other injury. The head wound was quite clearly the cause of death.

I stood, and Holmes turned from the fireplace as if he had been simply waiting for me to finish.

Miller stepped up next to me. "You two don't appear to have stumbled upon any revelations?"

Holmes grunted and shook his head, staring curiously down at the macabre tableau in front of him.

"Sorry to disappoint you," I apologized. Miller did look disappointed, as if his hopes of seeing Holmes's magic tricks in person had been dashed. "As far as I can tell," I continued, "he was killed by some large, heavy object."

"Was there a fight beforehand?" Miller asked, looking at Holmes.

Surprisingly, Holmes said nothing.

"There's no defensive wounds – meaning, it doesn't look as if he tried to block any blows or punch at his attacker, but it's still hard to say conclusively what led up to the murder," I supplied.

Holmes drew his gaze away, glancing dispassionately around the room before staring for a moment through the doorway to the hall. Abruptly, he exited the room.

"Excuse me," I muttered, following quickly.

He was halfway up the stairs when I reached the foyer. I bounded up the steps to catch up with him.

He knocked lightly on Emma's door which was opened by a robe-clad Agatha who allowed us entry.

Emma was sitting by her fireplace, with a low fire crackling for comfort. Agatha retook her seat next to her on the ottoman and wound their arms together.

"May I sit?" Holmes asked, gesturing to the chair next to her.

"Of course."

He sat, tugging off his right glove. He tapped his bare fingers against his knee. "You found him, yes?"

"Yes," she answered somberly, "and I kept the rest away."

"Can you tell me exactly what happened?"

I wondered if he weren't being too insensitive to what she'd just been through, but she answered steadily. "I heard a crash around 1 am, like some glass breaking. It startled me."

"But you didn't go to investigate right away?"

"No, I -" she broke off, looking frustrated with herself, "I suppose," she continued, "that 'startled' isn't the right word. It frightened me, so I didn't get up right away. I thought maybe we had imagined it, so I waited. I heard nothing else, but eventually, my curiosity got the better of me."

"We?"

"Agatha was here as well."

Holmes glanced at the doting maid. "Does Agatha often sleep in here with you?"

"No, I ..." A look passed between the two girls. "I'm teaching Agatha to read," Emma admitted. "She doesn't have much time during the day, so we often stay up late reading together. She doesn't want anyone to know."

Holmes looked at the maid with renewed interest. "It's nothing at all to be ashamed of," he reassured softly.

Agatha looked flustered. "If I can't do it, sir, I'd rather others not make it a joke."

A sad look passed over my friend's face at that. "I see," he murmured.

"I told my lady not to go down there," the maid continued, emboldened by our acceptance of her presence.

"Why didn't you wake one of the men of the house?" I asked.

The fluffy white cat emerged from under the bed and wound itself around Emma's legs. She petted its fur absently. "My father has less physical strength than I do. The servants are down in their quarters, and if I'd rung the bell and sent them up here without warning of an intruder, I would never forgive myself if they had been set upon and harmed."

"You didn't think to fetch your brother?"

"I do not -" her face twisted, "*did* not-" she corrected, "ever think of my brother as a source of help."

"No one else heard anything?" Holmes asked.

"Jonathan did. He was standing at the upper landing when I came out of my room. I told him to return to his chambers and lock the door. And I heard Florence moving about her room, humming to herself."

"And Jonathan listened?"

"Yes, he's a good boy. I went down the stairs and into the drawing room. I didn't notice anything amiss at first until I saw the vase of flowers spilled on the ground near the hearth. Then I saw him."

"A minute," Holmes stopped her. "If Florence was awake, do you think it odd that she heard nothing?"

"Her room is farther back while mine is right above the sitting room; Jonathan's is near mine as well. Plus, she was humming which means she was knitting. She often goes into her own world when she's at work."

Holmes nodded. "Did you touch him, move anything?"

"No, sir. I had no desire to touch anything in that room."

"But you have blood here." Holmes reached over and took a hold of her wrist, turning her palm up. There was blood on her hand.

Emma looked confused. "But how? I leaned over him for a moment but – oh, my hem," she reached down and gathered the bottom of her robe. There was blood soaked into the bottom.

Agatha quickly gathered a new robe which Emma stood and changed into with a brief stop behind her dressing screen.

She sat down again, wiping at her hand with a piece of cloth. "Do you know what he was killed with?" she asked.

"The murder weapon was the brass clock, I believe." Holmes leaned back. "Someone did an admirable job of wiping it down, on the victim's jacket, no less, but there were still faint bloodstains in the wood grain of the clock face."

"Someone wiped it down?"

"Yes, in fact, someone went through some great effort to clean up any clues that could aid me. Even the footprints were wiped away."

She frowned. "That must have been done while I was cowering here."

"They weren't able to clean up the vase before they heard you coming. In fact, I suspect it may have been knocked over during the cover-up."

"So the sound I heard was not his murder?" She paused, a look of pained relief crossing her face. "So he was already dead before I was even roused?"

"Very likely. Only a few minutes, but there was nothing you could have done had you hastened."

She digested that, her fist clenching and unclenching in her lap. "If it were a blow to the head, then it must be a man?" she finally observed.

"The odds favor it; the sort of strength needed for one killing blow heavily implicates a male suspect."

She fell silent for a long while, clutching at the cloth in her hand. "I know you must think me very cold, sitting here theorizing with you after my brother's death," she said at last. "But we never got on well with each other and in the last few years, he became intolerable. He resented me, my presence, my father's attachment to me. I believe once he even ... well, he even tried to set me up with one of the servants. One of the stable boys he used to cavort with tried some untoward things with me, and I always suspected my brother had encouraged it in some spiteful attempt to ruin me."

I shifted on my feet uncomfortably. "My goodness."

"Little Richard was no gentleman," Agatha interjected with venom. "He once-" she broke off, turning red.

Holmes held up a reassuring hand. "That's sufficient, Agatha. We understand boys like him."

"I know we're meant to always love our family but it's hard to feel anything but …" Emma struggled for the right word.

"Apathy?" Holmes supplied gently, "Maybe even relief at their death?"

"That's near it, yes."

I looked sharply at my friend, wondering at his tone.

"The rest of the household hasn't seen the body?" he asked more impersonally.

"No, once I discovered him, I called William and told him to fetch the police and then go round and speak to you two. I was quiet about it and stayed in the hall until the police arrived."

She kept wiping at her pink-stained palm. Holmes retrieved his handkerchief, dipped it into the nearly empty carafe of water on the table, and took her hand in his, wiping at the stain. "You've shown great emotional fortitude in the face of very unpleasant gore."

"I'm not the fainting sort."

Holmes made a distracted noise. "You're not wearing a corset."

"I-what?" Emma spluttered, and both girls visibly tensed.

"Holmes!" I gave him a not so discreet nudge.

He looked up, flushing a bit at his own loose tongue. "I only meant," he laughed ruefully, "– forgive me –I only meant that the restrictive nature of the corset likely leads to the common fainting spells women succumb to more than any actual overwhelming emotional distress. I, at times, forget not to think out loud. I apologize."

The girls relaxed, but Agatha narrowed her eyes at him. "You're an odd man, sir."

Holmes chuckled, letting go of Emma's hand and refolding his handkerchief with the wet portion tucked away. "So I've been told."

We left them there after I recommended a small dose of spirits to help them both sleep and went down the stairs and towards the ground-level master bedrooms. We were admitted by Mrs. Swift, holding young Jonathan in her arms. On seeing her struggle, Holmes took the boy from her – to my great surprise – and followed her to the small sitting room where Mr. Swift was staring into the empty fireplace, a blanket over his lap.

"Do you need help with the fire?" I asked and dutifully went to work when the woman nodded gratefully.

Holmes sat, readjusting the half-sleeping, sniffling boy in his arms.

"I'm sorry for your loss," Holmes said softly. "And I'm sorry I did not help you in time."

"That damned boy! Got himself killed," Swift exclaimed, clenching his fist. I could hear the crack in his voice that he was trying to conceal. Holmes glanced at the lady of the house, taking in the drawn look on her face, the dark circles smudging her eyes.

"You speak as if you know what happened," Holmes urged gently. "Do you believe your son's past foibles came back to haunt him?"

"What do you think?" Mrs. Swift answered, her voice level.

Holmes looked a tad startled by her blunt question. "I agree. All clues point to your son racking up gambling debt, getting in with the wrong crowd, and being killed by a shady acquaintance. The only issue is … well, to be blunt, what is the point of his death? What does the killer gain? And how did they get into the house?"

"Perhaps my son was going to reveal something. And perhaps he let them into the house," the lady answered simply.

"Yes, that could be true," Holmes muttered but still looked unconvinced. "I must tell you," he started cautiously, "that I did find some evidence that your son may have been involved with a petty band of burglars, mainly consisting of various servants around the town. We believe they stole and pawned items to fund their lifestyles and pay off debts."

"Why do you believe my son was involved in that?"

"They all had a similar tattoo -"

"I told you, Eloise!" Mr. Swift broke in loudly. Jonathan wriggled in Holmes's lap. He shushed the boy absently. "I told you when he came back with that obnoxious tattoo that he was up to no good!"

"Well, he's up to nothing now," she shot back, voice strained.

Holmes looked back at the doorway to the lady's bedroom. "May I?" he asked, nodding at the sleeping child. She waved her hand in permission.

As Holmes went to deposit the boy onto her bed, I asked if Dr. Rikes had been called. Upon hearing he had not, I administered some morphine to the older man that was stocked in his night table and advised the lady of the house to get as much sleep as she could. She too asked when the body would be removed.

I told her the same timeline I had told Emma, and she turned her head to hide her weeping as Holmes returned. He looked uncomfortable and we made an unobtrusive exit.

Holmes retrieved his coats and hat, speaking only briefly to the constable before following me outside.

"My thoughts still stand," Holmes said as we made our way a discreet distance down the pavement to find a cab. "This murder does not make much sense. Little Richard may have indeed had information that the rest of his cadre would have wanted secret, but he had nothing to gain from revealing it and did not seem to be undergoing any penance for his past that might motivate some to come clean. I wish I could understand better. I wish I could have prevented this." His voice had taken on that familiar castigating tone that I recognized easily. When faced with perceived failure, Holmes was his own harshest critic.

We finally came across a four-wheeler, and Holmes fell into deep thought as the driver leisurely carried us back to the inn. When we entered his room, William was there, drinking tea and munching on a nice loaf of bread with cheese. He blushed, jumping up from the table and gesturing. Holmes waved him down.

"It's all right," he signed. "Eat as much as you want. You can stay here the night too since there are very few cabs around at this time."

Breaking off a piece of the bread, Holmes popped it into his mouth as the young man retook his seat. "I think I need to get a better grasp on who may be involved in this little larceny pastime. I might visit Satine again and see if I can at least sketch a picture of Richard's frequent companion."

I thought of the way Satine had sidled up to Holmes. "I wish you wouldn't," I huffed, "I didn't care for the way he approached you."

Holmes laughed, "Your protectiveness is very much appreciated, old friend, but men like Satine are harmless. They simply want a reaction. I can handle myself. You needn't come with me; I know you find those places intolerable."

I took a seat across from William, helping myself to the tea and a chunk of cheese. "I don't see how you do not. All those smells and all that noise. I would think you especially would find it unbearable."

Holmes shrugged out of his coats. "It's amazing what one can grow accustomed to. In any case, I may also visit some of the other burglary sites as well and see if there are any particular servants under suspicion, including Bamford. I'm interested in the young girl Richard was carrying on with."

He set up a pillow and blanket on the lounge chair for William, and I took it as my cue to retire for the night.

Chapter Thirteen

The next day, I opted to accompany Holmes back to The Fox Tail anyway, partly to avoid a lackluster afternoon sitting in my inn room and partly to provide a buffer between the two men.

In the daytime, the pub was even more depressing. In the main room, the bright sunlight highlighted the faded stain of the wood floor, and only a few, despondent and unhappy men were scattered at different tables, nursing their drinks. The ring downstairs was empty except for a few people readying the bar and tables for the upcoming night's festivities. The odour was not as bad but now lingered with a musky old-food smell that made me crinkle my nose.

Holmes asked the bartender at the small makeshift serving area if Satine was there, and the man scurried off to fetch him.

He sniffed the air as well, face twisting with displeasure, then seemed to remember something. "Did you smell a particular scent in the sitting room? By little Richard's body?" he asked, leaning on the creaky wood of the bar.

"The smell of blood can be off-putting-"

"No ... It smelled like Florence."

I considered this. "Well, it is her house, Holmes. It wouldn't be unheard of for her scent to linger."

"She said she didn't wear perfume. That first night on the stairs. Yet, I could swear it was the same scent I smelled that night. A vaguely cinnamon aroma."

"Well, just because a woman doesn't wear perfume doesn't mean she does not have scents on her. Maybe a hair powder. Mary uses a very nicely almond scented bandoline in her hair, for instance."

He stopped me with a deadpan look. "Yes, Watson. Thank you so much for your brief lesson on women's grooming habits."

"Well, it's just you've never …" I floundered, "well, you've never lived with a woman so how am I to know if you're familiar with their daily ablutions?""

He narrowed his eyes at me, looking annoyed. "I've lived with women before."

"Yes, but I mean," I was spluttering, uncomfortable. Finally, I sighed with exasperation. In this rare case, I was the authority, so I embraced it. "It's different," I declared with finality.

Holmes gave me an odd look, a cross between irritation and embarrassment, and straightened from the counter. "If you insist."

I shrugged. In any case, I had no time to continue the debate, catching a glance of the ferret-like little Frenchman making his way through the old rickety tables.

Satine rushed up to my friend, clapping his hands excitedly. "It is monsieur Holmes! You come again to make me some money? You look so *splendide* in the ring! I can hardly think of anything else!" He gripped my friend companionably by the shoulders, then slipped a hand to the back of my friend's neck in a gesture entirely too familiar. On impulse, I nearly took hold of his wrist to thrust the hand away. I held back, but my fingers flexed with the thought of grinding those bones together in my grip.

Holmes, for his part, took the manhandling with equanimity, smiling wryly and pulling away. "Not today, Satine. I apologize. But I did make you a pretty penny, hmm? Would you be grateful enough to do me a kindness in return? A favor, if you will?"

"As I said before, little bird, I will do anything for you. I'm afraid Madeline is not here this early." He gave my friend a sly look. "I know you are fond of her, you spent quite some time in her company the other night."

Holmes frowned. "Half an hour is hardly a long time," he said before he could catch himself. A flush crept up his neck when he realized his mistake. "In any case," he continued quickly, "I'm here on a different mission. I was wondering if you could describe some of little Richard Swift's companions – if there were multiple – as I sketched out their likeness?"

"Ah, you are playing police today? How fun. I will make the time to sit with you, yes."

I glanced around at the nearly empty space. It seemed to me that he had plenty of time on his hands at the moment.

He led us over to a small wobbly table with 3 chairs crowded around it. I seated myself between the two men just to avoid any time-consuming carry-ons by the overly enthralled man.

"You mentioned that young Swift had a consistent companion. Can you describe him for me?" Holmes pulled out a few loose pieces of stationary and 2 sharpened charcoal pencils. He licked the tip of one and looked at our weasel of a host expectantly.

"Oui, he had a face like yours."

Holmes frowned. "You mean the shape?"

Satine brought his palms up to his face like wings. "High cheekbones." He then gestured to his forehead and the curve of his own jaw. "Here and here very nice. Like a painting."

Holmes looked a little ruffled, apparently unused to that peculiar compliment. "What did his eyes look like?"

"Round. Long eyelashes. Eyebrows straight and thick."

Holmes spent a few minutes sketching with confident, light strokes, asking numerous questions about nose and chin shape. He held up the picture when he was done and Satine nodded enthusiastically. "Oui, oui. Like that. Uncanny."

We spent another two hours at that stained table as Holmes drew sketch after sketch, five in total.

At the end, Holmes pulled out a folded up piece of paper and smoothed it out for our host to see. It was a drawing of the Caduceus tattoo. "Did all these men have a tattoo that looked like this?"

"Yes. You are a very good artist."

Holmes fanned out the pictures he'd drawn and took a moment to examine them. "Were there any other guests of Richard Swift?" he asked at last.

"No," Satine shook his head, "that is all I remember."

We didn't go directly to the Swift home. We went back to Mrs. Lawry and sketched her descriptions of her few servants. We did the same at the Bamford's and a few more houses that allowed us entry in the neighborhood. In the end, it was growing dark, and we had 13 sketches in our possession.

Then we were off to the Swifts. Florence answered the door when we knocked. Holmes frowned questioningly at her. She let us in and explained, "I know it's customary to have a butler see you in, but we no longer employ a butler." Her tone was wry.

"What happened to your butler?" I asked.

She shrugged. "My father let him go. He also let my lady's-maid go without warning. When I press him on it, I get no coherent answer." She paused and then gestured us towards the sitting room. "My father's mind is slipping further and further every day. They were simply victims of his paranoia."

"I hope they are able to find their way," I commented as I sat.

She shrugged again, which I felt did her no favors.

Holmes pulled out his bundle of papers. "We won't take up much of your time, but we were wondering if you could look at these drawings and tell us who you are familiar with."

"If I can be of any help."

Holmes spread out the sketches on the table before us. Florence spent some time examining them, even picking them up and tilting her head this way and that way. It seemed a bit affected, an attempt to appear contemplative. Finally, she pointed at one drawing, "That man is the valet that we let go without reference. I believe he relocated to Scotland." She slid that paper to the side to reveal the one beneath it. "That is the stable boy we also let go without reference; I'm not sure what became of him. And this," she picked up another, "This is the brother of that poor young girl that little Richard … well, the girl who was removed to Bath." Holmes took the three she identified and placed them on top of the pile.

He gave Florence a contrite look, but I saw keen observation underneath his expression. "I apologize for not giving my condolences about your brother."

Florence nodded, folding her hands in her lap. She swallowed back some emotion and then commented calmly, "I was a bit surprised you did not come to interview me."

Holmes held up a conciliatory hand. "It wasn't a slight. Emma had made it clear that you had not seen the body, so I felt it better not to bother you."

I thought I saw a flash of irritation on her face. "How kind of you." I wondered for the first time if there wasn't some underlying jealousy between the sisters that was not evident at first. Florence, I suspect, did not really appreciate coming second to her older, less refined sister.

Holmes must have caught the look as well, because, in a move obviously meant to placate her, he asked, "Did you have any insight that would help us?"

She smiled. "Not particularly."

Holmes glanced at me and then neatly folded his papers. "I'm not always good with sensitivity, as the doctor never hesitates to point out, so forgive me for the question, but how do you feel about your brother's death?" He looked up as he delivered the question, his hawk-like gaze quick and intense.

For her part, Florence didn't waver under the examination. She chose her words carefully. "Richard and I got on simply because we didn't speak. I think about the man he could have been and mourn that. But I also realize that one's actions have consequences."

Holmes peered curiously at her. "You think his murder is due to his long acquaintance with criminals?"

"What else could it be?"

"Indeed," he murmured and then fell into a thoughtful silence that neither I nor Florence interrupted. When his expression cleared, he glanced down at her décolletage for longer than is appropriate.

I was on the verge of nudging him when Florence brought her hand to her chest and pulled a necklace chain from the top of her dress. "Are you looking at my locket?" she asked with no censor in her voice.

Holmes nodded. "I presume you have a picture of Doctor Rikes tucked away there?"

She smiled. "Have you ever been in love?"

I saw a muscle twitch in my friend's jaw. He perhaps took a moment too long to answer, but I hoped our host didn't notice.

"No."

She narrowed her eyes at him. "I'm not sure I believe you." So perhaps she did notice. "But, if true, then I supposed you wouldn't understand."

"Understand what?"

"The need to keep your true love close to you at all times. That's the point of the locket. To rest near your heart." She pressed the little trinket to her heart to illustrate.

Holmes didn't look impressed. "Forgive me again, but Rikes is a bit older than you."

"Mature, you mean."

"And a lowly doctor."

"Oh, I don't think doctors are lowly." She cast a pleasant look in my direction.

"Very true," Holmes conceded, "but society does."

"His field isn't …" she trailed off, realizing that now she was in danger of insulting me by clarifying that Rikes's area of medicine was somehow more respectable than mine.

"Your family is fine with you tying yourself to a man of lesser status and means than you? Certainly, you come from a family of considerable wealth. You have, I presume, the expectation of a large inheritance," Holmes pressed, his voice unyielding. I wondered if Holmes disliked Miss Florence; his demeanor seemed to imply a negative feeling towards her. I also tried not to react to his mention of her inheritance knowing, as he did, that this was not true.

Florence frowned. "Rikes is a good man. And my father has always been free from the prejudices and narrow-minded thinking common to the wealthy. All he cares about is our compatibility."

"That's very generous of him."

This time, she peered curiously at him. She suddenly looked like a predator catching sight of a vulnerable prey. The look surprised me, and I found myself shifting unconsciously towards Holmes.

"You know Doctor Rikes?" she asked.

Holmes, while lacking many social graces, was not oblivious to shifts in mood. He stared at her levelly, refusing to reveal anything. "Yes, we met each other in my relative youth. At the start of my career – or hobby, really, at the time."

"If you insist," she agreed lightly but with a definite malicious edge as if humoring him. I struggled to keep my face neutral. "If you know him," she continued, "you know he's the epitome of a gentleman. And our feelings for each other compensate for any inequality of standing. Strong feelings have the extraordinary power to do that, as you know."

Holmes inclined his head. "As I said, I do not know."

"If you insist."

The gently mocking response grated on the detective's nerves. His leg jiggled impatiently, and then he stood. "Thank you for your time. Is your sister nearby?"

That look of jealous irritation appeared and disappeared in a blink of an eye. "I believe she's in her atrium."

We declined her offer of escort and made our way through the music room and out onto the patio. As we walked, I asked Holmes why he seemed on guard with the younger daughter.

He brushed me off. "It's nothing. She's a child simply not used to being second favored."

I rather thought Holmes had that backward. "So you do admit that you favor the sister?"

"I favor no one. I appreciate that Emma is easier to read. This makes my job simpler." He smiled. "Appeals to that lazy streak that so frustrated you when we roomed together. Quite frankly, I find Florence irritating for the same reason I find many women irritating – society has successfully beaten into them the exasperating ability to hide what they're really thinking."

"That's unfair of you, Holmes. You're too quick to view women harshly."

"I don't view women harshly. I view society harshly. A woman isn't meant to show anger or strong emotion without receiving scorn and censor. I have had female clients express the same emotional reaction to missing jewelry as they do to their husbands beating them.

It makes it hard to help, but it's not their fault. The horrors that women have learned to submit to without complaint make them too unknowable for my limited patience. Their reactions – or lack thereof – are illogical to me."

"You would think that would inspire more sympathy from you," I muttered.

Holmes stopped right outside the atrium. He gave me a heated look. "When have I failed to show sympathy for any of my clients when they deserve it?"

"You have always expressed sympathy, but to speak so practically of something-"

"I will always speak practically. No need to have an overly emotional reaction to something."

"No need to have an overly emotional reaction to something?" I repeated. "Then aren't you just like the women you find so inscrutable?"

Something dark passed over his face, but he held it back by smiling at me in an overly pleasant way. "The difference is, I'm the one deducing and rarely find myself at the receiving end. If I ever do find myself in that position, I would not be surprised if I proved to be a source of frustration. In fact, I'd venture to guess I've been that very thing to you yourself, haven't I, doctor?"

"You won't distract me from my point."

His smile fell. "What's your point then?"

"That you find women unreadable because they have been conditioned to hide their deep wells of sincere emotion. I argue that you yourself are quite the same."

He pushed into the atrium without response, thus proving my point. It was nearly pitch black, but there was a faint glow that we followed to a corner nearly hidden by plants. We only avoided bumping into the flower pots and upending a few by sheer luck.

Emma was sitting at a small table near the hanging English ivy plants. The atrium was lit only by the candles at her table. She sat wrapped in a shawl, a copy of Bury's *A Selection of Hexandrian Plants Belonging to the Natural Orders of Amaryllidae and Liliacae* open on her lap. She looked up at our arrival, and I was surprised by the dark circles under her eyes made starker by the shadowed flame of her candle.

Holmes felt it appropriate to comment on them. "You look tired, Emma. I take it you haven't been sleeping?"

To her credit, she took no offense. "I have had some fitful slumber of late," she confirmed, closing her book and setting it on the small table to her side.

"That's understandable," Holmes said, reaching over and turning the book towards himself as if the cover was fascinating. "It would be difficult to stay in a house plagued by ghostly activity. Please tell me what has happened?"

"How did you-"

"Simple. You are here when the atrium is not properly lighted for nighttime reading. You are also immersing yourself in a scientific tome that you have clearly read before. This is obviously for comfort and to keep your mindset firmly on the natural."

"Well, you're correct. I am here because the house has become unbearable." She stood and picked up her candle.

"In what way?" I asked.

"I hear noises, like knocking deep in the walls. Last night, early in the twilight hours of the morning, I heard wailing. As if someone singing and crying at the same time. It was horrific."

"From inside the house?" Holmes pressed.

"The wailing? No. Maybe. My first instinct is that it was coming from the yard, but the more I think about it, the less clear I become."

Holmes nodded. "That's a common problem with trying to recall sensory details."

"I know it's absurd, but a part of me wonders if my father is not right about the house. But then – ghosts don't murder people with heavy ornaments, do they?"

"That does seem a bit too earthly for a spirit. Are you sure the knocking came from inside?"

"It came from the wall that connects my room and my sister's room."

"Did Florence hear it?"

"Yes, she met me on the landing because she was woken by it as well."

"We just spoke to Florence. She made no mention of this."

Emma shrugged. "She is convinced it was just a normal house noise that we don't understand. But it sounded to me exactly like a person knocking. I hate being less logical than her, but I can't pretend it sounded like anything else."

Holmes hummed under his breath in that way he was prone to when something interesting had occurred but he wasn't sure exactly what it was yet.

"Let's go inside, gentleman," she offered. "It's drafty out here, and I feel horrid not offering you a place to sit. It also looks like it will rain soon, and I'd like to be safely inside before the weather turns."

"That would be lovely, Emma. We also have some sketches we'd like you to look at and the light might suit us better inside," Holmes agreed, smiling pleasantly.

We followed her out of the atrium. Casting a look back through the windowed walls, I shuddered at how dark and ominous the inside of it looked at night, like something out of a Grimm fairytale.

It was then that I saw a ghostly transparent figure flitter across the glass, rippling like a wraith across the surface of water.

I wasn't the only one who saw it; Emma stumbled backward, dropping her candle where it nearly landed on Holmes's foot. He made a noise of excitement and spun around, eyes scanning the house.

"Holmes!" I exclaimed, gooseflesh on my arms and my hair standing on end.

"Doctor, what was that?" Emma asked, her voice high and shrill with fear. "Was that a ghost?"

"Of course not," I reassured, but my voice was wavering. Holmes had stepped further onto the grass, staring hard at the house.

"What is it, Holmes? What do you see?"

"It wasn't a ghost, Watson."

"I know that!" I spluttered and it wasn't a lie. Objectively, I knew that it was not a ghost. But that did not prevent my heart from beating hard in my throat.

Holmes turned to the young woman. "There's no need to be afraid, Emma. That was not a ghost. It was just a trick."

"A trick?"

"Yes, let's get into the house before it begins to rain and I can explain it to you and allay your fears."

We were met halfway to the house by William, gesturing wildly. I wondered how Holmes could even see him that well in the darkness, but Holmes and the boy engaged in a deep signed conversation for some minutes before he turned back to us and translated for my benefit. "He says Mr. Swift is in a panic because he heard some strange noises and saw a ghost through his window, near the stables."

Emma was already walking towards the house, leaving us to trail behind.

"Our ghost?"

"Depends on your perspective on that," Holmes murmured. "In

reality, it's likely multiple people playing the same trick in different places to give the illusion of quickly moving ghosts."

"What trick?"

Holmes didn't get a chance to answer because we entered the music room and were striding urgently to Mr. Swift's chambers to make sure the old man was all right.

Emma let herself in without knocking. Mr. and Mrs. Swift were in the small connecting room. Swift was almost slack in his wheelchair, a glass of brandy nearly empty next to him on the table. Mrs. Swift was holding his hand, perched on the edge of the wingback chair next to him.

"Mr. Holmes!" the woman exclaimed, rising while keeping her husband's hand in her grip. "I didn't realize you were here."

Holmes nodded brusquely. "Can you relay to me exactly what happened?" he asked.

She let go of her husband's hand and placed it gently on his lap. "It may go against decorum, but please step into my bedroom so we can talk without disturbing him."

"Did you give him brandy to calm him?" I asked as we followed her into her chamber.

"Yes, he was spooked into near incoherence."

"Spooked by what?" Holmes repeated, a note of impatience in his voice.

"We were in his room. I was helping him into his bedclothes – he likes to read in bed for a while before sleeping – and then he gripped my arm so hard that I nearly cried." She lifted the sleeve of her robe and shift; there was an angry red mark around her forearm. Emma gasped and rubbed at the skin comfortingly. "He kept saying *do you see it? Do you see it?* over and over. It took me a moment to realize he was looking over my shoulder at the window. When I turned, I saw a strange, nearly transparent figure floating in the distance, near the stables."

"You're sure it was nearly transparent?"

"Absolutely."

Holmes peered at her intently. "What do you think you were looking at?"

Mrs. Swift answered without hesitation. "Some trick, like an illusion."

Holmes nodded. "Very astute of you. Indeed it was. Have any of you heard of Pepper's Ghost?"

Emma and I nodded, but Mrs. Swift shook her head.

"Simple trick sometimes used in theater. A plane of glass and a torch is all you really need. It works like this." He stepped away from us, preparing to literally walk us through the mechanics. I smiled, privately amused – and perhaps comforted – by my friend's familiar habit towards the theatrical in his lessons. "Say I was standing here in ghostly costume. My companion, Watson, would angle a piece of glass at a 45-degree angle towards the empty corner of the room and shine a light on me. My form, using the light, would project from the glass and take ghostly form in that empty corner."

"Oh, I heard of this connected to some Christmas play, yes?" Emma queried.

Holmes nodded. "Yes, that is where it got its name. The trick itself has been around since the 16th century. *Magia Naturalis.*"

"So someone is trying to drive my husband to madness?" Mrs. Swift asked, a dangerous edge to her voice. "Who would do such a thing to a sick man?"

"The most obvious answer is that someone wishes to ensure that your husband's mental state is called into question. Perhaps to invalidate some of his decisions of late." Holmes gave the woman a knowing look at which she drew in a deep breath.

She glanced at Emma and then back at Holmes. "If any of my children wished to use some legal loophole to contest my husband's will, this would not be the way to do so. My husband altered his will over two years ago. Well before any of this started."

"Papa altered his will?" Emma asked.

Her mother took a gentle hold of her arm. "Don't worry yourself, dear. It was about your brother."

Emma nodded but frowned, obviously attempting to weave in this new information to her analysis of the events now transpiring. It was a look quite similar to one I'd seen on Holmes's face while ruminating on the developments of a case. I was taken aback for a moment. I turned to my friend and saw that he too was processing, turning over the details in his mind. Mrs. Swift was quite correct – why would this tack be chosen when the timing would work against them? If one wanted to claim mental deterioration, wouldn't it have been prudent to do so at the time the will was changed?

"Perhaps they only recently found out about the will. This may be a desperate attempt," Holmes commented as if reading my mind.

"I just don't believe it, sir. No offense." Mrs. Swift shook her head.

Holmes didn't address her doubts. "Do you mind if I take a look around your husband's room? Perhaps the rest of the house as well?"

"Yes, of course."

"Watson, take Miss Emma into the sitting room and show her the sketches." He pulled out the papers from his coat pocket. "I'll meet you two there when I'm finished."

We bid Mrs. Swift adieu, leaving Holmes there with her to examine the rooms first. I hoped Mr. Swift's presence – even unconscious as he was – was sufficient enough to alleviate any concerns about propriety, but I'm sure the thought had not even occurred to the single-minded detective.

As Emma and I made our way towards the sitting room, I asked her about the butler and Florence's lady's-maid.

"Oh, I'm not sure what happened there, doctor. I simply came home from my music lessons and heard that both had been asked to leave. Very strange, because Marie was a very sweet girl. I could see no reason for her to be let go. Indeed, I find it hard to believe she could be under suspicion for anything at all. But my father's reason is slipping, whether by natural causes or outside forces or both, so it may have simply been a whim."

"Have you heard what's become of them?"

"I sent word for Marie at the closest shelter and asked her what happened, reassuring her that I would give her a glowing recommendation. She wrote back that she was well and that she had found employment already a few towns over. Apparently, my mother had given her a recommendation and set her up with a family she knows."

"So your mother does not believe either of them should have been removed?"

"Of course not." We entered the sitting room and she pulled the bell to call us up some hot tea. We spent some time going over the sketches but she gave me no new information on them. We conversed, sipping our hot drinks. Now that I was more accustomed to her, I found Emma's company refreshingly candid and hearty. She was a well-read and highly intelligent girl with a mind that leaned to the scientific, though she spoke of botany and the natural world with an awe that hinted at an artistic side.

I could see why Holmes liked her, despite his refusal to admit it, and why he seemed to fall into a comfortable rapport with her almost immediately. Indeed, they were not the same in many ways – Emma was open about her thoughts and feelings in a stark, blunt way whereas my friend hoarded his internal world like a dragon clutching at his treasure – but overall they shared important qualities.

Speaking of Holmes, I kept expecting him to make an appearance, but his absence grew into a tangible presence.

After a long hour had ticked by, with my constant, worried glances at the clock, Jonathan burst into the room, swinging the door wide enough to clang against a small table and nearly upend a vase of flowers. Emma caught it with catlike reflexes.

"Doctor! There's a body outside!"

I sprang upwards, heart leaping into my throat. Dear God, was it Holmes?

"A body?" I demanded. "Where? Who?"

"Out by the stables. I can see it through the patio windows, just a lump. But it's a body, sir!"

I pushed past him and rushed through the house towards the music room, Jonathan and Emma hot on my heels. The French doors were open and banging in the wind, outside the rain was pelting down hard, but I barreled outwards, slipping and sliding on the grass as I rushed towards the stables. I could see the lump Jonathan was referring to and saw that it was indeed a body. Jonathan tripped and fell with a thud next to me.

Skidding to a stop, I rolled the wet form over and nearly choked. It was Holmes! He groaned, and I thanked God he was alive. He was sans jacket, soaked to the bone. Emma reached us, an umbrella that she must have snatched up some time as we were running through the house, in her hand. She tilted it over us. Her dress was sodden at the hem, her shoulders damp with wayward rain.

"Holmes!" I shook him, and with a loud start, he sprung up and gasped loudly, his gloved hands scrambling at his neck.

"Holmes! Holmes, it's me!" I pressed his hands away and noticed the dishevelment of his collar and what I could barely perceive in the darkness were bruises around his neck.

He stopped panicking, but he was still coughing roughly and shivering.

"We have to get him inside!" With Emma's help, we got him to his feet. He was limping a bit; Emma slung one of his arms over her shoulder and snaked a supportive hand around his waist. Surprisingly, he didn't shrug her off even though she was half his size and likely not really bearing much of his weight, and with my help, we got him into the music room onto the settee that Jonathan pushed closer to the fireplace. It wasn't lit, but the helpful young boy began piling wood on immediately.

My friend was wheezing and in the helpful light of the room, I could see a long, thin bruising indent around his neck.

"Dear God, Holmes, did someone try to garrote you?"

Despite being soaking wet and struggling to breathe, he managed to give me an incredulous look. "Always one to state the obvious, Watson," he croaked.

Emma brazenly undid his tie and pushed his collar down further. "He's bleeding."

Holmes shook his head. I noticed him tense against her actions, a minute reaction that no one else would have noticed but I understood it as discomfort. "No, he didn't break the skin."

"He did," I disagreed. Without the rain to wash away the blood, a small part of his neck was oozing. I examined it gently. "It's not deep, but you may need a stitch or two. Hold this to it." I handed him my handkerchief. He pressed it to his neck.

Emma poured him a glass of brandy and urged him to sip it. "You must be freezing. I can gather you some of my brother's dry clothes."

Holmes made a look of distaste, and despite the way his trousers and shirt must have been uncomfortably clinging to him, he shook his head. "Give me a moment to dry off a bit, and I'll be all right."

She looked unconvinced, but gathered a small blanket from the divan and draped it around his shoulders.

"What happened out there, Holmes?"

He took another larger sip of his drink. He put his glass aside and reached down to undo his sodden boot laces. Emma knelt down to help him, and he pulled his foot away from the girl abruptly. She jumped up, realizing her error.

"Jonathan, help Mr. Holmes with his other boot so his feet can get warm."

We got his boots and socks off and, apparently immune to how strange it was to sit in a stranger's house barefoot, he finally told us what happened.

"I thought I saw a figure near the stables, so I went out to look around-"

"In the rain?" I interrupted.

"Yes, in the rain," he answered testily. "By the time I got there, I had lost him, but I wondered what the lurker might have been looking for. I lingered too long, hoping to see some clues."

"In the rain?" I interrupted again.

Holmes glared. "Learn a new question, Watson. Yes, in the rain. I see now that this was not only futile but foolish. I didn't hear the person come up behind me because of said rain. He attempted to slip a piece of wire around my neck, but I twisted away. Unfortunately, the wet grass worked against me, and I nearly slipped. He got a hold of my coat, and we tussled ... My coat," he grimaced, "I lost my coat. Did you see it outside?"

Jonathan glanced at the doorway. "It may be out there, sir, but it's still raining ..."

Holmes sighed, clearly pained; it was a very nice coat.

"In any case, he managed to get the wire around my neck."

"That's odd, Holmes. I've hardly ever seen anyone get the best of you in a fight."

Holmes looked a bit self-conscious. "Who said he got the best of me in the fight? I'm pretty sure I broke his wrist and possibly a few fingers."

"Is that why he didn't finish the job?"

"I presume. I did pass out for a bit. He may have thought he succeeded."

I moved the handkerchief to see if the bleeding had slowed. It had. "How did he not succeed? The garrote looks like it only broke the skin in one small place."

He slipped off his glove – which I only now noticed was torn – and held up a bruised and sliced hand. He moved it up towards his neck, miming how he had raised a palm between the wire and his neck.

I gasped and grabbed his hand, examining it. There was also some bleeding, and these cuts would certainly need stitches.

"I need my medical bag at the inn."

"It's fine, Watson. The leather of the gloves did wonders to protect my skin. Though I will now have to purchase another pair."

I stood to pour some alcohol on my handkerchief. Little Jonathan stepped between Holmes's knees, looking at his hand and hissing with childlike sympathy. Holmes allowed him, leaning over the boy and reassuring him that he was all right. "Barely stings," he commented. "It'll be good as new in a day or two."

I pressed the cloth to his hand, doing my best to disinfect the cuts until I could get to my bag. Holmes didn't react but when I dabbed at his neck, he jerked away and glared at me. I handed the cloth to the little boy and showed him how to dab gently at the cut. Holmes submitted to his clumsy ministrations but gave me an annoyed look.

"Does it feel better?" Jonathan asked.

Holmes nodded, "Yes, you're a doctor in the making."

"Why would someone try to hurt you, Mr. Holmes?" Emma asked.

"I'm not sure. By all accounts, it doesn't make sense. I can see no motivation for it."

"This little criminal gang who killed Richard may be trying to warn you from investigating any further," I commented.

"I suppose. Not the best way to get me to stop," Holmes muttered darkly.

"Well, not everyone is as excited by death threats as you are, Holmes."

He grinned at me, that charming twinkle only a privileged few were privy to lighting up in his eyes. "One can never be bored when someone's trying to kill them."

"Are you sure you don't need medical help, sir?" Emma asked.

Holmes gently removed Jonathan and stood, unwinding himself from the throw cover. "I've suffered far worse, my lady," he dismissed. "However, a warm bath would do me good."

I gathered his papers as he put on his shoes, stuffing his wet socks into his pocket. I was glad to be off, eager to wrap his hand in gauze to help him heal.

"We'll clean your coat as soon as we retrieve it, Mr. Holmes."

Ever fastidious about his appearance, Holmes cast a longing look out of the French windows and nodded his thanks. Seemed an odd thing, to me, to be upset about while sporting garrote marks on one's neck, but Holmes was always an odd one.

Chapter Fourteen

Holmes informed me that night that he had discovered more in the Swift's grounds than he had disclosed.

"Why did you keep details to yourself?" I asked. "Do you suspect young Emma?"

Holmes sighed, throwing himself onto the settee and tugging at his tie. "It is not that I suspect her outright, but this whole affair is complicated, and I feel it's helpful to keep some particulars close to the chest when one isn't entirely sure of what parts all the characters are playing in a story."

"And what did you discover?"

He stood and began undoing his wet cuffs. "There rain nearly derailed me, but I was able to trace the escape of two men, both average height, one wearing a size 8 and the other wearing a size 11 shoe, through the underbrush to the left of the stables. The trail eventually became muddy, but I assume that they made their way back towards town. I suspect they were carrying pieces of a plane of glass. Most likely used to create the Pepper's ghost illusion. The boots seemed well-worn, indicating our quarries are not well-off."

I watched him nudge each of his own boots off with a toe and turn on the hot water tap to the bath.

"But if they fled, who attacked you?"

The detective paused at this, pursing his lips. "Indeed. That is the question. And it implies there is a third party. But why did this third man not escape with his clan? That is a question I plan to ruminate on in the bath with a nice pipe in hand."

I took that as my cue to leave and settled into bed after washing my face and stoking the fire that had been graciously lit by the staff.

We spent the next morning visiting Miller and attempting to

connect names to the faces we had sketched with our friend Satine's aid.

The officer could not help us in our endeavor to identify any of Little Richard's former compatriots, giving us a contrite look and explaining that the details of servants was not something he was usually concerned with. He advised us that our best bet would be to go straight to the source and visit a few of the more well to-do houses and match sketches to actual faces. Holmes looked annoyed at this hurdle; he himself was a living encyclopedia of Londoners, being as familiar with the street urchins of Whitechapel as he was with the residents of Belgrave Square.

The residents were also not forthcoming, barring us from entry at the very idea that we would like to investigate their staff. I could see Holmes's ire rising with each scandalized response and closed door. The old widow Lawry was the only one with any information that was useful at all. None of the sketches matched her small, mostly female, contingent of servants, but she did seem to recognize one sketch as a boy whom she had found loitering about as if familiar with her maid. Her maid was no longer with her, having disappeared a little over a year before. Lawry believed she had eloped with another young gentleman and made her way with him to America. When pressed for more information about him, Lawry insisted that she had never seen him before and once she had warned her girl away from him, never saw him again.

I suspected the boy had used the maid to gain details about the widow's safe, and Holmes agreed with me as we alighted into the carriage after we bid her adieu.

"How the deuce does it help us?" he demanded. "We already know there was a petty theft ring that the oldest Swift boy was involved in. But we still don't know why they – if it was them – killed him or why they are still lurking about. Perhaps playing ghostly tricks on the Swift patriarch, of all absurd things. Or maybe it's two completely different cases …" he trailed off with an annoyed huff.

He was still in a bad mood when we returned to the inn and found Emma waiting for us in his rooms. She was tidying up Holmes's whirlwind mess of papers and cigarettes when we entered. Holmes, upon hearing we had a visitor, had put on a pleasanter expression, though I could see the tightness of his movements that spoke of his impatience.

She dropped some newspapers she was straightening and flushed at being caught at what could be perceived as snooping. Holmes made no comment, however, and swept into the chaotic space with that confidence that so easily controlled situations and people.

He dropped his sketches onto the newly cleared coffee table and removed his scarf. "Miss Emma! What brings you to our neat little home away from home?"

She watched his fingers work at the knot of his scarf and then reached over and picked up a black bundle from a chair. It was Holmes's frock coat.

The detective let out a noise of happy satisfaction and plucked it from her like a man reuniting with a long-lost child.

"I had it cleaned for you," she explained.

He was examining it carefully. When he came to the inside seam, he let out an annoyed sigh. "It's ripped here."

Emma made a disconcerted noise. "I'm so sorry. If I had known, I would have sent it to a tailor-"

"Do not stress yourself, Miss Emma," Holmes cut her off. "I wasn't expressing annoyance at you, merely the situation. I can easily repair it with a borrowed needle and thread from the proprietors here."

"I could manage that for you," she offered, but Holmes waved her off.

"No need. I can work a needle very well." He smiled slyly at her. "I can cook too, when necessary. Even though Watson likes to deny this."

Emma glanced at me for confirmation, and I shrugged. To be honest, Holmes could whip together some appetizing food, but he also had many missteps over the years, including nearly burning down Mrs. Hudson's kitchen when trying to cook some lamb shanks. "He can make a very admirable crème brûlée," I agreed.

"Speaking of," Holmes interjected while folding the outer coat gently over the back of his chair, "Watson and I were just about to have dinner. Would you like to join us?"

We only went as far as the inn's restaurant, settling into that same comfortable table next to the hearth. It was late, so it was blessedly quiet. Emma tucked into her potatoes and roast beef with a refreshing gusto, and I found it amusing to try to make her laugh so that she held her hand up over her mouth nervously. I saw Holmes watching her carefully, picking delicately at his own food. He appeared simultaneously distracted and intently focused on her which could be a dangerous combination.

She asked about cases I had not yet published, and I used her to test out my narrative of our latest case the year last with the strange red-headed league.

At the dénouement, she laughed. "All that and they were simply digging into a bank vault."

"The simplest answer is often correct," Holmes explained gently.

She nodded. "Yes, Occam's razor," she commented, earning a surprised and impressed look from Holmes. At his expression, she explained, "I've read Isaac Newton, Mr. Holmes. And many other books. I'm familiar with the rule of simplicity. It seems to me, however, that many of your cases do not have simple explanations."

"Do you feel this ending is too simple?" I asked eagerly. Holmes gave me a scolding look, aware of the nature of my interest. I shrugged. "A good writer is always interested in the opinions of the reading public." I realized too late that I had set up a strike with my use of "good writer" and cringed, waiting for the expected jibe.

Surprisingly, Holmes controlled himself and gave me a crooked half smirk in its stead. I still understood.

Emma interrupted our silent conversation. "No, I do not believe it's too simple. In fact, I think, in this case, simplicity is helpful considered the strangeness of the rest of the story. Honestly, that contrast also highlights your friend's talents." She turned to said friend. "You must have a very strong imagination to envision events so clearly."

Holmes gave her a tight smile. "I don't imagine. I deduce."

"But surely-"

"I look at details and can tell you exactly what transpired based on those facts. I do not need to imagine anything."

"You must envision it, though? Imagination must come into play."

"It does not."

She fell silent, glancing between us curiously. She used her thumb to spin the small ring on her index finger absently, a clear nervous tell. "Forgive me," she began hesitantly, "but why does my assertion bother you so?"

"It does not. I simply insist on accuracy."

"As do I." She said this with no antagonism but instead of sort of hopeless confusion. I took a bite of my steak, enjoying this back and forth from the safety of my status as a neutral, third party. Holmes shot me a glance that seemed to say he found my amusement unamusing.

"Take perspective, for example," Emma continued, "In Watson's stories, he tells me the facts of events quite explicitly. But my mind still works to envision the scenes, specifically from his perspective. *A Study in Scarlet* would seem very different from your perspective, and I would no doubt imagine it differently."

"But the facts are the same."

She sighed. "I feel you're missing my point on purpose. I'm not implying anything that negates your deductive abilities. But there's subjectivity in everything. My brother's murder appeared one way to the murderer and differently to my brother, I'm sure."

Holmes nodded. "But the facts of his murder are the same from an outside, objective perspective."

"True. And I appreciate that you play the part of that objective, outside perspective. But to say that no imagination is necessary on your part to recreate it in your mind feels frankly dishonest."

I looked between the two, wondering at their forthright and unemotional discussion of her brother's murder.

Holmes put his knife and fork down and took on that detached lecturer's voice I was so familiar with when he wanted to distance himself from a situation. "If what I see is the truth, it requires no imagination. Perhaps if I attempted to step into the role of the murderer – or the victim – that would require imagination. I would need to adopt their mindset, one that is not my own. But I do not attempt to do that."

She ruminated on that. "I see. So from an outside perspective, how did my brother's face look when he was dealt that blow?"

"I would ima-" he broke off, face flushing. A hush fell over the table for a horrible moment. I nearly choked on my steak at the sight of my friend's embarrassment at being caught out so. I wiped my mouth on my napkin and looked to the young girl, wondering if she realized the import of what she had just done.

Surprisingly, there was no triumph on her face. There was no indication that she had meant to win anything in this discussion. If anything, she looked confused by the whole encounter.

Holmes bit the inside of his lip and pushed his plate away from him slowly. She had upset him, and I felt my heart sink with disappointment. The evening had been going so well.

She fidgeted with her own napkin, suddenly looking distressed. "Forgive me, Mr. Holmes. I did not mean to argue with you at all. At times, I cannot help pressing a point. I know it's a very unattractive quality."

I expected the detective to excuse himself and leave. To my surprise – and relief – he cleared his throat and smiled at her. "Do you like wine?" he asked.

She gaped at him for a moment, obviously working through this social cue that was strange to her. It was clear to me that Holmes wished to move past the conflict without the pain of apologizing or being apologized to. This was odd of him; if Holmes wanted to discontinue a conversation, he tended to do so simply by abruptly exiting even if it came across as rude.

She glanced at me, and I nodded minutely to her. "Yes," she replied, "I like a sweet wine."

"They have a nice, very sweet red here. It's not vintage or expensive but delicious." He gestured to the barmaid and had her fetch us a bottle.

As Holmes poured us our cups, I caught Emma's eyes and shook my head, hoping she got my hint. To divert even more effectively, I spoke up, "If you thought those other adventures were interesting, just wait until I tell you about the giant rat of Sumatra."

Emma's eyebrows raised with surprise. Her gaze darted between me leaning towards her conspiratorially and Holmes giving me an amused and long-suffering look.

"I would very much like to hear it," she said, but her scrutiny was on the detective as if trying to gauge his agreement.

He rolled his eyes but it was good-naturedly. Picking up his wine glass, he leaned back as if to give me the stage.

I regaled her, spinning her one of my finest tales, watching closely to make sure nothing became too gruesome for her. She listened raptly, never flinching even as I described that monstrous thing we ended up chasing through the London underground. I was halfway through describing how my friend had looked, dirty and bedraggled, climbing out of the rank sewers when Holmes pushed his chair away from the table with a rueful glance in my direction.

"Well, this is a moment I have no desire to relive, so if you'll excuse me, I admit I'm very tired." He looked at Emma. "Watson here will attend to you. It is late, so please let him escort you to find a cab." He bid us goodnight in that brusque manner that left no room for protestation and alighted the stairs.

Emma watched after him, and I was struck by the expression on her face. Barring the crude way he'd phrased it, I wondered if her brother hadn't been spot on in his assessment of his sister's feelings towards Holmes. It wasn't that unusual; my roommate possessed charm, blinding intelligence, and arguably good looks, but most women were drawn to the challenge more than all else. I could easily recognize the determination in their approach to him, the idea that they could be the extraordinary one to break through his cool exterior driving their actions more than any real warmth of feeling.

But Miss Emma's face was bare of all that, smeared only with a pained longing that caused a strangled well of sympathy to lurch up in my chest. She caught me looking at her and flushed brightly.

"Don't be offended," I waved off, clearing my throat. "Holmes often reaches his limit of conversation and needs his pipe and solitude or else he becomes unbearable company."

"I understand that. I often feel the same way. I believe this may be the longest social interaction I've enjoyed in quite some time, doctor."

I pressed my hand to my chest in exaggerated pleasure. "I'll take that as a compliment."

She smiled. "It's merely the truth."

She seemed in no hurry to leave, and I was still working on my glass of wine, so I asked her the usual things about her upbringing and her education, all of which she answered perfunctorily. Obviously not one for small talk, I took a guess and ventured to ask her about where her interest in flowers originated.

Her face lit up. "Oh, I have always loved beautiful things, very simply. However, many beautiful things have become tainted in my eyes by the people around them. Take art, for example. I love paintings, but paintings carry implications of class, education, money … I cannot visit a museum without being aware of my status in society, and I cannot simply view a work of art without feeling forced to dissect it. Art becomes an exercise in vanity so easily. The same with music. This is why I do not play for anyone; even at those horrid parties I'm occasionally forced to attend, I refuse to play for an audience. My music is mine. As are my flowers. I do not want them tangled with society." She grew quiet a moment, twirling her ring again. "Forgive me, doctor. I speak too much but often find it hard to articulate what I'm really thinking in any way that is understandable. I feel like I'm miming behind a thin sheet, hoping others can follow."

"You're not alone in that, I daresay. I think many of us, to varying degrees, feel this way. My wife is very similar. In my company, she speaks freely but she often struggles to find the words to express herself clearly."

"As a writer, you should be well suited to help her. A nice complement."

"I try, but as you said, it's all a mime show really, isn't it?"

She nodded. "We're all alone. Ultimately. Stuck in this," she pressed at the flesh of her hand, "and fundamentally separate from others. We know our loved ones at a remove. Always looking at a shell and not the true thing."

"Nicely put."

She shrugged. "And sometimes even we don't know ourselves."

"For some, that's the only way they survive."

Her eyes flitted to the staircase Holmes had disappeared up a moment ago. "Yes, I think that may be truer than we realize."

I was protective of Holmes, and it was late, so I called the barmaid over to settle the bill and helped Emma gather her things.

The night was cold but dry, so we chose to walk for a while. Instead of picking up the conversation from before, she strolled silently next to me for a long time before commenting with dry amusement, "Mr. Holmes seems much attached to his coat."

"Ha! Yes. He's a strangely fastidious man. Always well put together."

"From your stories, I pictured him to be much more…" she waved her hands about, searching for the right word, "… bohème."

I snorted. "You should see his rooms."

"I just did."

I pointed back in the vague direction of the inn. "That? Oh, that's neat, Miss Emma. That's him putting forth effort."

"Oh. Oh my." She fell silent, likely trying to imagine how any one's rooms could look worse than the disarray she'd just seen. "I wonder about that," she finally murmured, as if speaking to herself. "Seems contradictory to be so careful about personal appearance but surround yourself with chaos. Both in terms of his lodgings and his work, I suppose."

"After years of living and working beside him, I've come to look at it this way – Holmes can't bear the thought of appearing anything other than completely unflappable. Personal appearance plays into that. Messiness implies distraction, perhaps even confusion or stress. But his environment is simply his kingdom. He would say there's a method to his madness. And indeed, he often knows exactly where everything is at, even when it makes no sense."

"Like affixing his correspondence to the mantelpiece with a knife?"

"Yes, like that."

We walked peacefully for a moment before she asked, "Is he though?"

"I beg your pardon?"

"Is he unflappable?"

I had been privy to some of Holmes's worst failures and seen the shame and embarrassment he would have hidden from others.

"No one is unflappable," I answered diplomatically.

Once it became clear that her coat was no longer shielding her from the cold, I fetched a cab for her and made sure she was bundled into the carriage. I assured her that we would keep her apprised of the case, and she frowned.

"Holmes believes my brother was killed by his questionable associates, doesn't he?"

"It's the simplest explanation."

"But it doesn't actually explain much, does it?"

I considered how to respond. "Yes," I ventured, "you're correct. That is why my friend hasn't made any definite statements about the case. He too is dissatisfied with that reasoning, as obvious as it seems to be. But we will get to the bottom of things. Trust me."

She didn't looked convinced, but nodded and ordered the driver on his way. I watched her four-wheeler rattle down the street before leisurely making my way back to my rooms.

It was silent behind Holmes's door; I resisted the urge to confer with him and left him to his pipe and meditations and instead got comfortable in my own rooms, barefoot and sleeveless next to a roaring fire.

I was in the middle of enjoying some roasted chestnuts I had procured from a vendor down the street and a dog-eared copy of Shelly's newest work when I heard some rather strange grunting muffled by the wall. In normal cases, I would not poke my nose into other people's private business but seeing as these grunts seemed to be coming from the wall separating me from Holmes, I stood and ventured to lean towards it, trying to ascertain what that blasted man could possibly be doing so loudly.

There was a ringing crash and loud repetitive thuds. I'm afraid it took me an embarrassingly long time to realize what was happening before I sprang into action, fumbling for my revolver in the drawer and rushing out of my room. Holmes's door was locked and a few attempts to put my shoulder to it made no difference. I resorted to blowing the lock off with a deafening report of my gun and slammed into the room to see my friend being attacked by three men.

The room was in disarray, the bath was full, but water was splashed all around the carpets and the screen knocked over. Chairs and items were disrupted, strewing papers and Holmes's assortment of used cups and cigarettes across the room.

Holmes was pressed on top of the table with all three men holding him down. He twisted and kicked to free himself, scrabbling at the hand wrapped around his throat.

I let off another shot at the ceiling, and two of the men let up, rushing towards the open window. This time I shot at them, but my bullet splintered the wood of the frame, and they were gone. The last man, the one engaged in trying to break my friend's neck, was slower to react, and as he turned aside to follow his compatriots, Holmes slid to the floor gasping, hooked an ankle around his foot, and sent the intruder sprawling.

They both scrambled to their feet but Holmes, with an extremely quick burst of violence, pushed him forward into the stone ledge of the mantelpiece. His head made contact with a resounding crack, and then he lay limply at my friend's feet.

My heart was racing,kno but as the adrenaline ebbed, I was able to take stock of the situation. Holmes was bare and wet except a pair of hastily shucked on trousers. It was obvious the men had entered the room through the window, giving Holmes only enough warning to exit the bath and pull on the bare minimum of clothing. The disastrous state of the room implied a rough fight, and I could see Holmes favoring his side.

"Are you all right?" I exclaimed, fully entering the room.

Holmes reached up and felt the back of his head tenderly, flinching. "Yes, quite all right," he hissed, voice raw. He stepped over the unconscious man to an upturned side drawer and pulled out his cuffs.

"I thought you didn't bring those," I asked stupidly.

He shot me an exasperated look. "I wasn't going to show them to a child."

Before he could lean down to restrain the prisoner, the door behind me creaked. I realized we had an audience; the innkeeper and his wife, along with a few of the barmaids were peering into the room, alarmed by the ruckus.

Holmes noticed them too, quickly stepping backwards and out of view of the women. I pulled the door closed to just a gap and spoke to the proprietor. "I'm sorry for the disturbance, sir. Could you be kind enough to alert the local police? We'll compensate you for your trouble and damages, of course."

The man nodded and hustled the women out of the hallway as I closed the door.

Holmes had secured the man's wrists but was now gathering some clothes. As he righted the bath screen and disappeared behind it, he bid me to check on the man's injury. "Is he alive?"

I rolled him over and checked his pulse. "Yes, though you're lucky, Holmes. A head injury like that could have killed this man instantly."

There was a muffled comment I couldn't hear from behind the screen. He emerged a second later in dry trousers, buttoning his waistcoat.

"He may be alive, but do you think he will regain consciousness? I have some questions for him." He sat and slipped on some socks.

"I'm not sure. Brain injuries are tricky. Is this the man that attacked you at the house?" I asked. I analyzed the face before me; young, lower class by the state of his clothes.

Holmes shook his head. "No, his hand isn't broken." He rubbed his neck ruefully. "But I think one of the others might have been. I twisted his fingers, and he made a very interesting noise." He looked up from where he was lacing his boots, looking a little too pleased with himself, then stood and with a sudden burst of worried energy, nearly flung himself across the room to look under his bed.

"What's wrong?"

He didn't answer, but popped up with his violin case in hand. He sighed with relief to see it had been unharmed in the tussle.

I kept an eye on our prisoner, worried at his lack of response. It seemed Holmes had given him quite a knock on the head. If he lived, it may be a while before he regained consciousness.

After half of an hour, there was a brief knock on the door, and one of the barmaids opened it tentatively, eyes downcast until she noticed Holmes was fully dressed this time. "The police are here, sirs." She stepped aside, and the constable and two bobbies slid in, casting quick and appraising glances at the mess.

Miller looked around with a wry and critical eye, ascertaining the order of events quickly. "They assaulted you while you were in the bath? How ungentlemanly," he commented absurdly.

Holmes laughed.

"This man needs a hospital right away," I interjected. "He has a massive head injury, and I fear for the worst."

Holmes looked sobered at that but not guilty. I understood the conflict, as a doctor.

Miller obliged, and he and his men set to work bundling up the assailant and carting him to the closest hospital.

"How is the state of your neck?" I asked the detective once he had submitted to the police questioning and we were left alone.

Holmes glanced around at the wreck and began righting some furniture. "It's been subjected to worse," he dismissed. I wondered if he was referring to the previous garroting he'd barely avoided or some other incident. Either way, it was troubling to hear him be so nonchalant about injury.

"May I examine it?"

I could tell he did not want me to. His fist tightened but to appear reasonable, he obliged. The skin was not bruised too badly, and I suspect the struggling I had witnessed was more due to being held down by three large men than being choked, thankfully.

"We need to speak to the patient as soon as possible."

I frowned. "I agree, but that blow to the head was severe, Holmes."

He righted an overturned chair. "Do you think he'll live?" His tone was casual, but I could sense his concern.

"Very likely, but if his brain is swelling, he will not be ready to speak to anyone for quite some time."

He sighed. "Then tomorrow, I want to visit any tattoo parlors in the area. I suspect there are few which will be helpful in narrowing down where those boys all got that distinctive tattoo."

"Yes. But it may be a shot in the dark to presume they would keep diligent records of clients."

Holmes shrugged. "Sometimes we must walk every road to find our destination, Watson."

Chapter Fifteen

Our plans were halted by some unexpected developments. We had arisen quite late the next day, though the dark arcs under Holmes's eyes informed me that he may not have slept at all. He would never admit it, but being subjected to multiple attempts on one's life likely took a toll.

Holmes presumed that the closest tattooist would be in Stroud, so we made our way down the main road of Cheltenham to find some breakfast and get some fresh air before officially starting the day.

"I received a telegram from Miller today," he finally said, voice subdued. "My attacker didn't last through the night."

His tone made it difficult for me to know what to say. "It wasn't your fault. You acted in self-defense."

"I don't feel guilty. At least not inordinately so. I get no satisfaction from anyone's death, but the bruising on my neck reminds me that he would have had no qualms about killing me. I am disappointed that a prime source of information has once again slipped through my fingers."

"Have we identified him?"

"Not yet."

I nodded. There hadn't been anything I could have done for the man, so I tried to push it from my mind and focus on the case.

After a long while, I changed the subject. "Not to be ungrateful for the peaceful walk and briskly invigorating fresh air, Holmes, but why did we not break our fast at the inn?"

As if to exemplify my statement, he took a deep breath as if savoring the lack of fog so common in the city. "You yourself may not be a great light, Watson, but you are an exceptional conductor."

"I beg your pardon?"

He wiped at the light moisture at his temple from the early

morning drizzle. "I would like to, as the Americans say, bounce some ideas off of you."

"Ah."

"I keep turning over the facts of the case in my own mind, but it may be useful to filter it through a third party."

I nodded, sidestepping and tipping my hat at a young woman passing by. "As a writer, I find it useful to hear my writing read out loud to me. It allows me to hear the flow of sentences and follow the plot from a more objective standpoint."

He shook his head, frowning. "I don't need an objective standpoint. I need connections that will make the logic of these events clear."

"It wasn't a direct comparison," I grumbled.

He gave me a conciliatory look. "Of course." Despite his stated desire to speak to me, he fell into silence for a few long minutes as we made our way down the cobbled streets.

At last, with that same placating tone, he spoke, "It was a strategy my brother taught me when I was young. When I faced hard puzzles or confusing events, he would painstakingly walk me through all the details, all the actions that led up to it, in an effort to understand it. And therefore control it or prevent it or even manipulate it. He had other motives for the exercise, but I find it beneficial now in my chosen field." He shrugged, "I'm a little out of practice – my mind detects and correlates clues on a rapid pace now – but occasionally I find it to be, and I don't admit this lightly, a comforting habit."

"Then I am happy to be of service to you. As always."

He smiled at that and then began a clinical summation of the case. "A few months ago, Mr. Swift begins to notice odd happenings in the house. He writes to Harris, who eventually comes to speak to us."

"But the odd happenings up to that point are subtle. None of the rest of the family notices," I interrupted.

Surprisingly, he did not look irritated by my input. "Indeed. We arrive, and it becomes immediately clear to me that someone in the house is aware of my methods and trying to mislead me. Which also means that they would be adept at covering over those small clues I rely on to make my bread and butter and my not inconsiderable reputation."

"Sterling reputation," I clarified with some cheek.

He winked at me. "At least professionally." Sobering, he continued, "We also know that items were going missing from the house and replaced with fakes. Now all of this is easily explained by Richard the second; he cavorts with the working class, and they scheme to steal items from the middle class and wealthy estates and use those ill-gotten gains for gambling and drinking and other," he waved his hand with a bit of discomfort, "pleasant activities. The noises Mr. Swift hears are simply the thefts taking place, the false clues and meticulous clean-ups are the work of the young master, finding an extra avenue of gratification in trying to toy with me."

"He was certainly arrogant enough to believe himself very clever."

He tsked. "He didn't strike me as clever. However, looks can be deceiving … But then he dies. This can also be explained by the fact that young Swift's servant co-conspirators had been let go. He no longer had the advantage of partners handily located right in the house, and I believe carrying off his family's possessions on his own became too much trouble. This may have led him to either back out of the scheme, much to the anger of his partners, or attempt to let others into the house to act as accomplices. Either way, he runs afoul of those who have much more on the line than the wealthy cad about, and it ends in his violent demise. An act of unpremeditated passion."

I hummed in discontent. "While the chains of your logic are

strong, the murder of Richard still feels subject to too much speculation in the stead of real evidence."

"I agree. The solution works, but that does not make it a reality. And then we have the more overt attempts at creating the illusion of a haunting."

I stopped our movement with a hand against his arm. "This is the point that confuses me, Holmes. At this juncture, if no other action had taken place, we may have been forced to cede to the theory that fit all the facts and written off the murder as a natural consequence of Swift's illegal mischiefs."

"Yes," he tapped his finger against my lapel, "so why the cheap Pepper's ghost stunt? Why the attempts on my life?"

I lifted my shoulder in a gesture of helpless confusion. "Well, the attempts on your life could be the murderers of young Swift warning you away from looking into his death."

"That is very true. But combined with the pained wailing and theatrics, the story gets muddy."

"Maybe they are two different cases?"

He leaned his head back to the sky and rotated his shoulders like a man readying for a fight. "That would be coincidental."

"You don't believe in coincidences."

He sighed. "Not as a general rule. But I haven't taken it off the table. It could indeed be two different mysteries." He made a sharp slicing motion with his gloved hand, speaking with no shortage of frustration, "But then we must face the fact that we are left with the original mystery – the matter we have been called here for – still much as it was when arrived. What is the source of the items moving and disappearing? What is the source of noises in the night-"

"No," I interjected, "that was the thefts."

Holmes stepped fully in front of me, arching an eyebrow

meaningfully. "Was it? So we are conveniently called here to investigate a possible haunting that is actually thieves doing their work at night, but while we are still here, someone begins faking a haunting?"

I ran a hand across my forehead, my head starting to pound. "So you do not believe the 'hauntings' were the criminals pilfering the house under the watchful guide of young Swift?"

"Herein lies the problem." He used his hands to create an imaginary timeline. "We have to deduce when the noises, etcetera, shifted from criminal activity to the ghostly tricks ostensibly aimed at the elder Mr. Swift. And the answer to that is simple."

"It is?"

He nodded slowly at me, as if speaking to a young child. "How did young Swift aid his comrades?"

"He let them into the house."

A sharp, disappointed shake of his head. "No."

"Oh," I pressed my fingers to the bridge of my nose, "the two servants who were dismissed. He never had to let anyone into the house. That's right. So when they left, Swift lost his accomplices."

"At that point, the Swift house was no longer a target. Young Swift helped the servants steal the items from the house and partook of a percentage of the profits to pay off his gambling debts. But left with no accomplices, Swift may have thought it too risky – or frankly, not worth the effort – to continue. He removed himself from the game."

"And that led to his death?"

He shrugged and we continued walking towards a busier intersection. I could smell bread baking somewhere in the distance and my stomach rumbled appreciatively.

"As I said, that answer is still unclear. As are the attacks on me. But we know that when the servants were released from their posts, the unexplainable things that occurred in the home from there on out may very well be a completely different case."

"That certainly complicates things."

"Certainly, but we have at least a part of our problem organized and put in its place."

"I still don't understand if the details that Swift wrote to Harris about were connected to an issue that had already resolved itself – the release of the thieving servants – then why would our secondary culprit, whatever their motives, continue their plan while we are here? Had they laid low, surely we would have left under the assumption that Swift was just an old man suffering under imagined terrors."

Holmes was quiet for a long time before commenting soberly, "I get the impression that someone enjoys our presence."

"This is a game to them?"

"I do not believe it's a game, but I think they feel confident in their plans and perhaps find our confusion thrilling." There was a suggestion of something deeper than irritation in his voice at the very idea. "And that complicates things. Multiple motivations are harder to untangle."

I wondered if it did not also have a detrimental effect on my friend, whose pride and vanity did not take patronization or insult lightly. I kept that to myself though, aiming my nose towards the smell of freshly baked bread and coffee.

I never got my meal, however. When we stepped onto the intersection between a small farmer's eatery and some haberdasheries, my friend stole forward with a sharp cry and bought a morning edition of *Cirencester Times and Cotswold Advertiser* from a flustered news vendor.

"Watson!" he exclaimed but made no further effort to elucidate on what had caught his attention. He scanned a story with the look of a bloodhound and then pressed the paper at me with a sparkle of excitement in his eyes.

I smoothed out the paper and read the piece on the bottom of the front page:

Murder at the Browning Estate!

It was a relatively small article about the death of a kitchen girl by the young footman of the house by the name of March. The article was to the point, seemingly more interested in the wealth and renown of the family than the death of a lowly servant.

I glanced up at Holmes, confused.

Holmes's smile dimmed when he saw my lack of understanding. "A possible lead, Watson. And a good one, at that."

"You think this footman is part of the burglary ring?"

"It's a strong possibility."

I thought it just as likely it was an assignation between servants gone wrong, but I had learned a long time ago to trust Holmes and his suspicions. "That may be, Holmes, but if memory serves me correct – and it's a pretty vivid memory – the Browning household is the one who attempted to set the dogs on us when we came around asking questions last time. Mr. Browning is a very wealthy and very prominent man in the area – even in London."

"Yes, he was a judge. Retired now but no less powerful. Still worth a quick pop over. What's the worst that can happen?"

"He can set the dogs on us."

Holmes laughed. "I adore dogs. Let's fetch a cab."

I sniffed the air mournfully, seeing my chance to have some delicious breakfast slipping through my fingers.

The Browning house made the Swift grounds look quaint. It sprawled out across a well-kept lawn and was accessible by a long walkway that trailed past a peaceful tributary of the creek. I kept my ears open for any pattering sound of dogs' paws, still on edge from that threat the last time we were here.

We did not even get as far as the door this time. We were stopped by a handful of officers barring the way. Even Holmes's well-known name met with no reaction.

Holmes looked annoyed. "Is Constable Miller inside? If you ask him, I'm sure he'll allow me entry."

The officer shook his head. "No, it's not possible, sir. Judge Browning has given us strict orders to keep the number of people in his house to a minimum."

"Even you?" Holmes asked. "It seems odd an officer of the law would allow his authority to be dictated by a civilian."

"A judge, sir," the officer responded, glaring at my friend. I suspected my friend had hit close to the truth there but instead of inspiring rebellion, it only served to make the officers more stubborn to create an illusion of control.

"Can you at least ask Miller if he would mind coming out here to me?"

The prominent officer in the group glanced towards the house but then shook his head. "Look, sir, I know who you are. Your name is familiar to me. I also know that Miller admires you, but I will not risk my job by defying orders. I'm sure the Constable would be agreeable to meeting with you later at the police station where he can answer any of your questions." With that, he stepped back, forming a neat barricade and clearly dismissing us. Being dismissed was not something Holmes usually took lightly.

To my surprise, though, he merely inclined his head politely and turned away, hustling me along.

"This is not an unexpected development, Watson. Judge Browning is still a very prominent figure. His years as a judge aligned him closely with the police commissioner, both Warren and Anderson. It isn't an overstatement to say he has considerable sway in who is promoted, demoted, and even fired."

Holmes, no stranger to influential government personages, looked unimpressed.

Roughly halfway down the walkway, when we were out of sight of the officers, Holmes pulled me suddenly to the side and through the thorny hedge lining the side yard.

I hissed as a thin branch or two scraped at my face, glaring at Holmes as we emerged onto the lawn. He didn't pay me any mind, once again pulling me, this time downwards to make sure we were out of view of the tall windows looking into what appeared to be a spacious music room.

Creeping our way along, we traversed the side of the house and turned a corner towards the back, near the kitchen door. At any moment, I was certain I would feel the sharp bite of dog's teeth in my leg, but the beasts must have been locked away for the sake of the police.

Holmes darted to the small door, used by servants to enter and exit the downstairs kitchen.

"Holmes," I whispered, "do you even know where we are going?"

"Miss Monk was a kitchen servant. Balance of probability says that if she stumbled upon another servant pilfering, it was because she was going about some of her own duties. And the closest valuables to a kitchen are generally silverware and china sets locked up in an adjoining room."

"There may be police there."

"Indeed, therefore we should exercise caution." He put his finger to his lips and picked the lock quickly after pressing his ears to the door for a bit.

It swung open soundlessly to a small but clean and well-stocked kitchen. It was empty, so we went in, treading lightly on the freshly cleaned wood floors. Holmes glanced around, running a finger over the countertop and humming curiously. There was a large stew pot in the sink. Holmes examined it for a long time before bopping his head in the direction of the next room which, if he was correct, would be the scene of the girl's death.

He once again put his ear to the door and then tried the handle. It opened easily, creaking enough to make me flinch. We waited a moment, but when it seemed the sound had gone undetected, we stepped into the empty room that held the dinnerware and wine. The door on the other side of the room, leading into the main part of the house, was thankfully closed.

I wondered why there were not more officers here, taking notes of clues, but I reminded myself that the deaths in the servant class were not often taken as seriously as they should be.

The room was lined with tall, glass-encased cabinets filled with nice dinnerware sets, various crystals, and wine bottles. Not being a connoisseur, I could still tell that many of the items, and most of the wine, were high quality and therefore expensive.

Holmes stepped over to the cabinet on the right, pointing at the floor meaningfully. I was practiced enough to understand what he had noticed; the cabinet was slightly out of place on the carpet, as if it had been jostled.

Holmes examined the decorative molding carefully for some minutes and then nodded. "Someone hit their head here, very roughly," he whispered. "A short person, likely a woman. I suspect this is how Miss Monk came to her untimely end." He wedged a finger into the cabinet door, and it swung open easily, unlocked. Holmes cocked an eyebrow at me and bent to examine the latch.

"The lock has been picked-" he started but then inhaled a sharp breath and stood up straight, his head swinging towards the main door.

I was standing near the entrance to the kitchen, and Holmes made it to me in two steps and shoved me out. "Go," he ordered, closing the door on my face just as I heard the other door opening.

I stood dumbly in the kitchen for a moment, debating what to do. I heard raised voices and what sounded like a tussle and the thought of leaving Holmes there caught as a red-handed intruder warred with the practicality of getting away. There was nothing I could do for him, so I quickly exited the kitchen and, attempting the same stealth that had brought us into the house, crossed under the music room windows, fought my way through the hedge, and tried to appear collected as I started back up the drive to see what had happened to the detective.

The hullabaloo in the house must not have reached the officers outside because they looked exasperated at my return, one of them already holding up a forbidding hand to block my progress.

Before I could state my case, Miller emerged from the imposing front door and stalked towards me like a man who already knew I was there.

"Doctor Watson," he said, an odd tone to his voice, "Fancy meeting you here." He sighed. "Your companion is inside. Let him through," he waved at the human barricade in front of me.

They parted, frowning at my smug look as I passed them. In retrospect, I should not have been so smug, and I was soon to find out that Holmes and I were not welcome guests by any stretch of the imagination.

I was shown into a large drawing room and met the not unusual sight of Holmes front and center in the room, surrounded by officers and what I assumed was the master of the house. In this case, however, instead of holding court, Holmes looked on trial and was well into a heated argument with the older man in front of him.

Browning was a stately figure, likely late in his 60's, with a handsome shock of white hair and deep green eyes. Beyond that, however, his face was etched with frown lines and a general impression of a man who smiled little. He was barking authoritatively at my friend as if he were an ill-behaved schoolboy. Holmes appeared to be barely holding on to his decorum.

"You impertinent young boy, scuttling around another man's house where you are not wanted like a pig snuffling out truffles! The few shillings your work demands does not allow you to impose yourself on people above your station," the retired judge sneered and then seemed to grow even angrier at Holmes's lack of response. Looking at Miller, the irate man continued, "And you, Constable. You let you and your men be made a fool of by some jackanape know-it-all?"

Miller looked like a man trying to escape a trap who sees no way out.

Holmes interjected in an attempt to spare him. "Sir, I was merely investigating-"

"Meddling!" Browning cut him off. "Trying to make a scandal of a simple affair."

Holmes drew in a breath, ignoring the rude interruption. "I'm not sure it is a simple affair, sir."

"I didn't ask you what you think, did I? Servants cavort inappropriately with each other all the time, it's in their blood. Once the body of this trollop was removed and her lover arrested, I see no reason to continue discussing this. My house is clean of the rubbish, and I am done."

"And do you have any evidence that the two servants were-"

"I do not need to provide you with any evidence."

"I was only attempting to-"

"Trespass," the judge interrupted coldly.

I had never known anyone, not even the numerous criminals we'd encountered in the long course of our work together, who had the audacity to cut off Holmes more than once.

I saw a look of unrestrained anger mar my friend's face before he took a deep breath and began again, his tone forcefully conciliatory, "Trespassing was only an inevitable side-effect of my primary goal which is to help you investigate this murder and shed some light on young Miss Monk's tragic demise."

"As I said, what occurred here was simply two lower servants playing at St. George when the household was asleep."

Holmes made a look of distaste. "And this lover's meeting would naturally end in her death? What a cynical view." He turned to Miller, "Have you spoken to the boy yet? What does he say occurred here?"

"Constable!" Judge Browning snapped. "I did not employ a cheap amateur detective to snoop around my business. You will keep details of this crime to yourself as a professional should. By all accounts, you should be arresting this man on charges of trespassing."

"If I were to ever be arrested, sir, I assure you would not be on the embarrassingly pedestrian charge of trespassing," Holmes quipped, attempting to use his not inconsiderable charm (which he possessed when he wanted to possess it) to alleviate the tension.

It did not work. "Miller?" Browning prompted expectantly.

Miller stammered, obviously caught between someone he respected and someone he feared. Holmes too seemed to struggle with the dilemma of demanding answers to his questions and putting Miller in an awkward spot.

I stepped forward, putting up a placating hand. "Gentlemen, I am sure the whole affair is very upsetting, but we did not mean to offend you."

"Oh, you did not care," the judge fairly spat. He was likely right, knowing Holmes, but I kept my hand up, bearing forward with my apology nonetheless.

"We were only concerned with the truth and that may have blinded us to the respect we should have shown to your property and wishes. We will gladly take our leave." I tipped my hat.

I turned to leave, Holmes following unhappily, but we were stopped once again.

"No, you will not leave," Browning said. "Mister Holmes was trespassing on my property, meddling with a scene of a crime, and interfering with officers in the course of their duties." He looked expectantly at Miller whose face had lost all colour.

"Well, surely, sir-" he stammered and then fell silent when Browning's expression remained unmoved.

Holmes, sensing that the whole affair was decidedly turning against him, softened his face and his voice. "I do apologize for my behavior, sir. My companion and I will take our leave and be sure to refrain from bothering you again."

He turned to make a swift exit and was barred by the two policemen at the door.

"Oh, this is unbelievable," he muttered under his breath and turned to look at Miller. "You cannot seriously consider arresting me."

"He is not considering it. He is doing it. Miller." Browning gestured towards my friend then glanced at me. "This one can go free. He at least had the civility of pretending to come through my front door."

Holmes stared down a pale-faced Miller and then glanced quickly around at the multiple doorways, clearly judging the possibility and wisdom of escape. Seeming to come to a decision, he clenched his jaw so tight I could swear I could hear his teeth grinding together, and nodded.

"All right then," he said to the constable, "I'm in your custody, if that pleases you." The last part was meant to sting, and I could see it did by the look of dismay on Miller's face.

An officer stepped forward, pulling out a pair of cuffs.

"Really?" I protested. "Is all that necessary?"

"It is. Restrain him and remove him from my house." Browning turned away, dismissing us.

The police officer dutifully shackled Holmes's wrist, struggling to avoid looking at the detective's face peering down at him with undisguised condescension as the poor boy fumbled with the catch.

Holmes held his head up during the march outside and to the police cab, but I'm sure the whole thing was a source of mortification for someone with his prideful nature.

I followed at his elbow.

"This is not at all what I want, Mr. Holmes," Miller said from his other side.

"I'm sure it's not," Holmes sneered then tempered his tone with some effort. "Will you allow Watson some leeway to make inquiries during my confinement?"

"Of course, sir. Anything you'd like."

"I'd like to be released from these ridiculous handcuffs and allowed to go about my business," he jibed with some heat. Then to me, "Watson, can you find your way into the mortuary and look at the body of my attacker and this Miss Monk?"

"Yes, that should be no problem. I'm a doctor, after all."

"Good. And then will you also interview Mr. March and get his account of what happened last night?" He cast a questioning glance at Miller who answered for me.

"Yes, I can allow that as long as we're quiet about it."

We had reached the police escort, and Holmes hopped into the carriage, ignoring Miller's outstretched hand. "I'm relying on you,

Watson. Take good notes."

I did not envy Miller being stuck in a cab with Holmes at the moment, but ultimately, it had been the constable's choice. I watched it rattle off with a mild sense of panic at being left entirely on my own. I had accepted long ago that I was no investigator. I enjoyed the help I could provide my friend at times, but being thrust into the role of detective myself was daunting.

I took a deep breath, deciding to start in by examining the bodies of the deceased, medicine being the field I was most comfortable with.

But first, I hoped Holmes wouldn't mind if I stopped for some breakfast. Food is fuel for the spirit, after all.

The mortuary was in Pitchcombe. It was a small facility but well-kept and clean. Both bodies had already been washed, a fact that would have frustrated Holmes, but I was certain I would not have been able to extrapolate any useful information from dirt under fingernails or peculiar scents on their skin as my companion would have, so it was no big loss to me.

The doctor who allowed me entry – a Doctor Davies – uncovered the small, pale body of Miss Monk. Even after all these years as a physician, the sight of a corpse always gave me pause. The look of it was bizarre, like a thing rather than the remains of a living person. To me, it was unsettling and unnatural and even more so when the body in question was so young.

Miss Monk looked to be only around 20 years of age, slender and short but not frail. Her face was wide and proud, and I could easily see how pretty she had been in life with her soft brow and full lips. Her auburn hair was severely slicked backward, and there were no visible marks on her.

"Did you conduct an autopsy?" I asked.

Davies shook his head. "No, the cause of death was fairly obvious, and her family did not request one."

"She has family?"

"Yes, they are in Reading, so we've only spoken by telephone. They are on their way to take custody of her body. It is a small comfort to know she will be buried with some dignity, even if the ceremony is modest."

"What was the cause of death?"

He gestured to her head, and I gently helped him turn her over. Her injuries bore out Davies's conclusion; a large bruise across the nape of her neck where she had struck her head on a heavy mahogany cabinet in which the expensive silverware had been kept. Her neck was broken, and the skull likely fractured. Thankfully, it would have been a quick death.

"Poor girl," I murmured. "Was there any evidence of other violence?"

"Her wrist was slightly bruised, as if she had been yanked around by someone."

"Just one wrist?" I asked, moving downwards and looking for myself. I turned her right hand over and noted the red marks there, clearly the imprint of fingerprints.

"Yes, just the one hand."

"As if someone had held her to keep her from leaving," I commented, "but did not attempt to completely restrain her."

"A common mark on women who are being commandeered by a man, but not usually a sign of murderous intent."

"Any signs of interference?"

"No, none. And no indication of any conjugal congress at all. She was fully clothed at the time of her death, as well."

"Could be that was the point of contention. Some men do not

take lightly to being rebuffed, especially by women of her status. They often feel entitled to them."

"That's possible," Davies conceded with a shrug.

"Do you have the other body I spoke of?"

"Yes," he moved off to another slab, and I followed. Pulling the sheet back, I immediately recognized the man who met his end in our rooms. He too looked to be around 20, perhaps 25, years old.

"His injury was slower to kill him. A very sharp trauma to his temple – a very dangerous area to injure – caused hemorrhaging and brain swelling. He was in a coma for most of the night but died early this morning. Am I correct in assuming you were present when he was injured?"

"I was. He broke into my friend's room and was in the process of attacking him. He was pushed into the edge of the fireplace. An unfortunate accident."

"Ah ... your friend Sherlock Holmes?"

I glanced up at him, trying to gauge the nature of his interest. "Yes. That's correct."

He smiled. "I hope it's not too forward to compliment you on your writings, Doctor Watson. Where is the detective?"

"He, uh, had some other avenues of inquiry he wanted to follow," I lied.

Davies looked disappointed. "Ah, a shame. I would have loved to make his acquaintance."

I pulled the sheet back over the man. "Many say that until they meet him," I joked. "Do we know the identity of this man yet?"

"Yes, we do. This is mister Jeremy Combes. He was a valet for a family closer to Cheltenham, the Ganforth house. Small estate. They identified him and told me that they had not seen him in about two months."

"Did they let him go?"

"No, they claim he merely disappeared."

"And they did not call the police to report him missing?"

"They said they simply thought he had found more lucrative work elsewhere, perhaps not as on the up-and-up as housework, and left to avoid explaining himself."

"Was he a good worker?"

"They had no major complaints."

I hummed thoughtfully and then bid the man adieu.

"Is that all you needed?" he asked as I turned to go.

I tipped my hat, "You've been of great help. Many thanks."

The air outside had gotten blustery, and I pulled my collar up high and looked for a cab to bring me back to the police station to interview our killer and check on how Holmes was faring. It had been two hours and while that may have been an endurable stretch of time to me, I suspected Holmes was already bursting at the seams. I could imagine him pacing the confines of his cell like a restless tiger.

Miller met me in his office, apologizing profusely still. I waved him off and demanded to see Holmes.

The constable shook his head. "I'd rather get the interview with March out of the way. The sooner it's done, the sooner I can breathe easy about getting caught allowing you in here." Seeing my look of irritation, he pleaded with me, "Please, doctor. Your friend is well, if not restless. Besides, I'm sure he will be interested in the details of your discussion."

"Have you interviewed March yet?"

"I have. His story does not match Browning's suppositions. He admits to stealing and being caught by the girl. She was doing something in the kitchen and found him in the adjoining room. He claims her death was an accident."

"Where is he now?"

"I have put him in the main interrogation room. I'll escort you there now."

Mr. March had his head down on his folded arms, the weak lamplight above him casting a sickly yellow glow across the sparse room. He didn't raise his head until I took the rickety seat on the other side of the table.

He was a young man, perhaps 17 years of age. The dark, fine curl of his hair actually reminded me a bit of Holmes, as did his light, nearly grey eyes. He was a handsome boy, but his face was streaked with tears and his eyes swollen and red.

He looked curious to see me. "You're not a peeler."

I shook my head. "I'm not. My name is Doctor Watson."

"Your name is familiar."

"Really? Strange," I commented, "In any case, I want to ask you a few questions."

"A doctor is asking me questions? Why? Are you trying to help me?"

"Do you think you deserve help?"

This started a fresh torrent of tears. "I reckon I don't, sir. But I really didn't mean to hurt her."

"What was your relationship with Miss Monk?"

"Relationship? Just about none, sir. She was proper like. Very by the book. I think she was supporting her family with her wages, so she was wary of losing her post. She was fond of following the rules, to the letter, you know? Speaking to the male members of the house, even other servants, wasn't something she did unless it was about our duties."

"Maybe you should have followed her example," I commented dryly.

He brought his restrained hands to his face, sobbing in a way that would normally grate on my nerves. I felt a bit of pity for him, however, despite my better judgment.

"You're right, sir. I should have kept my head down and done my work."

"But you didn't?"

"No, another servant told me about a little scheme some other working folk had going on. I refused at first, but I saw the money they were pocketing, and the temptation got too much for me."

"What was the scheme?"

He shrugged. "Nothing very special. We stole items. We did it smart like, though. Slowly. We got duplicates done when we could by a man in Stroud who was good at that sort of thing. One of the other servants, from a different house, knew him. The duplicates made it possible for some missing things to go undetected. Other things were small items that we figured wouldn't be missed."

"When did this scheme begin?"

"About a year ago."

"And it is an ongoing industry?"

He nodded. "I was simply trying to take a bottle of wine and a few pieces of silverware. I didn't think anyone would notice. I could sell them for a little profit and maybe have a nice night out."

"You mean gambling? Drinking?"

"No, sir. I wanted to take a girl I fancy to the theater. Maybe a nice enough dinner so she wouldn't think badly of me."

"And how did Miss Monk get involved?"

"She must have been in the kitchen. Sometimes she does that, you know. After lights out, if she felt there was still some work to be done, she'd stay up late, cleaning. I didn't hear her in the kitchen. If I had-" he broke off again, and I patiently gave him a moment to contain himself after handing him my handkerchief.

"I didn't mean to kill her. I didn't even mean to hurt her. But she burst in demanding to know what I was doing. When she saw me with the cabinet open, she got right angry with me. Ordered me to put the items back and promised she'd be speaking to the master about this. I grabbed her wrist, only to try to plead with her, but she twisted away, pulling. I got angry. I let her go, but I also kind of pushed at the same time." He fell silent, breathing heavily. Then, "She hit the cabinet so hard. I swear the whole house should have heard it. Her face went slack, just like she was no longer there. I tried to catch her as she fell but … I didn't mean it. I can't believe this is happening to me."

"Happening to you, Mr. March? Miss Monk is dead," I scolded.

"I'll be too in no time!" he shouted. "A man of my class will see the gallows. No trial will save me. I deserve it anyway. Maybe it's for the best. I can't stop seeing her face."

"How many other people were involved in this scheme?"

"I'm not sure. I knew of about 10, but I think there were more. It was like a chain, not everyone knew everyone, but we were all connected."

"How about Richard Swift?"

He sniffled, "The classy bloke? Yeah, he was involved with some of his own servants. I think he owed people money. I can't remember the servants' names. One was Nichols, I think. But the other ones are in the wind, as far as I know."

"Which are in the wind? Specifically, the ones who worked at the Swift estate?"

He nodded. "About two of them, I think. The family let them go, and that was the last we heard of them."

"Did you know if any items were coming from the Swift house after that?"

"I don't think so. I don't think the young master of the house really wanted to get his hands too dirty."

"How were the profits split?"

"Evenly."

"Evenly? Across all 10 members, no matter where the items came from?"

"Yes, that is how we developed loyalty. Our success was the group's success. It worked out well, and it also spread out the money so that it was less likely any one of us would be caught with a large sum at one time."

"Did you know anything about a servant named Jeremy Combes?"

"His name sounds a bit familiar, but I don't think I ever met him. Why?"

"Do you know if he happened to be in the wind as well?"

He shrugged. "I'm not sure."

I tapped the table and rose. "Thank you for being honest."

As I was opening the door, he stopped me. "Will that be a mark in my favor, sir?"

"I beg your pardon?"

"That I was honest and helped you? Could that keep me from the noose?"

I was silent, unsure what to say. Finally, I simply tipped my chin at him and left, trying to ignore the fresh wave of chest-deep sobbing I heard behind me.

Miller was waiting for me and took me further back into the station without a word.

Holmes was seated at a table in another small room off the antechamber of jail cells. It was a dingy room, barely lit, and must have served as a secondary interrogation room when the need arose.

He was still handcuffed, and the look upon his face was absolutely murderous, his hair in disarray from where he had obviously been running his fingers through it in frustration. I would have laughed at the picture he painted, but I knew it would be a risk to my life to do so at the moment.

The door shut behind me, and I rocked up on my heels, tsking. "I always suspected it would come to this. You, my dearest friend, on that side of the table and myself here." I sat down across from him, affecting a look of exaggerated disappointment. "Once that brilliant mind of yours grew bored of being on the right side of the law and turned itself to criminal endeavors."

He didn't smile, but I saw my jibe worked to soften his mood, and a flicker of amusement could be detected around his sharp eyes. He sighed and leaned his head back, the line of his proud mouth still stern. "I assure you, Watson, had I ever any serious inclination to turn to criminal endeavors, no beetle crusher would ever be quick enough to get me into this room nor keep me here."

For a fact, I wondered why he was still even here now. I knew Holmes could work his way out of handcuffs; I'd seen him do it once before. I'd also seen him escape from a straightjacket, during one of his curious moods inspired by a young magician he'd come across, by popping his arm out of the socket, much to my medical displeasure. He had been forced, at last, to give in and ask me to help him put the joint back in its place, and I believe the embarrassment from that is the only thing that kept him from trying it again.

I assumed he did not wish to make Constable Miller's life any more stressful, but I felt a pang at the sour turn the relationship had taken considering Miller's admiration of the consulting detective. I hoped Holmes would not hold it against him for too long.

"How much longer do they intend to keep you here?" I asked.

Holmes shrugged, but it was a bit petulant. "About an hour, I believe. Miller is trying his best to at least appear to consider my arrest a serious matter. I, for one, suspect the fat-pocketed retired Tory that demanded my detainment has already forgotten about me. But Miller is understandably precious about his job, so …" he shrugged again.

"Well, in any case, it's very admirable that you have stayed put for his sake."

That, at last, earned a wide smile. "I can be considerate when the mood strikes me." He brought his shackled hands up onto the table, leaning forward. "Now, tell me what you learned."

I relayed to him all I had learned, patiently answering any question he interrupted with. When I was done, he leaned back and bit the inside of his lip.

"Do you want to visit the Ganforth house?" I asked.

He shook his head. "No, I suspect that would not provide me with any new information."

"Did anything I discovered help you?"

"Hmmm, possibly. At least we now know we are correct about the burglary ring. We also know that the Swift house was no longer a party to it once the servants were removed. It's not revolutionary information, but at least it provides more certainty to that theory."

"I am going to ask Miller to release you-"

"No need," he interrupted, bobbing his head towards the door that was opening.

Miller entered, looking harassed and worried. "Mr. Holmes, my apologies," he said, hastening to undo the detective's shackles. "We have kept you here without cause, and you have my sincerest apologies. I cannot express how deep my regret is."

Holmes stood as soon as he was released, staring curiously down at the strangely nervous man.

"What will you tell Mr. Browning now that you've released me without charge?"

"I'm sure Browning will reach an understanding of what took place here."

"Ha!" Holmes burst out with sudden amusement. "I see you've received some communiqué from my brother, eh?"

Miller stammered. "Had I known of your relation, Mr. Holmes, I would have never considered Browning's request. I assure you. I'm merely a constable, sir, my work is not as secure as some, and I'm not at liberty to ignore those above me."

Holmes pressed his hand to his shoulder. "I understand, constable. I never meant for my brother to strong-arm you with his influence, but I can't say I'm not thankful for it. Though," he added irritably, "he could have been quicker with his interference."

I hardly thought that was true; the speed with which the elder Holmes had somehow learned of his brother's detainment and arranged his release seemed supernaturally fast to me.

"He must care a great deal about you."

Holmes snorted. "In his way," he confirmed obliquely. "May I?" He gestured towards the door and therefore freedom and wasted no time moving past the constable and out of the station, his long legs outpacing me easily.

Once on the safety of the pavement, he took a deep fortifying breath as if he had been a prisoner in solitary confinement for years. I ignored his dramatics.

I asked him what our next step was. He seemed disinclined to continue our quest to find the tattoo artist as we had discussed the day before.

"I think a change of scenery might be good for us, Watson. I have plans to room somewhere else tonight."

"We're leaving the inn?"

"No, but we are sleeping elsewhere."

I peered curiously at him before venturing a guess. "You want to stay at the Swift home tonight, don't you? Trying to catch our culprit in the act?"

He nodded. "There's hope for you yet, Watson," he smiled.

Chapter Sixteen

We arrived at the Swift's around 6 o'clock without any polite advanced warning. Standing in the foyer, Holmes requested – in that authoritative manner that made his requests a mere formality – that we be allowed to stay the night.

The lady of the house looked a bit flustered at the demand. "You're very welcome, but we have not made any preparations to make your stay comfortable." She looked thoughtful, "If you are hoping to catch our 'ghosts' in the act, I'm expecting that you would prefer to sleep in my husband's room? I can easily move him tonight into my chambers."

Holmes shook his head. "No, we'd prefer the sitting-room, if that's agreeable to you."

"The sitting-room?" she asked, "There really is no comfortable way to recline there."

"We won't be sleeping." He gave her a quick disarming smile.

"Oh, well. I suppose I have no real objections. Dinner will be served at 7 o'clock."

"That's not necessary," my friend waved off, already peering around her. There were sounds of laughter coming from the sitting-room.

"I really must insist on this point, sir," she ordered, pushing a stray blond wisp back behind her ear. I was once again struck by how lovely she was. "I cannot have guests in my house while the family dines without them."

Seeing perhaps that this battle wasn't imperative to fight at this very moment, Holmes nodded. "We'll consider it."

She gestured for us to walk with her. "We're all playing some parlor games. Jonathan has been having a hard time of it lately, nightmares and fits of crying. He and his brother weren't close but that hardly inures a young boy to grief ... or fear."

Looking closely at the woman in front of me, I now noticed the strain of her own grief on her face, subtly etched in the smudges under her eyes and pronounced cheekbones that spoke of a rapid loss of weight. In our intellectual quest for the truth, I think Holmes and I had rather forgotten that this woman had lost a son. It was easy to imagine that no one could miss the unpleasant young man, but a mother's love was not so easily swayed.

Holmes seemed to come to the same conclusion and softened his tone. "It's a hard thing to lose someone, and even more difficult to have their death occur under such brutal circumstances. Coupled with this other matter weighing heavily on the family, it is understandable that a young boy would suffer in his endurance. Indeed, it would be understandable for any of you of to be suffering."

She nodded. "It is an unpleasant sensation, knowing something dark is surrounding your family. Any aid we can give you to get to the bottom of this, to discover who has targeted our family with inexplicable malevolence, is freely offered, Mister Holmes. Please join us."

We followed her into the sitting-room, where little Jonathan stood circled by his family and Doctor Rikes, his eyes closed; upon hearing my friend's voice, he opened his eyes and broke away from the center of the group.

He swung himself into the detective's arms in a way that perhaps did not display the best manners, but Holmes did not seem to mind.

"Are you here to banish the ghosts?" the boy asked eagerly.

Holmes let Emma take his hat and walking stick then plopped the boy down on an armchair with an exaggerated grunt. He leaned over him, hands braced on his thighs. "I am here, young man, to do whatever necessary to bring peace to your house, but I assure you, there are no ghosts to banish. Trust me?"

The boy didn't look too convinced, but he nodded quickly as if loathe to disappoint anyone.

The detective nodded at Rikes and then leaned over once again to take Mr. Swift's hand. "Sir, I'm at your disposal. Your kind wife has allowed us to intrude for the night. I hope it does not inconvenience you."

Swift clearly did not know who Holmes was. He glanced at his wife uncertainly but nodded. "Yes, yes. Of course. For an old friend like you and, erm," he looked back at me, obviously at a loss, "your companion, it's the least I could do."

Rikes had come to my elbow, and I heard him let out a long breath, clearly distressed by the deterioration of his patient. "He's getting worse and worse every day," he murmured low enough for my ears only as we watched Holmes converse with the man, gracefully smoothing over his gaps in memory and humouring him in a gentle way that spoke of the detective's veiled but deep aptitude for empathy.

"We're playing a game, Mr. Holmes," Florence interrupted, a twinkle in her eye, "Would you and the doctor like to join us?"

I could clearly see they were playing Wink Murder, and Holmes grimaced and demurred. "Perhaps another time, but don't let our presence interrupt-"

"Oh, no, you must play," she insisted, grabbing onto my arm as the easier target and pulling me into the quickly reassembling circle. Holmes did not move until Jonathan tugged at his hand. I could see he had no patience for this, but he allowed a few rounds to go by before trying to untangle himself.

"We have a real detective here and no one has chosen him,"

Florence pressed, that twinkle growing at the look of consternation on Holmes's face. "We simply must see if we can fool him."

"I'm sure you can," he jested, stepping out of the circle. He was promptly drawn back in, bearing the grip on his arm by the younger daughter with barely contained irritation that I only recognized from years of familiarity with the man.

"Please, there's a few more minutes before dinner. Let us have a bit of sport with you."

He acquiesced with a sigh and stepped into the center of the group, closing his eyes dutifully. Florence, the ringleader of this endeavor, took it upon herself to choose the murderer, circling the group once, twice, then once in reverse, before patting Emma on the head and retaking her place. "Ready, detective."

Holmes opened his eyes, glanced at Florence, and then pointed confidently to Emma.

"Correct," Mrs. Swift exclaimed. "How did you arrive at the answer so quickly?"

"Elementary and not particularly exciting." Once again, he attempted to remove himself.

"No, no. Once more, please. Indulge us. Let's make it more difficult. Everyone, close your eyes. Only the person I select will know that they are the murderer."

We all cooperated, closing our eyes and waiting a few moments. I tried to do as Holmes would and track her movements, but I found they made no sense. I could clearly hear her move around the circle once and then twice, but it also seemed she moved about the rest of the room, stopping behind me and also by the fireplace. I suspected she was making some random movements to throw Holmes off her scent.

After a moment, her voice rang out, "Ready, again, sir."

Holmes cracked one eye open before opening both, an amused look on his face. He pointed at once at Florence. "You chose yourself as the murderer." He turned his head to regard me pensively, "Is that allowed?"

The women laughed. "There's no stated rule against it," Emma exclaimed. "You found her out, but I still think my sister deserves some applause for her cleverness."

Florence made a mock courtesy as the rest of the group clapped.

"Who did Florence kill?" Mr. Swift cried, confused.

"No one, dear, it's just a game," his wife kissed him on the cheek reassuringly.

There was an unspoken agreement that the game had run its course, so we all settled for a moment, waiting to be called to dinner. Rikes sat on the footstool near us, glancing at the two girls near the fireplace, both writing in well-worn leather journals. I could see Emma casting curious glances towards us, but she kept her distance.

"The women in the house are putting on an admirable show of courage, but the death of the young master is wearing on them. Or, at least, the unanswered questions surrounding the death are wearing on them," Rikes commented.

I shook my head, "Mrs. Swift is genuinely upset. Despite Richard's demeanor, she was his mother. If a man does not even have his mother to mourn him, it is truly disgraceful."

"The sisters are not deeply affected by it. They admitted as much to us," Holmes murmured, pitching his voice to avoid being overhead. He was watching Florence scribbling away in her notebook, framed prettily by the soft light of the fireplace. "But that may be understandable. He had gone to great lengths to alienate himself from them, especially Miss Emma. At a certain point, even natural feeling may be scraped away by years of abrasive behavior."

"The boy was an ass," Rikes muttered out of the corner of his mouth. "I'm fairly surprised it took this long for someone to act against him ... forgive me for my bluntness."

Holmes's mouth twitched. "Forgiven and forgotten, Rikes. We were thinking the same thing as well."

"So, tell me, Sherlock, do you have any suspects?" The other doctor looked pleased with himself and more than a little tickled by the opportunity to use police jargon.

Holmes gave him an amused smile, looking genuinely affectionate for a moment. "My dear Rikes, what makes you so certain you aren't a suspect?"

The man chuckled. "If I were, then of course I would ask to try to judge your reaction. Is he on my trail or not?" he peered at Holmes mockingly, as if reading his face.

"I doubt you'd be able to learn anything from my reaction."

Rikes waved his hand airily, "Ah, I can read you like a book, Sherlock."

To my absolute shock, Holmes laughed. "My dear Boswell here can as well," he commented even though I believed it was entirely untrue. "I'm getting soft in my old age, obviously."

Abruptly, Mr. Swift rolled himself from the room, looking as if he had to attend to an urgent matter. Mrs. Swift glanced his way, but the action didn't seem to strike her as unusual.

Holmes stood and beckoned her over to a corner of the room. I followed, nodding at Rikes who gave me a little wave and transferred himself to my empty seat.

"Yes, Mr. Holmes?" the older woman asked once we were near the doorway and out of hearing of the rest of the company.

"My indelicacy is unavoidable, ma'am, but does Mr. Swift often ... well, what I mean to ask is for a man of his age ..." he trailed off, looking uncharacteristically awkward before glancing pointedly at me for help. It took me an embarrassing moment to understand where he was going.

"Oh," I muttered, then cleared my throat and assumed the role of doctor, "What my friend is pointing out is that men of his age often find themselves-"

"Yes," she cut me off, "my husband often needs to visit the modern convenience." Her mouth twisted into an amused smile at our obvious discomfort. I could now see where Emma might have gotten her forthrightness.

"Does he need to make use of it during the night?" Holmes asked.

She shook her head, "Rikes often gives him a bit of laudanum so he sleeps well. That is, he did sleep well until all of this began. But if we make sure he handles nature before he retires, he often can make it until morning. He only sleeps five to six hours a night now, in any case."

Holmes nodded, a look of interest on his face.

"Why do you ask, Mister Holmes?"

"Just curious if we would hear him moving about tonight. Or perhaps we'll hear someone else moving about."

"Someone else using the facilities? Well, the entire family has access to them."

"I don't necessarily refer to family," Holmes murmured absently.

"Good heavens, what does that mean?" she responded, clearly alarmed.

"Where is the toilet?" Holmes asked, ignoring her concern.

"There is a water closet and bath here on the first floor. There's a washroom with running water on the second floor, between Florence and Richard's room. Why?"

"Are the appliances loud when they are in use?"

"No, not at all. They were all installed before we bought the house, but it was clear no expense was spared. The doors and walls are built to ensure that noise is minimized."

"What are your thoughts on your husband's state of mind?" Holmes asked softly, changing subjects.

She sighed, pressed her palms together nervously. "I would think that would be a question best addressed to doctor Rikes, sir."

"I want to know what you think."

"I think he's falling further away from us every day. I believed before that his claims of mysterious noises and so forth were a symptom of his failing health. But then it occurred to me that it was possible the noises and so forth were actually causing his failing health. A chicken and the egg dilemma. I suppose now we know the answer – whichever it may be in this analogy, I'm not actually sure what correlates to what - " she trailed off, distracted, before continuing, "seeing as we were all witness to that horrible trick with the ghost."

The dinner bell was finally rung and once again Holmes resisted being included. He stayed persistent this time, and Mrs. Swift finally ceded only on the condition that we would allow some food to be brought to us. Florence volunteered to bring us a platter instead of relying on the cook.

We relocated to the seats by the hearth as they left.

"What is our plan, Holmes?"

"Simply to see if we encounter anything unusual. No one knew we were coming here, so if our mischief-makers decide to set up another trick to frighten anyone in this house, hopefully, we can intervene and, more importantly, catch the culprits."

"And if nothing happens?"

"Chalk it up to bad timing or ..." he trailed off.

"Or?" I encouraged.

"Or somehow they were aware of our plans to be here."

"I don't see how that's possible."

Florence returned with a platter of roast beef sandwiches, clearly put together from their meal, and a pot of very fragrant black tea. She had left her journal precariously on the side table next to my chair, and when I twisted to move it out of her way, it fell onto the floor.

"Oh, do not worry about that, Doctor Watson. I'll get it." She slid the platter onto the now empty table and then bent down to gather the book. I settled the tea more securely next to me as she rose, pocketing the notebook.

"Would you two like any extra blankets or pillows?"

"No, I think we'll be quite comfortable."

"Someone will come put the fire out after dinner. I hope your vigilance pays off, gentlemen. It would be nice to finally be free from this mystery." She bid us adieu pleasantly and closed the door behind her.

"Did you happen to spy anything in her journal, Watson?" Holmes asked, sipping his tea.

"No. Even if I had thought of it, the table blocked my view."

He made a sound of disappointment.

"Is her journal important?"

He shrugged. "You never know what's important until it reveals itself to you. Never hurts to do a little snooping even if it turns up nothing."

We spent another two hours there, but instead of discussing the case, Holmes took me on a lecture about Edward Elgar and his prediction for his future success. I did not know anything about the man beyond the fact that he was a composer, but Holmes could not be persuaded to speak of anything else. He often did this at certain junctures in a case; it was as if, after trailing a scent, he had come to a wall and simply needed to wait for a ladder to scale it. While waiting, he felt no need to keep sniffing the scent, seeing it as a waste of energy.

Around half-past 9 o'clock, Florence surprised us by returning to put out the fire.

"Is this not normally William's job?" I asked.

"William is busy putting the fires on in my parents' rooms. I thought I'd ease his workload a bit. I am assuming you want the fire off? It's a bit difficult to be stealth with too much light." She was already at work, so Holmes merely nodded, watching her. With the fire extinguished and the lights turned off, we were cast in near blackness.

"Will you pass along to your family that it would aid use greatly if all of you could stay in your rooms tonight?"

She nodded, nudged at the logs to make sure there were no embers, and then clanged the fire poker against the grate accidentally. Holmes flinched and stood, going to sit on the settee, spread out with his head back towards the ceiling.

She wished us a good night and departed. I turned my chair, comfortably warmed by my body, and peered at Holmes through the darkness, my eyes adjusting enough to see his outline.

"What now, Holmes?"

"Now, we wait."

We sat there for hours, listening to the wind pick up, the rain start and stop and start again. Up above us, I heard Emma's feline friend meowing plaintively and then shuffling and finally, the clink of what I presumed was a milk dish. As the night wore on, the rustle of the family lulled into silence, and then the other noises began.

There was nothing as dramatic as wailing or humming or the distant chanting of ghostly specters, but the house was a veritable symphony of pattering rain against the windows, wind groaning, and arrhythmic screeching from all around us.

The sound of the long, low creaks and groans made my shoulders tense, but Holmes remained placid.

"Wood breathes with the weather," he whispered, "It inhales when it's cold."

I was aware of how wood shrunk in cold temperatures, but the knowing didn't dispel the crawling, ominous feeling that sounds inspired. Added to that was the slight embarrassment I felt knowing Holmes had detected my fear.

It must have been close to one o'clock when I heard some soft footsteps from the foyer. Holmes was up and opening the door before I could make mention of it, but as he had not commanded me to follow, I stayed put, ears perked. I heard low voices but just as I was starting to rise to see who he was talking to, he re-entered and waved me back into my seat.

"Just Jonathan lurking. I think our presence has him too excited to sleep. I sent him back to his room with a stern command to stay there."

Before Holmes could settle fully back onto his seat, there was the distinct sound of a door opening, then a violent bang and a scream.

"That was Emma," Holmes shouted, and this time I did follow. He took the staircase to the first floor two at a time and fell to one knee by Emma's doorway. In the darkness, I could not see her on the floor at first. Holmes swept something up in his hand, which ended up being Emma's dropped candle. He lit it hastily and shone the light on the girl.

She was leaning up against the hall table, holding her head. I leaned down to her side and moved her hand, hissing at the trickle of blood oozing down the side of her face.

"What happened?" Holmes urged, setting the candle on the table, and taking her elbow in his hand.

She groaned and flinched when I probed around the cut. "Someone shoved at me. I hit my head."

There was the distinctive clang of the front door banging open. Holmes jerked in surprise and fairly flew down the stairs in pursuit of our fleeing assailant.

I heard a thud and then another ominous thud before silence fell. I could detect the downpour still pattering loudly from the open front door, but no footsteps. I would not have put it past Holmes to chase the intruder out into the rain and darkness. I helped Emma sit up against her doorframe, urging her to press my handkerchief against her temple.

Swiping up the candle, I lurched down the stairway. I lowered it to light my steps, and only barely avoided stumbling over Holmes's body at the bottom of the landing, sprawled across the foyer floor.

"Holmes!" I exclaimed, bending down next to him and using my fingers to probe for a head wound. He grunted and groaned, attempting to heave himself up to a sitting position.

"What happened?" I pressed, steadying his shoulder. As I suspected, the main doorway was open to the porch, the gentle pattering of rain angled into the house. In the light of the moon and the weak candle, Holmes looked gaunt and pained. Before he could answer me, there was a noise from the sitting room like a table wobbling on its legs. Holmes whipped his head towards the sound but made no move to rise. I sprang up, rushing towards the closed door – we had left it open, I was sure – and burst in to find the place exactly as it had been. There was no one.

The excitement of the moment deflated from me in a rush of disappointment, and I cursed myself at how stupid I had been. Of course, the intruder was not here; the front door would be the most obvious path of escape. I turned back and went once again to the side of my friend, still propped up on one elbow as if he could make no more effort to stand. In the merciless darkness, I could not tell what was wrong with him. The wind from outside was cold, pushing through the fabric of my shirt with persistent fingers.

Emma was bounding down the last two steps of the staircase, the glass of her night candle rattling dangerously. Florence was right behind her.

"Holmes," I asked, leaning down, "What happened? Are you injured?"

"The bloody man came out of nowhere," he growled through grit teeth, obviously too distracted by pain to temper his words in front of women.

"Are you all right?" Florence leaned down over him just as Mr. and Mrs. Swift emerged from their rooms.

"Of course," he mumbled and allowed me to help him rise. Mrs. Swift stepped in front of her husband's wheelchair and added the illumination of her candle to Emma's, shining more light on my friend's strained expression and the odd way he was hunching his back.

To my dismay, Holmes staggered against us, nearly collapsing. I grabbed at him, and my hand came away slick with blood. Emma screamed, clamping her palm over her mouth, and then aimed her candle towards the floor. A considerable pool of blood shone ominously between us, nearly touching the tips of Emma's toes. She drew back with a gasp.

My stomach dropped like lead. "Holmes, you're bleeding!"

"Astute observation, Watson. What a competent doctor you are," he murmured, and then his legs gave out beneath him completely.

Chapter Seventeen

I did not let him fall, grunting with exertion as I dropped my candle and tried to get my hands under his arms. Florence pressed herself forward and attempted to help me, smearing her entire front with blood in her kind but ultimately futile efforts.

"Bring him to my chambers," Mrs. Swift ordered, but I shook my head, half dragging the nearly unconscious man towards the sitting room. His booted feet scraping across the floor were unnaturally loud. "This is closer," I explained, panting with effort. Holmes was heavier than he looked.

Emma darted in, lighting the gaslight and the fireplace as I laid out my friend across the soft carpet. I couldn't be bothered to care about the mixed company and went to work undoing the detective's tie and buttons. Emma leaned down and asked me what I needed. In better light, I could see the cut on her temple was shallow but obviously painful and already beginning to swell. She would be sporting a large bruise for some time, I predicted, but she was lucky.

"Alcohol, bandages, anything to stop the bleeding."

Florence moved off, ostensibly to find me some supplies. I moved his shirt from his shoulder and steeled myself against the sight I uncovered. Holmes had been stabbed right under the curve of his left collarbone, in the delicate dip above his pectoral. Emma drew back, her face pale.

"One stab wound," I said, voice trembling despite my best efforts, "I would guess a short, double-bladed knife. It missed his heart, but there is damage and blood loss."

"Jonathan," Mrs. Swift turned to the young boy, whose presence I had not even noticed until that moment, "Take your father back to his rooms and then go to the kitchen and retrieve the bottle of brandy kept in the cupboard. You can reach it with the stool." She grabbed the boy's shoulder, forcing him to stop looking at the gruesome scene. "Stiff back, son, like a man. Yes, there you are. Now, do as I say. It's very important."

Mr. Swift allowed his son to roll him away, a sort of dazed look of confusion on his face. I couldn't spare a moment of sympathy for the man's rapidly declining mental health, too consumed with helping my dear friend.

Holmes was conscious, staring up with glossy eyes at the ceiling. I saw him attempt to turn his head to look around the room, but the effort proved too much, and he gasped for breath and clenched his jaw.

"Relax," I cooed gently, pressing a bit of his shirt against his shoulder to encourage clotting. "Just relax and let us help you."

His eyes flashed dangerously at me, but he said nothing, head beginning to loll.

Emma suddenly sprang. up straight. "Oh! Doctor Rikes!" She scurried to her feet.

"No, it will take too long to call another physician here. I just need-"

"Yes, I know, doctor," she interrupted, already halfway out the door. In the foyer, I saw her nearly slip on Holmes's blood, soaking her stockinged feet. "But he has left things here for us!" She disappeared around the banister towards her parents' ground floor room and reappeared a moment after, struggling with a medical bag.

My heart nearly leaped out of my throat at the sight of it. Florence and Jonathan flew back into the room as Emma upended the bag onto the floor next to me. Bandages, disinfectant – good man, Rikes, I thought, a doctor after my own heart – and, thankfully, some needle and thread.

I grabbed the disinfectant and a piece of clean bandage and poured a liberal amount on my friend's wound. He hissed loudly.

"Doctor, would this help?" Emma held up a small bottle of morphine and a syringe. I faltered but gave in, trying not to think on it too much.

I administered a dose into his arm, already dotted with old marks, and took up the needle and thread.

"I brought the brandy," Jonathan volunteered, holding out the half-empty bottle hopefully. I no longer needed it, but I took it anyway and popped off the cork, taking a long fortifying swig of it. Emma watched with wide eyes. I handed it to her, and she followed suit. I hoped it would help her as I worked to stitch up the wound; it was obvious that I would not be able to get her to leave even if I tried.

Florence and her mother, though, led Jonathan away and I heard the front door opening and closing repeatedly. I guessed they were still calling for a more well-supplied doctor, but I threaded the needle and went to work. The blood loss and the morphine had worked to send Holmes under and though he twitched occasionally as I pushed the metal loop through his skin, he never woke. Emma watched me work with a look of worry warring with curiosity, her fingers occasionally stealing into Holmes's slack hand as if she could not help but try to provide comfort.

I checked for major artery damage and cleaned the wound the best I could. The stitching took longer than I would have liked due to the shake in my fingers that my medical training and the brandy could not dispel. I was no stranger to blood, but I had never seen so much coming out of someone I cared so much about.

When I was done, I dabbed it with disinfectant and secured it with a bandage.

Emma left and returned with a long shawl. "A sling may help," she explained. I agreed, working the knotted shawl around his neck and sliding his arm into the fabric. I moved his shirt and coat back over his shoulder so that I could transport him back to our inn with some dignity.

Reading my mind, Emma asked, "You do not think it better to stay here?"

It may indeed have been wiser not to move him, but I shook my head vehemently; the very idea of remaining under this roof turned my stomach.

At the inn, I, at last, got him comfortable in the bed, fell onto the settee, and was promptly sucked under into a deep but restless sleep. Around 5am, I awoke in a numb daze, administered some more morphine, and checked his bandages. All the while, he slumbered with his chin lowered against his chest and his face slack. His breathing was deep and regular which was reassuring.

I drank a bit of whiskey to calm the pounding in my head and laid back down. When I awoke again, the angle of the grey sunlight peeking through the gaps of my curtains informed me that it was already midmorning. My heart lurched on first consciousness, as if grieving, before I remembered that my friend was alive and well.

Then it lurched again when I heard low voices. I sat up, and it took me an embarrassingly long time to register that Dr. Rikes was sitting by Holmes's bedside, conversing with the exhausted-looking detective in hushed tones.

Noticing my graceless exit from the arms of Morpheus, Rikes gave me a strained smile. "Ah, he lives," he exclaimed.

Holmes looked improved from the night before, but he was still pale. The other doctor stood to let me move to his side to change his bandage.

"I gave him some morphine about an hour ago. I figured I'd let you sleep," Rikes informed me from his spot at the foot of the bed. That would explain the bright look in my friend's eyes. He watched me work on his dressing and then tried to lift himself up to a more upright position, waving me off irritably when I tried to prevent him.

"I'm fine, doctor," he said absurdly and then rolled his eyes at my annoyed look.

Fighting him was useless, so I helped him sit up and rearrange his sling. His face was tight with pain, but he sighed happily once he was no longer flat on his back.

"Are you all right?" I murmured again, my sleep-addled mind unable to conjure up anything else.

He glared at me, adjusting the fabric of the sling around his neck. "Stop asking me that, Watson. I was stabbed. The answer is pretty obvious."

I sat down where Rikes had been. I did not intend the gesture to push the man out, but he glanced at his pocket watch and gathered his coat. "Well, I have a patient I need to see at one, so I must be off." He patted Holmes's bare foot. "I hope you recover soon. I'll wire you in London so we can meet up under better circumstances."

"Are you going somewhere?" I asked.

He and Holmes shared a meaningful look. Rikes cleared his throat. "I have to go to Dover for a few weeks."

"Aren't all your patients here?"

He drew in a breath and then smiled tightly at me. "It's a long story, Doctor Watson. Perhaps I'll be able to catch you up later. But, I must go, so I wish you a good day." One more tap on Holmes's foot, and he was out of the door.

I gave the detective a questioning look, but he was looking longingly at the empty whisky glass on the table next to the settee. I shook my head. "No, not with the morphine. But I'll ring up for some coffee and breakfast. It will help keep your strength up and quicken your recovery."

The fact that he did not argue with me was a bit worrisome. After I'd rung the bell and organized our food, I sat back down and ventured to ask a few questions.

"Did you see your attacker?"

He tsked weakly at me, but there was a glint of respect in his eyes. "My dear Watson, straight to the point, are we?"

"Oh, do you want me to fuss over you a bit more?"

"No, mother hen, I do not." He shifted, hissed, and then tried to cover his pain with a cough. "There is not much to tell. After we heard the door open, I descended the stairs to follow our suspect before I realized something very important."

"What was that?"

"If the person fleeing the house was the one who struck Emma, we would have passed them on the stairway."

The proprietor's daughter knocked and entered with our food and coffee on the breakfast tray. I was thankful for the brief interruption; Holmes's voice was strained, and her presence gave him a moment to rest. When she left, I placed a coffee cup on the table next to him and his plate of food on his lap. He struggled to eat his eggs and bacon with his right hand, being left-handed, but glared at me when I seemed inclined to help him.

"You realized the attacker could not have passed us, and then what happened?" I urged gently.

"Well, I stood there for a moment, debating the possibility that there were actually two intruders - one who attacked Emma and another one who came in the front door. Realizing this could be true, this meant that there must still be a threat lurking on the first floor with you and, as I would find out a second later, another threat that just entered the house." He reached for the coffee cup on the side table, but it was on his right side. I passed it to him, ignoring his look of frustration. He drank thankfully and held the cup in his lap. "When I turned to return to you, perhaps distracted by the idea of you and the young ladies being in danger, I barely caught the figure coming at me from the side."

"Which side?"

"The right, from the direction of the sitting room. I'm sure the knife was aimed for my heart, but I twisted at the last moment and felt the blade sink in. I pressed my only advantage, momentum, and twisted the attacker's arm against the elbow. It had the unfortunate side-effect of shifting the knife currently in my chest, but I heard him grunt in pain and pull the blade out. That was the part that hurt the most. I can't really describe it. In my shameful fog of pain, he kicked me in the back of the knee and fled."

"Fled where?"

Holmes was quiet for a long time. "I'm not sure," he finally admitted. "I tried to raise myself, but there was a lot of blood and dizziness hit me hard. That, combined with the darkness, makes it hard for me to say definitively which direction he went."

"And you're sure it was a man?"

"Yes, the angle of the knife supports that too. If a shorter person had stabbed me, the knife would have entered at an upright angle. The blade went straight in. Sure and true," he smiled wryly. Then his smile fell. "It was foolish to go down the stairs at all. I should have realized …" he trailed off, looking angry with himself.

I took his coffee cup and refilled it for him. "What were you talking to Rikes about?"

"He had heard of my mishap and simply wanted to see how I was faring."

"He seems an upstanding man," I commented.

He shrugged. "He is." Taking a long drink of his coffee, he squinted, thinking deeply. "I need to speak to Emma," he said at last. "Can you call for her?"

"Now, Holmes? It may be wise for you to rest. If you tax yourself-"

"I need to speak to her this instant. I did not have an opportunity to ask her about what happened when she was attacked."

"Holmes-"

"Please fetch her now."

"Would you at least like to get dressed?"

He waved me off as if the matter was trivial, though I suspected the effort of doing so was simply too much for him. "Just get her here; I'm sure she'll be understanding of my situation."

By the time I returned from sending off a quick note with the inn's errand boy, Holmes was asleep, leaning back against the headboard, the pulse at his neck beating strong but fast.

I rearranged the blanket over him for warmth and fussed a bit with his sling. He cracked his eyes open during my ministrations but promptly fell back to sleep.

I began to wonder if perhaps it was too late to send another note informing Miss Emma that it would be better for her to come at a later time, but there was a quick knock on the door, and the servant girl introduced our guest.

I stood, fumbling with the watch I'd been glancing at. "Oh, that was a speedy arrival!" I exclaimed and she blushed, pressing her gloved hands together. I noticed her gaze dart over to the sleeping occupant of the room and her blush deepened.

"I don't mean to intrude. The note sounded urgent."

"He made it seem very urgent," I assured, taking her by the shoulder and gently turning her. "However, I believe his zeal outpaced his stamina in this case-"

"My stamina is quite fine, Watson," Holmes snapped, his voice tired but irritable. He opened his eyes and turned his head to glare at me. "And I was not stabbed in the brain."

I was a bit dismayed at his simplistic view of physical trauma but refused to be drawn into a debate. I made a welcoming gesture with my hand, urging Emma further into the room.

"Come sit here," Holmes commanded, pointing at the chair at his side. Seeing her flush, he softened his voice. "Please, I have some important questions that I cannot rest without asking you. And Watson here can tell you all about the medicinal benefits of good rest." His eyes twinkled, and she finally moved forward and settled herself elegantly on the edge of the seat. Hands folded in her lap, I could tell she was making a valiant attempt to ignore my friend's state of half-dress. Holmes, for his part, did not care or perhaps even notice. Never one to be concerned with propriety, the man had taken clients at Baker Street in nothing but his shirtsleeves and dressing gown before.

Handing him his coffee cup and helping him light his cigarette seemed to put her more at ease, as though falling into the role of nurse allowed her to focus.

Taking a deep inhale, he took a long moment to examine her face and the bruising around her eye. "Has a physician looked at your head?" he asked.

I cursed myself for my rudeness and stepped to her side, turning her head and probing gently at the spot.

She winced but looked amused. "Yes, this morning."

"Was that doctor Rikes?" I asked.

"Yes."

Ah, so that was how the good man had heard of the previous night's drama. "Did he give you anything for the pain?"

"He gave me laudanum, but I'm not fond of the effects so it was a small dose. The pain is negligible, doctor. I'm not the one we should worry about," she observed meaningfully.

Holmes rolled his eyes good-naturedly. "If you're feeling up to it, may I ask you about what happened last night?"

"Of course."

"Why did you exit your room?"

"Someone knocked."

Holmes drew up at that, interest plain on his face. "Knocked on your bedroom door? In what manner?"

She reached over and mimicked a soft, three-count knock on the bedside table. "Precisely like that."

"And who did you think it was?"

"To be honest, I thought it was you."

"Me?"

"Or Doctor Watson. Who else would have been knocking on my door?"

"Your sister? Jonathan?"

"They usually just enter."

"Yes, I'm familiar with siblings who have no sense of privacy," Holmes commented drolly. "You lit your bedside candle and opened the door. What did you see?"

"Nothing."

"Nothing?"

"Well, I mean, I wasn't looking into the void. But there was no person there at all."

"But you stepped out?"

She looked embarrassed. "Yes. I know it was foolish, but I didn't even think about it. I stepped into the hall."

"Despite my strict orders to stay in your room?"

"I guess I didn't consider it leaving," she faltered and then clamped her mouth shut. "Yes," she conceded, looking irritated with herself, "despite your orders to stay put. It wasn't intentional. I assure you, I'm just as mad at myself as you are."

Holmes flexed the fingers in his sling. "I'm not mad at you at all, Miss Emma," he assured her softly. "Now, what did you see in the hall?"

"Again, nothing. No one was there."

"Someone must have been there. Someone knocked on your door."

"That goes without saying, but whoever knocked was not there."

"How far did the light of your candle reach?"

She thought for a while. "Not far."

"So could someone have been hiding in the shadows?"

"I suppose but that just seems like a childish prank."

"Not so childish when they struck you."

"Yes. Decidedly not," she commented, handing him his cup as he reached for it. I saw her eyes dart down and notice the old needle marks on his forearm and the delicate skin of his elbow bend, and she fumbled with the cup a bit.

I had witnessed Holmes express a wide range of emotions in my years living with him, but I rarely saw him appear self-conscious. I was shocked to see the feeling flitter across his face now.

He took the cup and cleared his throat. "Describe the attack for me."

"Well, once I saw the hall was empty – or at least, I perceived it as empty – I felt that perhaps I should not have been so quick to open my door, so I turned to go back in."

"Was your door still open?"

"Yes."

"Continue."

"Then I felt hands on my shoulders, shoving."

"Equal force from both hands?"

She thought back. "No, it seemed the hand on my right shoulder landed first and pushed with more force."

"Your candle was in your right hand?"

"Yes. I dropped it."

"Hmmm, perhaps that was intentional. Did this push seem to come from someone taller than you?"

"How would I ascertain that?"

"Did the hands seem to be bearing downwards on your shoulders or upwards?"

Her back arched as if remembering the moment. "Perhaps a bit downwards but not by much."

"So likely someone not much taller than yourself. And you were shoved into the doorframe?"

"No, that shove only succeeded in making me drop my candle. Then the hands shoved again. I was already ill-footed, unstable, and I was sent sprawling towards the hallway table. The edge of it hit my stomach, and as I fell further, my head hit the edge hard."

"Did it seem as if the intruder was aiming you towards the table? As opposed to the doorframe?"

"Yes, actually it did. The doorframe was closer."

"And you screamed."

"I didn't mean to."

"The sound of the table rattling, along with your exclamation of surprise and pain did its job."

"And what was that?"

"Luring us up the stairs."

She frowned. "But why?"

"So the second intruder could do his job. Luring me down the stairs."

"To hurt you?"

"To kill me, more precisely," he corrected with an inappropriate amount of liveliness.

"So you believe there were two intruders?" she asked.

"There were two intruders who escaped here," I gestured towards the window.

Holmes nodded. "Likely the same men."

"Why do they want to kill you?"

"Exposure of that burglary ring would have devastating effects on the servants involved. No one will employ them after; their lives are over."

I arched my brow disbelievingly. "So they add murder to their list of crimes?"

Holmes shrugged and then hissed in pain. Emma leaned over and adjusted the fabric of the sling around his neck. "Not beyond the realm of possibility. They already have with that poor servant at the Browning's house."

"I believe that was an accident," I insisted.

"I know you do, and I don't vehemently disagree. But the fact remains that faced with being found out, that young boy chose violence. Other members of their gang may be even quicker to do so."

"But March said there were some members in the wind."

"He may have lied to avoid being associated with them. Or perhaps they are, but that doesn't mean they still aren't at risk of me exposing them."

"There's no real fault in your reasoning, sir, but it feels

unsatisfactory," Emma offered hesitantly.

"Mmmm, I'm inclined to agree." He grunted, and I noticed he looked pale and tired.

I approached and leaned over him, pulling his coffee cup from his hand and urging him gently to lay back down. He must have been exhausted because he did not fight me.

"You're quite right, Watson," he mumbled. "A little rest may be in order. Does Miss Emma want her shawl back?"

I hadn't even remembered that his sling was makeshift from her clothing. She waved her hand as she stood. "No, not at all. It pleases me to know you're using it." She frowned at her own words. "Not, that it pleases me but, I suppose I mean that it makes me feel of use," she stammered.

I touched her gently on the shoulder both to reassure her and turn her away towards the door. "We understand perfectly well." I walked her to the door and stepped outside with her, leaving it ajar just enough to see the detective sleeping.

She turned and took one more glance inside at him. "How long will his recovery take, doctor?"

"For an ordinary person, three or four days before they could be relatively comfortable up and about, but roughly a month for a full recovery. For Holmes though, I'm sure he'll be out of bed tomorrow despite my stern protestations and then, despite that ill-advised movement, miraculously fully healed in two weeks because, I swear to God, sometimes I think that man isn't actually human."

She laughed at my affectionate tirade, glancing into the room. "I'm not sure that is something we should be complaining about in this instance."

I smiled, "Indeed. I'm very thankful for it right now."

When I re-entered the room, Holmes was once again awake.

"Were you feigning sleepiness to get rid of our guest?" I asked.

"Of course not," he mumbled, "It's just-" He grimaced, and I understood.

"I can give you some more morphine, if that would help."

He shook his head, "Rikes gave me a full dose only two hours ago."

"A small dose now would not hurt," I offered tentatively.

He clenched his jaw and shook his head more vehemently. "No, that is not necessary. But ... something sweet may soothe my spirits." He smiled pleadingly.

I cast my eyes to heaven at his unnecessary manipulation and rang the bell. "I think we could charm some apple cider cakes from our hosts." Our quest was easy as the inn had some leftover cake that they were willing to send up to us.

He shifted up the bed when the food was delivered. "I miss Mary," he commented apropos of nothing.

"My Mary?" I asked, confused, handing him the plate.

"She makes those delicious lemon raspberry petit fours."

I laughed, "I'll be sure to tell her that as soon as possible." I noticed a letter on the platter. "In fact," I said distractedly, "I haven't wired her yet this morning; maybe I'll include it. I'm sure the compliment will brighten her day. Holmes ... there's a telegram here for you from your brother."

Holmes paused in his enthusiastic eating and then waved his fork at me. "Read it to me."

"Are you sure?"

He shrugged.

I tore it open and read the brief missive: *Moriarty's number 2 removed. One corner of the web snipped. Return to London as soon as possible to do your duty and serve your Crown.*

Holmes snorted, and I raised my eyebrow. "Will you answer?"

"Not today. He has told me nothing I did not already know."

"Is Moriarty the case you're working on in London?"

He nodded.

"And you're sure you would not like my company?"

"I'm absolutely sure. The game is nearing its dénouement and that means it grows more dangerous. The precipice looms, but there is no need to pull you towards it."

Now here, dear reader, I feel it appropriate to confess that I was not completely ignorant of who Moriarty was before Holmes came to our house that fateful night before our escape to Switzerland. Holmes had spoken of him before briefly, and I was aware that he had tangled with the criminal in the past. I'd never seen the man firsthand; the closest I ever came to him was on one occasion when we were looking into the death of a prominent parliamentarian at an opium den. A slick, ominous black carriage had pulled up to that dingy Dorset Street lodging house and requested Holmes alight for a chat. He had spent a half an hour in that cab, much to my fearful dismay, and emerged unscathed but angrier than I had ever seen him. I never could press the story from him and only presume to this day that it was Moriarty himself and not one of his lieutenants that he had spoken to, but the parliamentarian's death was quickly attributed to cardiac failure, and we were barred from further investigation.

Holmes spent the weeks following full of cocaine and abusing his violin in ways that occasionally forced me from the house.

"In any case," he continued, "I have no time for Mycroft. That work is plodding along nicely, and the wheels in motion do not require my presence at the moment. Our current enigma, however, has become a bit personal."

"Our current enigma," I responded firmly, "will also have to wait."

"Watson-"

"*Doctor* Watson, Holmes. And I have to be firm on this. You cannot start running around until your shoulder is recovered. If you strain yourself too soon, you could cause permanent muscle damage. Do you understand me?"

He rolled his eyes, but the hauteur was undercut by how strained and tired he looked.

"You may think you can fight me on this matter, but if you choose to ignore your doctor's orders to rest, I will enjoy watching you promptly pass out once you try to emerge from that bed." In truth, I would enjoy nothing less, but it was no small feat trying to get Holmes to listen, so I needed to use all persuasion in my arsenal.

He glared at me and then turned away sullenly. "I defer to your expertise," he muttered. "Perhaps some more morphine would be welcome after all."

Chapter Eighteen

We spent the next three days confined to our rooms. Well, to be more accurate, Holmes spent the next three days confined to our rooms. I was free to leave, at times escaping my friend's understandably sour mood in the pretense of collecting newspapers and a variety of food for him.

Holmes's behavior was quiet but simmering which was one of the most dangerous mental spaces for him, from my experience. I weaned him off the morphine the best I could, and he did not fight me on it even when his breathing sped up and his face paled.

He took a few turns around the room every day under my watchful eye and tried his best to shave and wash, but I could see the minor effort tired him easily.

Because of this, the case stagnated. We heard nothing from the family; I imagine they thought they were being polite by giving the detective space to recover after being so injured under their roof, but I knew Holmes would have preferred updates, so I sent discreet telegrams to the family and received only vague responses such as *Nothing out of the ordinary here. Give Mister Holmes our regards* as if this attack only made them realize that they should not have called in the detective in the first place.

While I understood their regret, it was too late to handwave this mystery. Holmes would not leave, even for the benefit of his own health, and thus their tight-lipped strategy to prevent further harm to him only delayed our actual escape back to the safety of Baker Street.

It was on the fourth day that we were forced from this painful limbo by a development that was devastating. It came innocuously by note from Constable Miller, urging us to come to the Swift's with "absolute" haste.

Holmes was pushing the blankets from his legs in an instant but had to grab hold of the bedpost for a moment until he was steady on his feet. He was looking much improved, and I secretly patted myself on the back for plying him with hearty food and plenty of water these past few days.

"Are you sure you're feeling well enough for this?" I asked, my hand hovering close by as he moved from the foot of the bed to the washbasin.

His movements were steadier now, and I gathered some clothes for him as he shaved and went about his toilet.

"What do you think the urgency is all about?" I asked as I retrieved his boots from under the bed.

He wiped his face with a towel. "As I am regrettably not clairvoyant, Watson, I can't know until I'm there. But I do fear the worst. I find it strange already that we have heard no word from the family. It's out of character for Miss Emma to remain at a distance." I saw him glance down at the needle marks on his arm, most faded but a few were new ones still healing from the past few days, and pause for a moment, that brief look of self-consciousness flickering across his face.

I had often wondered about what type of woman could even begin to break through the impervious reserve my friend cultivated so carefully. I had always presumed – perhaps erroneously – that the woman in question would have to possess extraordinary, nay, preternatural beauty and intelligence to even turn his head. That belief had been solidified by my suspicions about his feelings towards the darling soprano Irene Alder.

That notion, however, was challenged during the one instance I actually laid eyes on her in the flesh. Holmes and I had been on a case in Paris, and one night he had compelled me into attendance to the opera without informing me that the singer was the lead. She was married at the time, which tempered a bit of my excitement when I realized the purpose of our night out, but was reappearing on stage for a limited engagement.

Holmes's face while we watched her performance dashed any hopes I had of finally seeing the more romantic side of my friend. He did not look at her like a man smitten, but like a researcher watching a science experiment in its final stages of development. After, he commented to me that she seemed, to his surprise, happily married and content, as if that was his sole point of curiosity.

That put me back at square one in my analysis of my flat mate's inner workings in relation to the fairer sex; I have not made any other leeway since then, except perhaps a glimmer of something between him and the admirable Miss Hunter, but that may have also been wishful thinking on my part.

But now he seemed oddly concerned with the young Emma's opinion and well-being. I knew not to voice my observations though, knowing it would only result in Holmes digging his heels in and refusing to admit anything to me. In any case, I was likely mistaken in my assessment, as usual.

He was able to pull on his own trousers, but picking up his shirt, he looked to be at a loss. He glanced at his sling and then at me, and I spared him the discomfiture of asking for help. It took some time and a few pained grunts, but we finally got him into his shirtsleeves and waistcoat, his sling once again securing minimal movement of his shoulder. I guided his good arm into his frock coat and left the other side simply hanging over his sling.

I buttoned his boots as he patted his pockets for his cigarettes and matches. When he stood finally, he huffed, "We've dawdled too long here, Watson, we must fetch a cab at once."

I ignored the censure in his tone, as if I were the reason our exit had taken so long, aware that he was simply frustrated by his lack of mobility. For a man like Holmes, restraint was unbearable, as he naturally leaned towards a nervous energy that kept him in motion.

He wouldn't speak to me as the hansom cab rattled along the street, preferring to stare out of the window with a consternated frown that was unlike him.

There were police all over the estate but this time Miller met us on the neat pathway leading up to the main doors.

"Ugly business in there," he gestured his head towards the house with that offhand tone that I knew many police officers – and, in fact, medical men – often adopted to endure the horrors their work inevitably led them to see. "Only one survivor. At least from the family."

I felt Holmes tense next to me, his back going as tight as a bow cord. There was a new paleness to his face that did not seem to be caused by physical pain.

"What has happened?" he asked at last, his voice precisely measured to show no emotion.

"We won't know for sure until the bodies are examined, but it looks to me to be a poisoning." He paused. "Well, there's nothing for it. You can look for yourself."

For the first time in all our cases together, I was under the distinct impression that Holmes did not want to look for himself. He stood rooted to the spot for a second or two longer than he would customarily, peering up at the house with a sort of tired wariness.

Then he strode up the steps with a purpose that belied his injury and his minute hesitation.

The foyer was empty besides a few straggling officers, and we were promptly led through the house towards the dining room where we had once shared a very nice meal with the family.

A young, fresh-faced but tired looking policeman was standing guard at the door but stepped aside wordlessly to let the constable and us inside.

It was a sickening tableau we came upon. Holmes took one step into the dining room and sucked in a breath as if he'd been struck in the chest.

"Christ, Sherlock," he muttered to himself under his breath, a tremulous note of self-castigation in his voice.

The dining room had been set for early dinner. Small serving bowls of roasted potatoes and roast beef rested in the middle of the table, and plates had been filled and tucked into. The wine glasses were half full, one overturned and leaking the bloodlike fluid across the white tablecloth, dripping steadily onto the floor.

Mr. Swift looked as if he were sleeping, head lowered onto his chest, but the pallor of his skin and the stillness of his chest immediately let me know he was dead. Jonathan was still in his seat, head heavy on the table, his plate shoved away as if swept aside by his arm. Lady Swift was lying at his feet, her chair overturned as if she had rushed to her son's side and had not made it to him before being struck down.

They were all deathly pale, eyes open hauntingly, but there was no blood or sign of external injury. They had the appearance of ghastly puppets someone had posed.

Holmes circled the table, his movements efficient but jerky as if it were taking a monumental effort to hold himself in check. He sniffed the food and wine, occasionally taking a small taste with his finger. He examined the bodies and the carpet. When he came upon Jonathan, he stilled, looking down at the young boy with a moment of undisguised sadness before gently reaching down and closing his eyes.

He took a deep breath before starting. "It is clear to me that your assessment of poison is correct, Constable. It appears that Jonathan was the first to be affected by whatever toxin was used. Mrs. Swift appears to have lurched out of her chair, likely trying to reach her struggling son but was overcome herself. The master of the house likely followed after, confused and terrified in his chair. The carpet tells this story and also lets us know that no one entered or exited the room once the food was served. Where are the daughters?"

"The younger was here. Apparently, she hadn't come down to dinner. She was near hysterical, so we sent her to a doctor to see if he could administer something to help calm her down. Also, quite frankly, just to get her out of the house. The older one is unaccounted for. She does not seem to be in the house, and we are not sure when she left."

"Who called for you?"

"One of the maids after Florence found the bodies."

"She didn't enter the room," Holmes stated.

"From what I could get from her, she stood in the doorway, saw her dead family, and broke down. I assume you'll want to speak to her?"

"Yes, the address to the doctor would be welcome."

"I have to tell you, these are not our only victims. The cook and a parlor maid were found dead in the kitchen. I presume that had tasted the food as well. Likely not targets themselves, but unintended casualties."

Holmes passed a distracted hand over his brow. "Was the maid a young blond girl? Particularly short?"

Miller shook his head. "No, sort of auburn, I think the term is. I think she's the one who cleans the house at night."

I breathed a sigh of relief that Agatha had not fallen victim to the murderer and then felt a pang of shame. A girl had still died. Holmes seemed to feel the same way, exhaling and nodded to himself.

Holmes began another round around the room, pulling out his magnifying glass and embarking on an examination of the room that was slow and methodical.

The young officer at the door stepped in. "Sir, there's a cab pulling up."

Holmes looked up at me. "Watson, can you go and see who's visiting while I finish up here and in the kitchen? I'm nearly finished."

I obeyed, thankful to exit that horrible room.

The cab was bearing no visitor after all. I encountered Emma coming across the wet lawn without an umbrella or shawl. "Doctor Watson, what's happening?" she asked, voice a bit shrill with worry as she glanced around at the bundles of officers invading her home.

I took her shoulders, dreading the prospect of telling her the news. "It's cold out here, miss. Take my jacket."

"I accidentally left my things in the cab when I saw the crowd," she said distractedly. "I do not want your jacket," she waved off irritably when I started to shrug out of my outer coat. "What has happened?"

"Where were you?"

"I visited my music teacher-"

I pulled her over towards the side of the house just as Holmes came out of the front door and strode across the lawn towards us. He'd left his own coats and hat inside, his hair dampening quickly in the light drizzle. His shirt-sleeves were shoved up and the fabric at his shoulders was wet against his skin. The elements would not be conducive to his recovery, I mentally lamented. He rotated his injured shoulder slowly, grimacing a bit. Emma pulled away from me.

"Mr. Holmes, what is going on? Doctor Watson refused to tell me."

Holmes cast me a rueful glance. "Why were you not at dinner?" he asked gently.

She spoke through clenched teeth. "I already told the doctor I went to a music lesson."

"It was not a scheduled music lesson, though?"

She frowned. "No, no. I wanted to discuss some difficulty I was having with a piece. And … then I was going to come and see if you and the doctor wished to have dinner with me again. I found it pleasant and wanted to see if you were feeling improved. Doctor Watson had informed me that the first stage of recovery for a wound like yours usually takes about 4 days, so I hoped I could call on you without interfering with your rest."

Holmes nodded. "Did anyone know you were leaving?"

"I told my parents, naturally."

"Was Florence already out?"

She looked confused. "Florence was home, I think. I didn't see her because she was in her room. Why do you ask? What's gone on? Is Florence hurt?"

Holmes reached out his right hand and took her by her elbow softly, "No, Florence is not hurt . However," he took a deep breath and tightened his hold on her, "your family was found here. The dinner was poisoned. Your parents, Jonathan, the cook, and the parlor-maid are dead."

All color drained from her face. She stumbled a bit and tried to dislodge my friend's hand. "What? What are you going on about? You can't be serious."

"I'm afraid it's true. You and Florence escaped but-"

"Mama?" she whispered and then swallowed. Holmes pulled her to the side, preparing for her to be sick. She waved him off but was breathing hard. "My mother and father?" Something horrible dawned on her face. "Jonathan!" her voice was strangled. "He's just a boy!"

She tried to step past Holmes, but he gripped her tighter. She weaved, and I moved closer to her in case she fainted. She did not, but she seemed to have a hard time staying upright. Holmes, surprisingly, drew her to him, letting her rest against him, his good arm tight around her. He flinched a bit at her weight against his injury, the sling pressed between them but did not adjust his grip.

She didn't cry, but she let him hold her, looking pathetically wet and haunted.

After a moment, he gently transferred her to my hold and told us he'd return soon before disappearing back into the house. I held her awkwardly, only one arm around her as she leaned into my side. After a moment, Agatha and William came around the flank of the house with umbrellas. Emma fell into her maid's arms and the two girls held each other tightly. William canted his umbrella over me so we could share.

He signed something at me, but I shook my head, unclear. He raised his hand up, signifying something tall. Oh. He was asking where Holmes was.

"He's inside," I nodded towards the house.

The man in question came back out, this time with his coats on.

"Arsenic," he declared. "There was an opened box of rat poison in the kitchen. I suspect it was in the wine since it's the one thing I can clearly see all victims partook of." He signed the best he could for the deaf young boy.

Agatha let out a sob, pressing Emma closer to her. William gestured towards himself and then mimed drinking. Holmes looked worried. "Did you drink the wine?" he asked urgently, gesturing the best he could with limited mobility. He moved his arm too roughly, hissing, and his jacket slipped off his shoulder. I pushed it back up and was startled at how heavy the coat was.

The boy shook his head, flung out a few more complicated hand signals, and Holmes sighed with relief. "He said he thought of stealing some wine but didn't want to get in trouble," he translated.

I patted the boy on the back. "Don't worry."

"I can hardly make heads or tails of anything in there," Holmes groused. "The police have trampled all over the place."

The boy pulled at his sleeve, signed to him. "No, no, you were right to go to the police first. That's what you're meant to do," Holmes reassured, signing back.

Emma pulled away from Agatha's embrace. "Where is my sister?"

"She was overexcited," I told her. "I believe she was brought to a doctor."

"I need to go see her."

Holmes stepped in front of her, blocking her way. "Absolutely not." He tempered his tone at the look of shock and grief on her upturned face. "She needs to rest, as do you. Please. Come back to the inn with us." He glanced at the others. "All of you, we have two rooms. We can move our things together and allow you and Agatha privacy." Emma looked ready to argue, but Agatha put a hand on her arm and seemed to communicate with her in some way beyond our understanding. This silent communique seemed more effective than Holmes's logic. She conceded to our plan with a sigh.

"May I see my family, one last time?" Her voice was small.

Holmes flinched and shook his head firmly. "Trust me, my lady. That is not a wise choice." He slid an arm around her, turning her from the house, giving Agatha a beseeching look over her head. The maid was quick and pressed herself once again to her lady's side, anchoring an arm around her waist and helping us guide her to our cab.

As I began to move off, Holmes clutched my sleeve and held me back. "It was not arsenic, Watson," he whispered. "It was nightshade used in the wine. The sweetness of the drink masks the poison."

"Nightshade? The plant?"

He nodded.

"But," I glanced at Agatha and Emma alighting into the carriage ahead of us, "that would mean-"

"Nothing," Holmes murmured, "Or everything. Never trust an obvious clue. I'm going to stay here for a bit longer. Settle the girls into your room – that seems easier since you're much neater than I am – and I'll be back at the inn once I've satisfied myself to everything I can learn here." Then, to my shock, he opened his frock coat and urged me to secrete the wine bottle he revealed into my own pockets. Putting a finger to his lips, he nodded.

I secured the purloined clue and tipped my hat, following the others into the cramped cab.

I deposited the girls in my room, listening to the cooing of Agatha as I packed up my few belongings to relocate to Holmes's chamber. Agatha was petting her lady's arm, murmuring comfort, but Emma stared out of the inn window into the drizzle and darkness of the small grassy yard behind our rooms.

"Who would do something like this?" she whispered, voice monotone.

I straightened from where I was leaning over my small travel bag. "I'm not sure Miss Emma, but I promise you that we will find out." I flushed as soon as the words were out of my mouth, shamed by our failures in this case.

Emma must have noticed. She sighed. "I don't blame you or Mr. Holmes for any of this. The detective was severely injured, and he's only human. I'm sure whoever did this was aware that he was laid up and chose their moment accordingly."

"Over the last four days, did you notice anything amiss?"

She began to answer, but I held up a hand. "Actually, let's wait on that. Let me send for some port to warm and relax you. I'm sure Holmes would want to question you in any case, so there's no need to make you endure that twice over."

After making sure they were ensconced in the armchairs near the fire, I left them alone to straighten up Holmes's room to accommodate me and William. William was already tidying everything and when I asked him if he was hungry, he nodded eagerly. I rang the bell for service and then heard movement in the all.

I opened the door and saw Holmes coming down the hallway, a white ball of fur in his one good arm. Florence trailed behind him. She looked as if she'd been crying but was composed now. I wondered if the doctor had given her something for her nerves.

Holmes came towards me. "I picked up Florence and Alice here because I didn't feel comfortable with them in the house." He jiggled the mellow cat in his arms. "Give me a moment, Watson."

He disappeared into my old room for long enough for me to receive the little meat pies and wine from the kitchen and settle the items on the table in his room. William dug in immediately.

Holmes returned with a dazed looking Emma in tow. He gestured her into the straight-back chair next to his unmade bed and settled on the edge. He looked wan and drawn, so I pressed some food in his hand and made him eat before allowing him to continue what I suspected would be a very uncomfortable interview.

He did not want to cooperate with me, but I suspect he knew it was quicker to comply, shoving the pie in his mouth with absolutely no manners at all and chewing fast. Emma was staring at the hands in her lap, oblivious to the world around her.

At last, she looked up just as Holmes was swallowing his mouthful with some difficulty. "How is your shoulder?" she asked.

Holmes looked stupefied by the concern. "My injury is nothing,

Miss Emma. You needn't worry about me. Let us focus more on you and what you have endured."

"I do not wish to focus on that," she murmured. "I don't want to think of it. It feels like a bad dream. As if I'll go home tomorrow and they're all still be there like before."

"Let us go from the beginning," Holmes began, voice monotone. "Over the past few days, did anything unusual continue to happen in the house?"

"No, not at all."

"Interesting. And how was your father?"

"I don't think he knew …" she took a fortifying breath, "He recognized my mother, but occasionally he forgot who his children were. He mistook me for my aunt once."

"Do you think his state of mind might be why the unusual occurrences stopped?"

She frowned. "Are you implying my father was behind them?"

"No, not at all. I'm implying that he was the target. But once he was no longer of sound mind, it was no longer necessary to carry on the hoax."

"So someone wished to convince my father the house was haunted just to end up killing him and the whole family? There's no logic to that."

"There's some," Holmes muttered as if in his own world.

"Would you care to elaborate?"

He continued on as if he hadn't heard her. "Why did you decide to go to visit your music teacher?"

She looked a bit embarrassed. "My real purpose was to visit you," she confessed, "but I thought stopping by my tutor would give me a pretense so I wasn't intruding."

"You would not have been intruding." His voice was gentle.

"You were trying to help us and were stabbed."

He gave her a patient look and continued his interrogation. "Did you eat before you left?"

"No, I stepped into a tea house near Vicarage Street and had some cakes."

"And then where did you go?"

"I went to my teacher's, and we spoke for about an hour. Then I came here, and I was told you had received a telegram and had left. At first, I thought maybe you had been called back to London, but you were not checked out of your rooms. I returned home, predicting that I'd find you there."

"Did you go into the kitchen at all before you left your home?"

"Yes."

"Explain to me everything you saw."

"I told the cook I wasn't going to dine with my family, so there was no need to set a place for me. She was standing at the range, seasoning the potatoes that she had removed from the oven. No one else was in the room. The pot roast was on the servant's dining table. She was wearing her usual apron and cap."

"Did the cook seem to be in good health?"

"Just as surly as ever."

"Was she eating? Drinking?"

"It looked as if she had set aside a bit of roast for herself. There was a plate of about four slices next to the platter."

"Enough for her and the parlor maid?"

"Marceline. Yes, I suppose there was enough for two people."

"Wine?"

"There was a glass full of something near her elbow, but I don't know if it was wine."

"What color was it?"

"I couldn't tell. It wasn't a wine glass; it was a mug, like for ale. I noticed it because the family never uses those cups."

"Was the cook the type to drink the family's wine?"

"To be frank, she may have been because we didn't really care. The servants have free reign of the kitchen. My mother is very generous and feels the servants should be able to eat what the family eats." She paused, swallowing back emotion. "*Was* very generous."

Holmes let a moment of sympathetic silence pass by. "So she may have been drinking the dinner wine in the mug?"

"If the wine is poisoned, then we already know she was, don't we, sir?"

He sighed but nodded. "That would be logical. Thank you for your help, Emma. I don't relish putting questions to one who is grieving, but at times it can't be helped."

She stood, twisting the ring on her finger. "Would you like me to fetch my sister?"

"No. I've burdened you both enough."

She left the room looking exhausted, but Holmes jumped up, pulled out a small bag that held some basics from his chemistry kit, and set everything up next to the tea platter. I handed him the stolen wine bottle and watched as he went about adding different chemicals.

William woke up, and the excitement of the little science lab wiped any trace of sleepiness from his face. He came and stood next to me as we watched the detective work.

"What are you looking for, Holmes?"

"Just making sure I'm correct about the lack of arsenic." He pointed to the plate where the wine had been burned off. "See? No residue. No arsenic. Other than that, I'm simply doing a few other tests to see …" he drew back after dropping a few white crystals in the water he was using to dilute the drops of wine. "That's odd. It seems there are traces of blood here."

"Blood?" I exclaimed. "How would blood have gotten into the wine bottle?"

"And enough for me to detect even when watered down." He leaned back, looking pensive and a bit confused.

"Could it be a mistake?"

"Not likely. In any case, blood can't poison anyone. It's just peculiar, to say the least."

"Can you detect the nightshade?"

"There's no way to test for it." He gathered up his supplies and carefully repacked them, still looking preoccupied. By now it was late, and Holmes urged both of his new roommates to retire for the night. I slept on the bed while William curled up on the settee with a copious amount of blankets.

Holmes sat in the armchair by the hearth, puffing intently on his favorite cherry pipe. I fell asleep to the comforting smell of his favorite shag tobacco and the sound of the fire crackling.

When I awoke, the room was chilly and that comforting smell had stagnated into something decidedly less pleasant. The moonlight cast a sickly blue glow, and Holmes was still seated in the armchair, his pipe sitting next to him on the small side table and his head back against floral upholstery. He was awake, staring into the cold, unlit fireplace.

"Holmes?" I slurred, still half asleep.

He rolled his head to look at me. I was shocked by how despondent he looked. I sat up.

"Holmes? What is the matter?"

He shook his head. "I'm an idiot, Watson," he whispered. "I've been too distracted. I haven't taken this case as seriously as I should have and now all those innocent people are dead."

"You've done the best you could."

On the settee, William snuffled and rolled over.

"I haven't, though," my friend insisted, voice quiet. "The mind must be clear to see the full details, and my mind has not been clear. I've been looking at the wrong part of the chessboard and let a rook sneak up on me. I knew who I was playing against, but I completely mistook their strategy. Indeed, even their goals."

"Who?"

"It was so obvious."

I sighed. "It's not obvious to me."

"I don't expect it to be," he responded absently and the comment stung. He didn't notice. "But I should have seen." He trailed off and then sighed, shifting in his seat. "Go to sleep," he commanded.

I didn't move, staring at his sharp features in the shadowed room.

He looked at me, face stern like a schoolmaster scolding an unruly boy. "I said go to sleep."

Dutifully, I laid back down. "Will Miss Florence and Emma be all right?" I asked the ceiling.

He took so long to answer that I had accepted that he was ignoring me. Then he said, "Yes. Don't worry about either of them. Go to sleep."

Chapter Nineteen

I jerked awake the next day like a man breaking the surface of the ocean after nearly drowning. I had been dreaming of something, but it instantly slipped away like a slick leviathan sliding back into its swamp.

I cast my eyes about, searching for Holmes as if I had lost him. He was nowhere to be seen; William was sitting in his spot at the hearth, fire already roaring and tea tray at his elbow.

"What time is it?" I asked before I remembered that the young boy was deaf.

"It's nearly noontime," Holmes announced as he came in the door even though it seemed impossible that he had heard my query.

"Where have you been?"

"I went to the house to see what the state of the police inquiry is. They've removed the bodies and have finished up their investigation, to use the word lightly. I suspect the ladies can return now."

I stumbled out of the bed, grasping for my robe. "Are you quite certain it's wise to let them return there?"

"At this juncture, it's not only wise, it's necessary," he shrugged, at odds with the sober demeanor of the night before. "They have to return at some point, in any case. Best get it done with."

"Necessary?" I echoed, but Holmes was at the tea tray pouring himself a full cup, swiping up some warm pastries, and eating with gusto. There was something about his manner that struck me with a shiver of excitement. It was clear he had a plan, and there was nothing that so sharpened my friend's performance than a clear goal.

He gestured some things at William that he did not bother translating for me and then popped another sweet in his mouth. The boy got up and began organizing himself as if to leave.

"Have you spoken to the ladies?" I asked, pouring my own cup and hoping the warmth would help to stop the pounding in my head.

"I have," he answered, sliding into the chair. Now that he was still, I could see the remnants of the night's self-recriminations on his face, etched deep in the lines around his wide mouth. "They are readying themselves to return home."

"And what are our plans?"

"What leads you to believe that I have plans?" he asked.

"Because I know you."

He laughed dryly. "I may have a plan, but my immediate goal is to bathe once I have sole occupancy of my room back."

There was a timid knock on the door and William opened it to Emma with her cat cradled in her arms. I bid her enter, and she came in and sat gently on the armchair across from Holmes. She declined the offer of our tea, insisting she'd eaten enough, and smiled faintly when Holmes reached over and scratched at the cat's head. The fluffy feline simply purred, completely at ease. Clearly, she had lived her whole life with her every need being cared for.

"Are you arranged to leave?" I asked her.

She nodded. "We only needed to repack my sister's small bag. I can't say I'm eager to return, but Florence says we should get it done and over as soon as possible."

"An imminently practical viewpoint," Holmes commented.

"I suppose. Florence can be very pragmatic at times. Usually when I am not. We complement each other in that way, I suppose." She trailed off and then continued softly, "Did they suffer at all? In the end?"

Holmes gazed at her for a long time and then lied, "No. Not at all. It would have been like going to sleep."

She patted the cat absently and then buried her face in its head, eyes wet.

Holmes leaned over and slid a hand around her forearm. I expected him to say something comforting, but he merely clasped at her gently.

That was how Florence came into the room, clearing her throat purposefully and pulling on her gloves. "Emma, are you ready to depart?"

She nodded and rose, casting Holmes an appreciative glance and sliding past her sister, who stood expectantly until Holmes came up to her side. Her eyes were clear but smudged with dark circles. I wondered if she had slept at all the night before.

Holmes stepped towards the doorframe and watched Emma meet up with William at the top of the landing.

"I'd like to thank you both for your hospitality," Florence said, following his gaze. "I've paid the bill for your rooms as well as your meals for the day. It's the least I could do ... I do worry for my sister, though."

Holmes turned a sharp eye to her. "What do you mean?"

Florence put her gloved hand to her stomach, the picture of sisterly concern. "She said some troubling things last night. I do think she's handling all this very poorly." Holmes's gaze became even sharper. He analyzed the side of Florence's face with an intensity that she did not notice only because she was still staring down the stairway after Emma.

"What sorts of things?"

"She blames herself, said that she was guilty. Heaven knows what she means. Grief does strange things to people."

Holmes was still staring thoughtfully at her. "Indeed. After your initial shock of emotion, you seem to be handling yourself very well."

"Thank you. It was a shock, finding them there. My mother's skin was already cold," she said sadly, swallowing hard, "but I must hold myself together in the days to come. Especially for my sister. She appears strong, but she is very fragile in many ways."

Holmes glanced down the hall where William and Emma were waiting. Emma was still pressing her face into the soft fur of her cat's neck. "I've noticed as much," he agreed but there was a curious tone in his voice, as if he was having a different conversation than Florence.

"Well," she continued, "in any case, I'll keep an eye on her the best I can until the grief – and the danger – has passed."

Holmes was quiet for a long while. I saw the gears turning in his mind. Finally, he murmured, "Indeed. Very loving of you."

"Well, she is my sister."

"Yes, she is."

A few moments after she left, Holmes asked me to help him remove his sling and shirts so he could bathe. I left him to it, making use of my own room to clean and freshen myself from the past few days' unpleasantness. When I was done, sipping on the remnants of the ladies' tea, Holmes tapped on the wall, and I reentered his room to help him get into his shirtsleeves and waistcoat again.

His hair was slicked back, and he smelled of his familiar neroli and lavender scent, and though his movements were still strained and, indeed, the act of being helped into his clothing humiliating, I was glad to see that his recovery was moving along nicely.

He surprised me by leaving as soon as he was dressed, refusing my company and telling me that he simply needed a walk to "clear his head". I didn't press the matter, and he disappeared for nearly two hours while I made due with afternoon tea and my overlooked Shelley novel.

He returned, hair wet with rain and a little flushed, sporting a black eye.

I stood, but he cast me a warning glance, removed his coats, and folded himself into his designated armchair.

I took my seat again, teacup balanced in my hands. After the initial shock of worry had passed, I could see now that he seemed strangely at ease.

"Did you go boxing?" I asked, hoping my tone was not as accusatory as I felt.

He gave me a withering glare. "Is this of some concern to you?"

"I thought you were going to clear your head?"

"Nothing like taking a few punches to clear one's mind."

Or giving them, I thought. "Is The Fox Tail even open this early?"

"You can always find someone willing to fight in a place like that."

"I suppose you come across people eager to fight you no matter where you are."

He laughed at my insult which only furthered my irritation. I wasn't sure why I was so cross with him. He was a grown man, and if he wanted to spend his time trading hits with some stranger while he was injured, it was no business of mine. But it rankled that he chose to engage in this when he couldn't even find the time to explain to me what our plans were for this case.

"You said you were going to walk to clear your mind?"

"I walked."

"To a boxing ring."

"Is that not walking?"

I put my teacup down with some noise. "Holmes, you were stabbed four days ago. How in the world would you think boxing is what you should be doing at this time in your recovery? You don't even have use of your dominant arm."

"It was a friendly bout, Watson. Please stop clucking. I did survive for twenty-seven years of my life before you entered it."

"Did you, though?"

"I'm here, aren't I?" He drank the cold tea he had left there that morning. "Enduring a few hits in a boxing ring is hardly the worse I've endured. I did need to clear my head but, unlike others, I cannot do so without filling it with some distraction."

I huffed but decided against pushing the argument. Instead, I asked, aiming for levity, "Did you at least win?"

He chuckled. "Not at all. But my opponent was good-natured enough to take it easy on me considering my disadvantage."

"Now that you've gotten that out of your system, would you care to enlighten me as to what our next step is in this murder case?"

"I plan to spend another night at the Swift's. I made a mistake last time; our visit was too announced. It's obvious our prey were aware of our presence and altered their plans accordingly. Instead of catching them, they took advantage of our visit to try to get rid of me."

"Are we going to break into the home?"

He shrugged enigmatically.

"You really aren't going to tell me what you're thinking, are you?"

"My dear Watson," he smiled weakly at me, "if I tell you and I end up being mistaken in some way, I'm not sure my ego could take the battering. Besides, you must admit that seeing the culmination of a case unfold in front of you is infinitely more entertaining. So why would I, as your dearest friend, deprive you of that pleasure?"

We didn't leave the inn until close to midnight, dressed in the darkest clothes we had on us. Holmes didn't speak at all during the ride to the house and instead of going to the front door, Holmes tiptoed around to the side of the house, scanning the top floor for something. After a moment, he leaned over and picked up a small pebble and lobbed it towards the house. It dinged off of one of the windows. A light came on. The window opened and Emma, hair prettily loose, peered downwards at us in confusion.

Holmes put a finger to his lips and then gestured towards the front of the house. She frowned but nodded, closing her window carefully without a sound.

We met her at the front door. She slipped out onto the porch silently, and we moved down towards the lawn.

"What is it, sir?" she whispered, clearly confused by our furtiveness. She wiggled a bit, stockinged feet cold against the stone.

Holmes leaned towards her. "William is around the corner there with a four-wheeler. Go to our inn and stay there."

She shook her head, "What? Why?"

Holmes pressed his finger to his lips again. "Trust me, please, Miss Emma. Go."

She glanced down at her robe but Holmes shook his head and gently pushed her. "William is the soul of discretion, and the inn knows you are coming. Please, this is urgent."

She finally acquiesced and slipped soundlessly down the path and disappeared around the stone fence.

Holmes walked up the porch and pressed his ear to the door before opening it slowly and slipping in. We stood in darkness for a moment before he turned on a small torch and nodded towards the sitting-room. At that doorway too, he stopped and appeared to listen before entering. He motioned me into one of the chairs and took a seat on the divan. Turning off his torch, he plunged us into darkness.

In the dark, we could hear outside noises, the rustling of the wind, the slight rain that started and stopped. Some other noises were difficult to decipher, seeming to well up from under us. The clock ticked on and how long those hours felt as we sat there! It passed midnight, it passed 1 am, and then at nearly a quarter past 3 in the darkness, I heard a loud grinding sound, like a wheel and gear turning. And then, in the very faint moonlight, it seemed to me that the fireplace was growing bigger.

No! Not bigger. It was moving forward, one corner opening into the room. I dared not move, taking the cues from my companion who still made no sound. The fireplace fell slowly back into place; a dark figure that I could only see because my eyesight had become so accustomed to the dark, had slunk halfway across the room before Holmes clicked on the table lamp, washing the room with startling light.

The man jumped; his face was vaguely recognizable to me, but I had no time to analyze it before I noted his hand going towards his inner coat pocket. Holmes was quicker though and already had my Webley pointed steadily at the man's chest.

"Do not," he commanded.

The man drew his hands up, but his eyes darted between us, calculating. "Do not," Holmes repeated, his voice quiet and commanding.

Holmes stood. "Turn around, put your hands high on the mantle."

The man obeyed, and Holmes nodded to me. Reaching into his coat pocket, I retrieved his pair of handcuffs. I moved cautiously to the intruder, divesting him of his gun and securing his hands. One of them was bandaged tight, and I realized he was the one who had attacked the detective near the stables. I tightened the cuffs roughly, glad at the hiss of pain it induced.

"Set him on the seat," Holmes commanded. Once I had moved back to my friend's side, Holmes – never as confident in his own marksmanship as he was in mine - handed me the gun and retook his own seat.

The intruder scowled at us. I recognized him then, the former valet that was sent away. The one supposedly in Scotland. Good lord, had he been here the whole time? Secreted away in a hiding place in the house?

Surprisingly, Holmes didn't say anything. He reached over and knocked on the wall with quick, loud raps and then pulled out a cigarette.

I wondered at this behavior, but before I could question him, I heard a door open softly and quick, stealthy footsteps coming down the stairs.

Florence entered the sitting-room, robe tied and hair pinned up as if she had not yet readied herself for bed. She turned on the lamp next to the door and frowned at our intruder, then started when she saw Holmes and me sitting on the settee.

"Florence," Holmes exclaimed cheerily. "I'm so pleased you joined us. Please have a seat."

She gave the handcuffed man a long, indecipherable look and then frowned at Holmes. "What exactly is going on here, sir? Who is this man?"

Holmes barked out a laugh. "No need for that now. Please sit." When she still did not take a seat, he lowered his voice dangerously. "I said to sit down."

She sat elegantly, perched on the edge of a hardback chair. She tightened her robe and folded her hands in her lap. "Now, can you inform me, sir, what you are doing in my house? Is Emma all right?"

Holmes stood. "Despite your best efforts, Emma is once again unharmed."

Something lifted from Florence's face. Instead of curious concern, her eyes went flat. I felt that I had just watched her turn off, like a switch had been flipped and anything resembling a human was at once removed.

Holmes walked over to the door and opened it. William, having carried out his duty of getting Emma in the waiting cab, now appeared like a soldier at attention.

Holmes stood at the doorway, his back nearly to Florence. I tensed, uncomfortable with the vulnerable stance, but Florence merely stared straight ahead, that strange dispassionate look never wavering.

The detective gestured at the young boy, clearly commanding him somehow. Once William had departed, Holmes turned, wetting a cigarette with his lips and striking a match on the wallpaper.

"Convenient to have your co-conspirator secreted away right here in the house, under everyone's noses. Must have made it very simple to come here and collude and cavort. Little Richard was an accident, hmm? Did he come upon you two?"

She still didn't answer; Holmes inhaled on his smoke and blew it towards her face. Despite the ungentlemanly action, I was pleased to see her flinch finally.

The detective moved away.

"Do you think this was a pact of love?" He addressed the young man now, nodding at the girl sitting so still and unmoved across from us. "How do you think she would feel about your grubby hands trying to touch her money? How long do you think you would have lasted? You're just one last thread to snip. Look at her. You know it's true." The boy lifted his chin defiantly, but I could see Holmes's words struck home. He turned his attention back to Florence, puffing placidly on his cigarette. "Did you know about the will? That your father had left all his estate to Emma?"

She tilted her head. "I'm not surprised." The flinty expression on her face never wavered. It was like a veil had been lifted from my eyes, and I finally saw her for what she was. It was horrific and infuriating to look at.

"Is that why you felt justified in killing her?" Holmes murmured, his voice pitched dangerously low. After a heavy pause, he continued, his voice strained a bit with anger and pain. "How did you justify little Jonathan?"

I looked closely for a reaction to that, but she leveled her gaze and didn't twitch a muscle.

"You were going to make Emma's death appear self-inflicted," Holmes continued, "A mistake. I would have known right away-"

"Right away?" she responded, a lilt of amusement in her clear voice that would have been attractive in any other situation. "You've been steps behind me this whole time."

Holmes conceded with a solemn nod. "I have. You wanted the whole family killed at the same time, but you were forced to kill your brother. That accident ended up being a blessing in disguise. It threw me on the wrong scent. That, coupled with your past criminal acquaintances being routinely set on me led me to believe the obvious thread. A burglary ring, a spoiled young man's past comes back to haunt him. But you must have known to continue with your plan would eliminate that possibility. You couldn't help yourself. You regrouped. Tell me, when you staged your sister's suicide, did you intend to frame her as well? A mentally sick young lady who took her own life in the face of her own familiaricide. Is the note already written?" He held out a languid hand to the man shackled next to him. "Give it to me."

The boy obeyed, his cuffs tinkling as he pulled the folded paper from his inside pocket. Holmes took it, his quick eyes scanning it.

"Pathetic attempt," he snorted. "Easy to detect the differences in her handwriting. It also reads false; these are not the words and thoughts of a suicidal person. It is a pretty tale you spin here, though. Emma, mistakenly believing her father had removed her from the will and desirous of its full amount, decides to drive her father to insanity and blame him for the death of the family. An exorcism of sorts by a deluded old man. However …" Holmes trailed off, a dark look crossing his face. Without another word, he passed the forgery over to me.

The rest read like a sordid Pennyback novel. Enter the infamous private detective and Emma becomes obsessed. She's desperate for his attention, but then her family's death shames her, makes her feel unworthy of my friend's affection, and she sets her mind to suicide as a dramatic penance. The words are flowery, embarrassing. I have the strong urge to start a fire and use the thing for kindling.

I shook my head. "This is preposterous. You've been reading too many romance novels, Miss Florence. Your writing reeks of cliché. And what of this: 'In their last moments, my family was closer to him than I realize now I'll ever be'?" I glanced at Holmes and registered his stony expression. Realization flooded me, and I felt the color leave my face.

Florence smirked. "I felt impelled to add that because I knew Holmes had stolen the poisoned bottle and would undoubtedly examine it. I had intended for Emma to be here and the dinner table to be the site of my father's murder-suicide. The blood was just a personal joke until I remembered that the detective here had invented a way to detect haemoglobin. A joke became a stupid mistake." She gave my friend a loathing glance, "She had seemed desperate to taste you, so I thought it would be fitting to give her that at her death. But then she had the pure, dumb luck of avoiding a nice, clean end by skipping out to her music teacher before dinner. Therefore, I had to alter the story a bit. Instead of my father killing himself and the whole family, I simply passed the blame onto Emma. Her motive was easy to create – I merely gave her mine. Thus the need for a new note. Had it worked, though, it would have explained everything even better than the original plan."

Holmes flushed at that. My face was hot with indignation. "Do you mean to tell me that you put Holmes's blood into the wine?"

"It was hard to resist the great big puddle of it in the foyer after you'd met the sharp end of an intruder's knife. It tasted a bit like copper when I licked it off my fingertips. I couldn't gather all of it without drawing attention to myself, but it was a nice addition. I still have some of it in a little ink jar in my rooms."

Holmes stared at her with barely contained loathing. His face was paled by the strange violation. After a long moment, he continued with a forced steadiness, "The other error I made – and the far worst one – was failing to see the darkest truth. I opted to believe, after the Pepper's Ghost misstep that solidified the possibility in my mind that you were, in fact, the culprit, that you were merely aiming to create doubt about your father's mental state to contest the will. I correctly deduced that your brother's death was an accident, but it did not occur to me it was only an accident of *timing*. You always meant to kill him, but you intended to eliminate the family in one fell swoop. The thing that pains me the most is that I cannot even chalk my mistakes up to inexperience. I've encountered creatures like you before. You aren't new. Quite frankly, you're not even that interesting."

She gave him a curious look, made all the worse by its sincerity. "Your naivety, therefore, caused my family's death. Will that follow you forever?"

Holmes clucked his tongue. "No, you caused your family's death. Just as you planned to cause the death of your co-conspirators and fawning beau over here as soon as you came into your money."

The young man glanced sharply at him, and Holmes once again addressed him, though he didn't turn his head but kept his gaze leveled on Florence as if she were a dangerous specimen behind a glass cage. "Oh, don't look at me like that. Look at her. Go on, look at her. She killed her 10-year-old brother because she couldn't abide the thought of sharing any of her wealth with him. Do you think you're special? I'd wager you yourself are in on the plan to off your little ring of actors and sidekicks. But of course," he added hastily with mock sureness, "the same plan could never be in motion to get rid of you. *You* – the last dangling thread in her scheme. Because she loves you, correct? Look at her. You really think she's capable of love?"

Holmes crushed his cigarette out on the bottom of his boot, dropping it unceremoniously onto the table next to him, and continued, "I'd also wager – if I was a betting man; that's more Watson's hobby – that she fully intends to plead ignorance to this whole thing. You're a vengeful former servant. Who's to say this wasn't simply an act of revenge? She'll see you hang, and she won't weep one tear for you, boy."

"You have no evidence that I had anything to do with any of this," Florence broke in. Her voice was sure, but there was finally a tremor there. Holmes had hit the mark, and her partner in crime was slipping away from her.

"I do, indeed." Holmes waved the paper in the air. "For one, the stationary you wrote this faux suicide note on is irrefutably from your desk. You see the slight darkening on the edge of the right side? Smell that faint aroma of soot? That's because Florence keeps her stationery on her desk, near her fireplace. Emma keeps hers inside her desk, safe from any outside pollutants. Any handwriting expert – which I am – can also tell the difference between this forgery and your sister's real penmanship. There's also the issue of Pepper's Ghost."

"What about Pepper's Ghost?" I asked.

"The angle and trajectory of the first illusion could only have originated from Florence's bedroom. You did not mean for us to see it, confident that we would spend more time in the corner of the atrium with Emma. The glass necessary for the illusion was easily lowered to your accomplices below and taken off the property. If it had not been raining, I would have been able to trace them. You've also incriminated yourself multiple times in this conversation."

"It will be my word against yours."

"Indeed, and that brings me to the most damning evidence of all … I'm Sherlock Holmes. My word *is* evidence."

She smiled, looking unworried. "You must be very pleased with yourself."

"Pleased?" Holmes folded the note and slipped it into his coat pocket, rotating his shoulder with a wince. "No, I'm far from pleased. There's no pleasure to be gained from what happened here. I feel that way because I'm human. But you are … just a thing occupying a human body. Aren't you?" He watched her carefully and then, apparently satisfied with what he saw, he continued as if discussing the weather, "Once a case is over, I wash my hands of it. I move on, but I think I'll actually enjoy watching you hang. I might make a weekend of it. A vacation, if you will. You, however," he directed his attention to the quiet, handcuffed man, "I could very well put in a word for leniency if you promise to tell the entire truth."

The man stared at the woman across from him, and I wondered if passion or logic would win out.

He nodded. So it was logic then. "I'll tell the police everything that has happened. I'd rather do time with hard labor than hang, sir. At least one holds out hope."

Florence made a scoffing sound, but I saw her face shade with worry. I wondered if Holmes would truly speak for this man who tried to stab him in the heart.

The detective nodded brusquely. "Just one more thing, if you will." He stood and walked to the fireplace. "Tell me exactly where the latch is here."

The handcuffs jingled a bit. "It's not a latch, per se. Press the third brick down, directly in the middle, exactly where the stone meets the wall."

Holmes did so and the fireplace swung open. He examined the brick, the wall, and then the floor carefully. "Splendid," he muttered, "there is no indentation or marking where the finger is pressed, no visible gap between the button and the wall, and no scrapes from the hearth on the floor. An absolute masterpiece of craftsmanship."

"We took care of the brick, to make sure it bore no marks of use," the criminal volunteered helpfully. "The rest is, as you say, craftsmanship."

Holmes disappeared for a moment into the opening, descending down some narrow stairs. I tightened my finger on the trigger, put on edge by his absence. He wasn't gone long, however, and squeezed back out, rotating his shoulder in his sling gingerly.

"Tight confines," he commented. "But enough room for a cot and some necessities. I imagine this was used to hide during the reformation but perhaps improved upon in later years." He nodded once more to himself as if satisfied and made his way towards the main door. "Hold them here, Watson, while I fetch the police."

After our villains had been carried away by the constabulary, Holmes sat on the settee in the Swift drawing-room, struggled to strike a match with one hand, and puffed broodingly on a cigarette. We could hear the police still moving about the house, questioning the few servants, mostly stable hands, about the events of the night.

I sat next to him, flinching at the rustling of the seat cushion under my weight, but the detective didn't seem perturbed by the interruption to his thought process.

I ventured forward, "I'm still a little confused."

He snorted. "A little?"

"How did this servant – Nichols – return to the house unnoticed from Scotland?"

"He was never in Scotland."

I nodded. "I was afraid of that."

"He's been here in the house the entire time."

"What a horrible thought."

"It's not a thought. It's a fact. That is where the two mysteries linked, and I was too stupid to notice it. Little Richard was not the only one cavorting with the servants, and when this Nichols was let go, Florence – in her anger at being denied something she wanted and perhaps annoyed by news of the will changing in her sister's favor – concocted a plan to hide her beau away here in the house and slowly chip away at her father's sanity."

"So Rikes?"

"Was never of interest to her. She used him as a façade to hide her real relationship – if you can call it that – with Nichols."

"Is that why he left?"

"Yes, I advised him to."

"Was the original intent ever to contest the will?"

"No. Another point of chagrin for me, her plan was never to contest the will. Her plan was to murder her family and blame it on her insane father exorcising the house of his imagined ghosts. And she would emerge having barely escaped. Sole heiress, tragic figure, an innocent young girl who had lost her entire family. Pepper's ghost was an act of hubris. We exited the atrium sooner than she expected we would, and her mother happened to be in the bedroom. Unintended witnesses to what was meant to be an ill father's hallucination."

"How was she going to explain her brother's death and the

attempts on your life?"

"The same way we may have been forced to explain them – the burglary ring. She knew of it, of course. After all, she was carrying on with Nichols. All of that could have been neatly explained, especially since the murder at the Browning estate made it more likely the whole scheme was going to come to light."

"But really her brother happened upon her and Nichols one night." I picked up the thread. "They killed him while Florence escaped, humming purposefully so that her sister would know she was in her room, while her suitor cleaned up."

"But he knocked over a vase."

"And slipped into the fireplace where he lived during the day."

"The fireplace always drew my attention. But I could not see any clear mechanism. It was carefully hidden and carefully used to prevent any clues. I could have found it, but it would have been a painstaking exercise in touching and pressing on every inch of the mantle and hearth and I did not ... I should have done it. I didn't take the case as seriously as I should have."

"You were distracted." ·

"I was stupid. And perhaps not as motivated by the death of young Swift as I should have been. It was easy – and satisfactory – to accept his murder as a natural consequence to his own actions."

"That doesn't sound like you."

He was quiet and then conceded. "You're right. I have been distracted of late. With things afoot in London, with news I received from my brother, with future plans looming ..."

"I know you told me to stay away for a while when we return, but you do not need to brave whatever dangers lay ahead alone. You are not alone."

"Neither are you. Speaking of, you may want to wire Mary and inform her of our imminent return. I'm sure she's been missing you." He stood and strode out of the sitting-room without a backward glance.

Emma was still awake, sitting bundled by the fireplace in Holmes's room when we returned. She stood when we entered, clasping her robe closed. "What has happened?"

Holmes didn't say anything. He stepped forward and held out the faux suicide note between two fingers. Emma took it warily, as if being offered a poisonous snake.

She unfolded it and read quickly. There was no response at first; then realization drew over her face like a shroud.

"You understand?" Holmes asked gently.

She looked up, gaping, and then nodded joltingly. Holmes reached over and removed the note from her hands, evidently eager to keep it as evidence.

"But she …" Emma trailed off.

I moved to the small sideboard and poured her a healthy glass of brandy. She tried to wave me off, but I pressed her to drink it. Her hand shook and she downed nearly the whole thing in one gulp. Coughing, she put the glass down and wavered. I took her elbow to steady her.

"But she …" she repeated, "She's my sister? She was … how?"

Holmes stepped forward and put a hand on her shoulder. I expected a rallying speech about logic and the nature of evil, but he gave her a sympathetic look. "There's nothing anyone can say that would make sense of this. What goes on in one's heart to allow such inhumanity is too strange to understand. To lack such natural …" he trailed off and then gently pulled her forward into his embrace.

There didn't seem to be anything else to say.

Chapter Twenty

Emma came to our room the next day and seemed surprised to find us packing.

"Are you leaving so soon?" Her voice was cracked and tired. She looked aged, worn out.

"For now," Holmes reassured. "We'll be back in time for the trial if we're asked to testify."

She pressed her hands together nervously. I could see she did not want us to go. I felt a surge of great compassion for her, all on her own now, going back to that great, empty house.

"Are you going to stay at the estate?" I asked.

She nodded confidently, though her eyes were troubled. "I won't let anything – I won't let *her* push me out of my home."

"You'll be all right," Holmes asserted, closing his bag.

"Will you?" she asked.

Holmes drew up short, looking flustered by the question. "Of course."

"Was it my sister? That night? Did she shove me so that her partner could hurt you?"

Holmes nodded. "There was no intruder on the first floor; only your sister. I suspected it then."

She stepped further into the room, glancing quickly between the two of us. "Will you visit? Later, I mean. When it's all said and done, I'd like to see both of you under pleasanter circumstances."

I wondered if she really wanted to see both of us, but kept my gaze even and valiantly refrained from glancing at my friend.

Holmes smiled. "It would be our pleasure, Emma. I have some pressing matters to attend to in London that may occupy me for some time. But once those are settled, I think Watson and I could do with some fresh air and rest."

"Nothing dangerous, I hope."

Holmes picked up his jacket, his movements suddenly strained. "Assuredly not," he lied. "Minor political business. My brother is in government, and he has some tasks for me. Quite boring matters, to be frank."

She nodded, unaware of the dishonesty.

"Will you take care of Agatha and William?" Holmes asked once he had his coat on, one side hanging over his restrained arm.

"Of course," she waved away, "They'll always have a home with me."

"That's good to hear." He picked up his bag, and I followed suit. "You may write me, if you please. We look forward to visiting you soon." Uncharacteristically, he faltered for a moment. "I want to apologize to you as well. I failed this case. I failed you." She didn't correct him, but I could see by the look on her face that she was distraught by his expression of guilt. "And for that, I will never truly forgive myself. Your family deserved better than me. Clearly, I am not the man from the pages of the doctor's stories, and I am ashamed you had to discover that firsthand."

"I think nothing of the sort," she whispered.

He stared hard at her, his quick eyes darting around her face as if looking for clues. Not for the first time, I wondered about Holmes's demeanor towards a young lady, but to my dismay, he nodded in goodbye and stepped around her.

The atmosphere in the cab was oppressive with the shadow of Holmes's self-recrimination.

It was only once we were safely bound on the train headed home that I dared to ask something I had been wondering. "Do you think Florence did hear about her father's change in the will? Is that what drove her over the edge?"

Holmes looked at me curiously. "What makes you so sure she was ever driven over the edge?"

"Well," I spluttered, "to do what she did surely implies some sort of madness."

"I'm not so sure. I think madness might be too kind of an excuse for her. I think Florence has always been Florence. The will may have motivated her, but I don't believe there was anything broken in that woman that wasn't there from the beginning."

It was a depressing thought and difficult to accept. "Just goes to show that you never really know anyone, I suppose."

Holmes gave me a strange look. "That may be true, to some degree. Fortunately, monsters like Florence are few and far between. The inner mysteries of most are much more mundane."

I thought of his words before: *the dreary mundane drama of the Holmes family.* I frowned and looked out at the scenery, feeling farther away from my friend than I ever had before.

Of course, he sensed my mood and shifted in his seat. "Remember," he said at last, "when we get back to London, you need to stay away for a bit. I have some work to do that will consume most of my time. Despite what I told the young lady, it may also prove a bit dangerous."

I nodded brusquely.

His face twisted into something I had never seen before; it might have been pain. He looked out the window and exhaled. When he spoke next, his face was flushed and his voice strained, as if his next words came at great cost to him.

"Watson, you've often noted that the vision in my left eye is weak. It's been that way since I was very young. It is the result of an injury. One of many past injuries, in truth. Sadly, this one left a lasting mark."

I looked him over. "What sort of injury?" I asked cautiously, already fearing the answer.

"When I was nearly seven years of age, my father struck me so hard that my head rebounded off the banister of the first-floor landing."

"Dear god," I murmured, pressing my hand to my forehead to shove down the overwhelming swell of emotion I experienced.

"It's nothing now," he dismissed. "That's why I did not tell you of my father's death or attend his funeral – Rikes told me of your conversation," he waved away my look of confusion, "and it troubled me that you were wounded by my reticence. But it is an odd and unpleasant thing to remember – I believe I nearly died - and I do not see the benefit of dwelling on it. You must understand."

I looked out of the window, taking a moment to level my emotions into something manageable. "I understand that," I conceded, "and it was never my intention to force you into confidences that made you uncomfortable."

He was looking at me carefully, with that intent and dispassionate gaze he usually reserved for interesting clients or his science experiments. "It was years ago, before you knew me, and yet you seem very affected by it," he commented curiously.

"Of course, I'm affected by it, Holmes. This may be hard for you to accept, but I am actually your friend because I care about you. Not simply because you drag me on exciting adventures."

He didn't look entirely convinced but shrugged. "I don't think about it now. So you shouldn't have to either. Put it out of your mind."

I doubted that he did not ever think of it. It seemed obvious that there were many memories that the detective had not succeeded in shutting away in some dark storage closet in that amazing brain of his.

"If I had confided in you about something like this, would you be affected by it?" I asked, despite the risk of a wounding answer.

He gazed at me for a long while before inhaling deeply and breaking eye contact. He stared out at the moving scenery and didn't respond.

I decided not to be hurt by his silence. I felt understandably awkward and tongue-tied. I did not know what to say to him. "I will never understand how parents can be cruel to their own children."

He kept his gaze trained out at the moving scenery of the countryside. "Distance can often offer us perspective necessary for full understanding. The separation from my father allowed me to see him more objectively; therefore, in my later years, far away from him, I knew him better than I could have while in subjective proximity to him. Before he died, I had learned to view him with a clear detached pity ... because he was unwell; I view past undesirable facets of myself with the same detachment." He turned and looked at me, gaze even. "I feel nothing when I think of him now - in the very rare instances I'm forced to think of him - because I have trained myself to feel nothing. It's simply a matter of removing oneself, in a sense."

"Simple as that?"

"Simple as that." Under my own unwavering stare, his face twitched, and he looked away once more. "You'd be amazed what one can face when they learn to control their emotional reactions. My mother tried to teach me this when I was younger, as did Mycroft. But as I said, I was too close to the matter to understand reason."

I twisted my cane between my hands. I needed to tread carefully here. Despite his declarations of dispassionate reason, I sensed a very strong emotional attachment to his mother and brother that I knew may make him disinclined to hear anyone at odds with them. "I mean no offense, Holmes, but I believe your mother and Mycroft might have been wrong," I ventured gently.

He digested that with equanimity. "McClaren agreed with you. But in any case, I'm sure you'll understand as a writer that chapters begin and end, and life is very similar. We may reopen parts we enjoy, but others can remain firmly shut."

Epilogue

My publisher has rejected my draft of this story. Holmes's death is still a fresh wound in England, and I was urged to choose a tale more uplifting. Therefore, I will put this away until a more appropriate time.

The little Christmas tale of the blue carbuncle may soothe the literary masses' feelings, so I turn my attention to finishing up those notes. Its recollection pains me; remembering the relaxed peace of that simple mystery, the theatrical flourish with which he had revealed that little vibrant blue gem, his own pale eyes sparkling with the delight. The holiday meal we'd shared together after.

Perhaps it is best for the public to remember him that way. It would be best for me as well, but we are beyond that point of delusion. For all Holmes's safeguards against being known, I did know him.

And I will treasure that intimacy – both the good and the bad – for the rest of my life.

Read on for an excerpt of the thrilling sequel to *The Specter of Painswick:*

The Byrne House Murders

Chapter 1

"How long does the test take to complete?"

Holmes, shirtsleeves pushed up to his elbows, carefully drew out a long pipette from his chemistry table. "Not long now."

"And it's definitive?"

He shifted on his stool, features drawn in concentration, cast in sharp shadows by the low gaslight and weak moonlight peeping through the curtains. "Perhaps not for official police."

"But for Sherlock Holmes, consulting detective?"

"Sufficiently definitive."

"And what do you think the result will be?"

"Will you be quiet, old man?" he snapped but with so little sincere heat that I did not take offense. "My thoughts will align with the evidence, as always."

The year was 1894, and I was on the edge of my seat – literally – watching Holmes carefully drop a pinch of white powder into the vial of clear liquid he held in one elegant but scarred hand. I shifted in my chair at the dining room table, engrossed in the careful and steady movements of my flatmate's fingers as he poured a small amount of the mixture onto what I suspected was one of Mrs. Hudson's decorative sugar spoons and held it carefully over the flame of his Bunsen burner.

The sight was so familiar to me that, for a moment, I could almost believe it was the old days, back in the first months of our new companionship, before my bitter-sweet departure upon the start of my marriage, before Reichenbach Falls, before my wife and little girl left me for those sweeter eternal meadowlands, and before Holmes reappeared in my life with a dramatic flourish that nearly stopped my heart in shock and relief.

Holmes himself had hardly aged. The stress of hunting down Professor Moriarty and braving through three years of self-imposed exile only manifested in a few relatively pleasant lines around his eyes. My own 40 years had resulted in a bit more softness around my middle and a smattering of grey hairs through my fair locks in a manner that I preferred to view as distinguished.

We had certainly circled back to the early days in terms of our living arrangements. Upon my friend's official return to the land of the living, I had quit my flat near Kensington and returned to my previous digs at Baker Street. Those first few months in my old room were surreal, to be sure. The comfort of familiarity warred with the pang of absence when I awoke, realizing I had kept space on the right side of the bed for Mary, as though she would once again slip in and press against me as she had for those few blessed years the universe saw fit to allow us blissful matrimony.

Then I would walk into the sitting room to the smell of Mrs. Hudson's delicious egg and toast breakfast with homemade marmalade and listen to Holmes slide his bow over the well-tuned strings of his violin, and it was as if the previous 10 years had been a strange fever dream.

But Holmes's melodies were more subdued now, less prone to that chaotic and gypsy-like wildness of his youth that occasionally bordered on grating, and the man himself was quieter as well. I would often catch him standing at the bow window, staring out, not at the hustle and bustle of the street below, but at the lazily drifting clouds or winking stars with the look of a man weighing and calculating the height and breadth of the universe and feeling bleakly unimpressed with it all.

Despite my desire to pretend otherwise, I was painfully aware of the pall that had been drawn over our once vibrant flat at this now well-known address. Holmes was not the same man he once was; despite being free of that blasted combination of morphine and cocaine, despite his life and reputation having been restored, and despite returning to the city of his heart, the once effervescent hues of his personality were now strangely sombre and muted. He reminded me of an old masterpiece, now singed around the edges. My own grief and, indeed, unaddressed hurt feelings at having been deceived by my friend's false death, did nothing to alleviate the feeling.

In the flush of a case, he seemed, not passionate, but content. However, it pained me to notice that he took on fewer and fewer clients and seemed uninterested in the drama of his dénouements. Once or twice, I had ventured to address the change, but the words always tangled on my tongue, awkward and heavy. I felt as if I was walking on a tight-rope, desperate to keep him near, fearful of any misstep that would push him away. I still kept that brief and carefully written note he had left for me on the cliffside in Switzerland, and the memory of the deep grief I had felt upon first reading it paralysed me into silence on any topic that felt unsafe to broach. It made no rational sense, as I'm sure Holmes would boldly tell me if I voiced these thoughts to him. I could imagine that twinkle of patient condescension in his eye as he cut through my irrationality with incontrovertible logic.

But this would pass, I assured myself. The solitude Holmes had been forced to endure and my dulled but still aching grief would fade more and more until we had returned to our previous version of normality. This is what I kept telling myself.

The liquid burnt out with an acrid smell. Holmes let out an unsurprised grunt. "Well, that's that then." He put down the warped spoon; I cringed at the destruction of our estimable landlady's silverware. She was still overjoyed at the return of her favourite tenant, so I doubted she'd raise hell about it, but I wondered how long she'd remain in this overly forgiving state. I made a mental note to find a replacement as soon as possible. Preferably before she realized the item was missing.

"So?" I prompted.

Holmes scooted back from his table, pushing down his shirt sleeves. "No poison. Mrs. Stevenson was not a victim of murder. She took her own life, as I suspected."

"So you did have an idea of what the result would be?" I asked, hoping I did not sound as irritated as I was.

"Not at all."

That was a bit nonsensical, but I let the matter drop, following his lead as he stood to gather his coats.

"I do not believe Mr. Stevenson will take this news well," I commented.

"It's easy to see why. He doesn't want to face the role he played in her misery and thus her death."

I faltered with my gloves. "Is that what you plan to express to him, Holmes?"

"It's the truth of the matter. And a truth he needs to face."

"Holmes-"

"I won't coddle the man," he said in an even measured tone that brooked no argument. "Perhaps he should have taken an honest look at his own behaviour long before this."

"The man grates on my nerves as well, Holmes, but delicacy should still be employed here."

A look of irritation crossed his face as he picked up his kid gloves and pulled them on. He declined to respond.

Honestly, I understood Holmes's feelings. Mr. Stevenson was a difficult man to like. He pointed fingers and whined about everything in his life. He was the picture of sullen bitterness, and his wife had been subjected to his constant needling complaints meant to inspire guilt about her every action. It had become clear she was despondently unhappy with the arranged marriage and yet had found no help or even a sympathetic ear.

Holmes bounded down the steps and stopped to speak to our landlady, assure her that no dinner would be necessary, and to wish her a goodnight. I followed slowly, preparing myself for the inevitably unpleasant task ahead.

Mr. Stevenson lived in the well-to-do Mayfair area, and the lights of his fashionable townhouse were ablaze when we rattled up to the kerb despite the late hour. Holmes tightened the collar of his frock coat against the misty chill of the cold spring night. Hatless, his hair quickly grew damp as he bounded up the porch steps and loudly rapped upon the pristine door.

It was opened by a morose footman, and we were wordlessly herded into the foyer. It was a brightly lit home, with an L-shaped staircase to our right leading up to the first and second floors of the tiered house. It was an impressive dwelling, expensively furnished in cream and beige hues with antique Edwardian furniture.

We were instructed to wait in the salon for our host. A beautiful cocker-spaniel lifted her head at us from her cosy position near the fireplace, and Holmes leaned down and rustled her soft fur before rising and staring curiously at the painting above the mantle.

Our client graced us with his presence after a few minutes. He was a short, soft-faced man of around forty-five. There was something unsettlingly untried about him, as if he had never known a day of stress or hard work. And indeed, considering the amount of money he had been born into, this was likely true. He was an almost comical contrast to the detective's sharply honed features. The confidence with which my friend carried himself was the polar opposite to the Lord's petulantly stooping carriage. He had been at least twenty years his wife's senior, and flush with enough wealth that he had his pick of women. However, he had only had eyes for one young lady and, despite her lack of interest, pursued her with the single-minded focus of a man who refused to be denied anything he wanted. In the end, her parents had been employed in his scheme, and with their insistence, an unhappy match had been set.

He waved us into the comfortable armchairs, decorated with beautifully brocaded throw pillows. Holmes unceremoniously placed the pillow in his chair onto the floor near his feet.

"So your conclusions, detective?" he asked, forgoing any other niceties.

Holmes clasped his hands together. "Your wife was not poisoned. She hung herself, as the physical evidence suggested."

The sullen man was quiet for so long that I began to wonder if he had forgotten we were present. Then, he persisted, "So Mr. Bailey had no hand in her death?"

"No. This was no masterminded murder plot by a spurned lover. Just a sad woman overcome by hopelessness."

Our client passed a frustrated hand across his brow. "I can't believe she would do this to me."

Holmes was quiet for a moment. The leather of his gloves squeaked as he flexed his fingers. Then he said, his voice carefully measured, "She told you she was going to do this."

"She only threatened to make me feel inadequate."

"If that were true, she would never have carried it out."

The man stood with a huff. "She wanted me to suffer, to make me a laughingstock. I will always be known as the man whose wife took her own life to get away from him."

Holmes and I shared an exasperated look behind the man's back. It was telling of his character that his main concern about his wife's death was how it would make him appear to society.

"Did she explain to you why she was unhappy?" Holmes inquired patiently.

Stevenson waved his hand with a violent, dismissive flourish. "She had a list of complaints."

"And did you take this list into consideration?"

The Lord turned from the fireplace to peer dumbly at my friend. "I'm afraid I don't understand."

The clock on the mantle ticked by as Holmes regarded our client with cold detachment. "Your wife communicated her feelings clearly which, I might add, is a luxury many people are not afforded when someone they love takes their own life," he said at last. "Did it not occur to you to engage in self-improvement to save your marriage?"

Stevenson twisted a loose wrist in the air, a gesture meant to encompass the whole of our surroundings. "Look at this house. At everything I offered her. I made sure to never lay a hand on her. I never looked at other women. What more did she want?"

"That's not a high bar," Holmes murmured.

Stevenson seemed to not hear the detective's mutterings. He pointed at the painting above the fireplace that Holmes had been staring at earlier. "I bought her that Goya there. I told her when I gifted it to her that I knew she would not appreciate it, but I was still going to lavish her with whatever money could buy to earn her love."

"You said this to her?" I spluttered, breaking my silence, "And you thought this was a useful approach?" I was dumbfounded by this. I tried to imagine gifting Mary something in that manner. Even Holmes, not the most romantic man by nature, winced with disbelief.

Our client looked between us as if confused by our reaction. Then, he asked, "Will you keep the details to yourself? I need time to create a story that does not cast me in such a weak light."

Holmes's lip curled in momentary disgust, and then he took a deep breath, measuring his tone into that wounding indifference that was so efficient at cutting people down to the quick. "Mr. Stevenson," he started, purposefully forgoing the man's title, "I wish with all my might that I could take leave of this home and no longer have any memory of you. I did not know your wife but, from what I can gather, she was a patient but sad woman. The natural melancholy of her disposition and the burden of enduring your company day after day simply bore too heavily upon her. You did not get her the help she desperately needed. Indeed, it seems you viewed her as no more than a pretty fixture to add to your décor. She made it clear to you, your parents, and her own parents that she did not wish to go through with this arranged marriage, and yet you did not heed her. Then you had the audacity to be surprised that you were living with a woman who did not love you, unmanfully casting yourself in the role of oppressed victim." He stood brusquely, straightening the lapels on his coat, delivering the final blow with a dull bluntness that made me cringe, "In my highly respected professional opinion, your wife was not murdered - but that does not mean she was not killed. Good day."

Our host looked gob-smacked.

As we made our way through the doorway into the foyer, he finally roused himself enough to yell out, "Do not expect a positive report of your services, Mr. Holmes! You have been unnecessarily rude and condescending to me."

Holmes turned at the doorway. "Oh, I believe it has been entirely necessary. Send payment to 221B as per our agreement."

I hid a smile as we jogged down the short porch steps and hailed a cab. Holmes worked on a flat rate (or no rate, if a supplicant was poor), but I knew he was apt to charge twice or even triple his normal asking if he took a special dislike to a client. The Lord had been one of those whose fee had been tripled, and the money was sorely needed.

Not that Holmes needed it, per se. His own fortunes since returning from the dead were quite healthy, and many of his recent cases had been matters of state which paid handsomely. Holmes did not favour this sort of work and only acquiesced on the urgings of his brother who was adept at running Holmes down with patriotic sentiments of King and Crown meant to guilt him into obedience.

I also suspected that, left to his own devices, Holmes would not partake in any cases at all. The private affairs he looked into in the last few months had been perfunctory, as if he knew he must keep working but found little enjoyment in it all. Indeed, without the substitute of morphine and cocaine, I believe he knew he had little choice but to accept clients if only to avoid complete idleness. It worried me beyond measure to witness this. Holmes's passion in his work had always felt like a fixed mark to me, unchanging and comforting. I wished to broach it but had not found the words to do so.

In any case, the money he had just earned from the case was substantial, and I felt a weight lift from me. I myself was doing well, in general, with my practice in Kensington. But I had recently made some unwise moves in the betting arena and had fallen into a small amount of gambling debt. Holmes would never do me the mortifyingly embarrassing insult of offering me money to cover my bills, but he had the habit of paying me a bit more than necessary for my expenses while accompanying him on cases and would treat me for some time to dinners that would allow me to save some of my own coin. He often showed that deep well of kindness he possessed in discreet actions rather than effusive verbal expressions.

A wet and unhappy cabby picked us up, and I was surprised when Holmes directed our driver to Simpsons instead of Kettner's seeing as he had expressed a desire for French fare earlier that day. I much preferred a more robust English dinner, and I wondered if he hadn't chosen our destination out of consideration for me.

"She was asking for help, Watson," he muttered without prompting as he leaned back in the damp carriage. "For two years, she was vocal and clear about what she was suffering, and she was summarily ignored. When one is on a precipice like that, they need immediate assistance, someone to pull them to safety. She had no one." Holmes's own past was largely obscured to me. I had glimpsed parts of it as if through a dirty window, but from the confidences he had deigned to express to me, I knew he had personal experience with this topic[1]. He gave me a look, as if realizing at the moment that I was aware of the full import of his words, and cleared his throat. He settled his gaze on the rain splattered window of our rattling four-wheeler.

"He is not a man who will ever see the part he played in his wife's misery," I dismissed sadly. "And even if he did, he would use it to court sympathy. Best put him out of our mind."

"Already done." He tapped the window to direct my attention to the warm light emanating from the welcoming windows of Simpsons. I looked forward to a quiet, relaxing dinner.

Alas, that was not meant to be.

---

1.   Holmes's past struggles with depression while at Oxford are discussed in my notes of another case *The Specter at Painswick*.

Made in United States
Orlando, FL
23 December 2024

56451129R00181